### *"You look like hell."*

Gen couldn't help but laugh. "I hope you don't expect me to say you look any better."

She was glad when he closed his eyes. He wouldn't see her rub her hands along her pants to wipe off the sudden perspiration. He wouldn't be close enough to hear the sudden staccato of her heart.

Good grief, she thought. He looks like day-old hamburger, and I'm about to swoon. Her hands were tingling all the way to her elbows, and she had done nothing more than push him back into bed. She wanted his teasing. She wanted, ridiculously enough, to settle herself on the side of his bed and just enjoy his company.

A man who was recovering from a head injury. The man she'd single-handedly put in the ICU.

Dear Reader,

This is definitely a month to celebrate, because Kathleen Korbel is back! This award-winning, bestselling author continues the saga of the Kendall family with *Some Men's Dreams,* a journey of the heart that will have you smiling through tears as you join Gen Kendall in meeting Dr. Jack O'Neill and his very special daughter, Elizabeth. Run—don't walk—to the store to get your copy of this genuine keeper.

Don't miss out on the rest of our books this month, either. Kylie Brant continues THE TREMAINE TRADITION with *Truth or Lies,* a dicey tale of love on both sides of the law. Then pick up RaeAnne Thayne's *Freefall* for a haunting, mysterious, page-turner of a romance. Round out the month with new books by favorites Beverly Bird, who's *Risking It All,* and Frances Housden, who'll introduce you to a *Heartbreak Hero,* and brand-new author Madalyn Reese, who gives you *No Place To Hide* from her talented debut.

And, as always, come back again next month, when Silhouette Intimate Moments offers you six more of the best and most exciting romances around.

Enjoy!

Leslie J. Wainger
Executive Editor

Please address questions and book requests to:
Silhouette Reader Service
U.S.: 3010 Walden Ave., P.O. Box 1325, Buffalo, NY 14269
Canadian: P.O. Box 609, Fort Erie, Ont. L2A 5X3

# Some Men's Dreams
## KATHLEEN KORBEL

Published by Silhouette Books

**America's Publisher of Contemporary Romance**

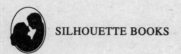 **SILHOUETTE BOOKS**

ISBN 0-373-27307-X

SOME MEN'S DREAMS

Visit Silhouette at www.eHarlequin.com

**Printed in U.S.A.**

**Books by Kathleen Korbel**

## *KATHLEEN KORBEL*

lives in St. Louis with her husband and two children. She devotes her time to enjoying her family, writing, avoiding anyone who tries to explain the intricacies of the computer and searching for the fabled housecleaning fairies. She's had her best luck with her writing—from which she's garnered a *Romantic Times* award for Best New Category Author of 1987, and the 1990 Romance Writers of America RITA® Award for Best Romantic Suspense, and the 1990 and 1992 RITA® Award for Best Long Category Romance—and with her family, without whom she couldn't have managed any of the rest. She hasn't given up on those fairies, though.

This is for the real Elizabeth
who faced what Elizabeth did with grace,
strength and insight:
who triumphs

I'm so very proud of you

# *Chapter 1*

Dr. Genevieve Kendall met the new chief of pediatric critical care at the house staff softball game. More to the point, she knocked him out.

Literally.

Dr. John Parker O'Neill, the handsome new *wunderkind* of medicine, who until very recently had made his name in Boston by effecting near-miraculous saves of desperately ill children, had this day decided to introduce himself to Chicago's Memorial Medical Center by pitching for the attending-physicians team that always challenged the residents on the field of battle the Saturday after Memorial Day.

He had, so far, pitched as near-perfect a game as anybody would have expected him to. By the time Gen showed up—late, because of a surprise admission she'd had to finish—he'd helped the attendings trounce the hapless residents by a score of fifteen to one. The residents promptly sent Gen in to pinch hit for their own sadly overmatched pitcher.

For Dr. O'Neill's part, he still looked unwrinkled and unflustered, standing out on the pitcher's mound in perfectly pressed khaki shorts and a peach Izod shirt, his hawk-like features tanned and smiling, his gray-fingered black hair tousled just slightly in the humid breeze of an early Chicago summer afternoon.

Gen, on the other hand, looked as if she'd just pulled a thirty-six-hour shift, which, in fact, she had. Stretching the kinks from a sleep-deprived body still encased in wrinkled, Snoopy-decorated scrubs, she tossed her thick chestnut braid over her shoulder and choked up on the softball bat.

"Come on, weenie pitcher!" she taunted, much to everyone's surprise. "See if you can reach the plate!"

Dr. O'Neill's smile, a thing of controlled beauty, widened a notch. He tossed the thick, scuffed ball a couple of times into his oiled and gleaming glove, and eyed his prey as if she were an amusing child.

His first pitch was wide. Gen waited until the ball safely thunked into the glove behind her to give her bat a few more practice swings.

"Big-time doctor can't even find the strike zone," she taunted, which drew howls of outrage from the infielders and another enigmatic smile from her foe.

His next pitch was as sweet a strike as is allowed in slow-pitch softball. Gen watched it arc into the afternoon sun and smiled with delight. She was winding up even before the ball reached its apex. Feet planted, left shoulder slightly forward, whole body tensed for contact. The ball dropped toward her, and she slammed into it as if it were the head of the last surgeon who had called her an idiot.

The crack of a solid hit could be heard into the next diamond. The ball shot straight back the way it had come. Gen never even got the chance to drop her bat or turn toward first base. She recognized imminent disaster before anyone else.

Even Dr. O'Neill.

"Oh, no," was all Gen got to say before the ball, with unerring accuracy, slammed into Dr. O'Neill's forehead and dropped him like a rock.

For a second there was dead silence on the field. Then mayhem. By the time everybody else had dropped gloves, balls, bats, toddlers and girlfriends, Gen was already on her knees in the dust alongside the supine physician.

"Oh, God, I've killed my chief of staff," she moaned, feeling for a pulse, praying for respiration. "And I haven't even been introduced."

He was ashen-colored and stone silent. He was, however, breathing. Gen could feel the flutter of air against her forearm as she reached to discover a heartily reassuring carotid pulse. His heart and lungs were working. Now they could only hope his brain was, too.

Gen barely noticed the people already jostling for position around her. She didn't pay attention to the forest of cell phones raised in an effort to call 911. She didn't attend to the babel of conflicting orders from the chief of every service except the two she needed most, trauma and neurosurgery.

"Pardon the cliché," she said, already having been stepped on twice and losing enough light to keep her from checking Dr. O'Neill's pupils. "But could you guys all move back enough to give the man some damn air?"

There was a rustle, another stunned silence and a small "Oh."

But a space cleared.

"Paramedics are on their way," somebody said. "Don't move him."

No kidding, Gen thought to herself. I bet that guy's a doctor.

"I just put him here," she snapped, even though she knew better. "I'm not going to move him now."

Somebody giggled, a high, scared sound. Gen thought she was going to throw up. Instead, she checked Dr. O'Neill's pupils. Equal, round, reactive to light. Another good sign. His irises were blue-green, as translucent as the Caribbean on a summer morning. The kind of irises that would look just great smiling over wine and flowers.

What a waste.

Now Gen wanted to giggle. This was just so absurd.

"What a perfect end to a perfect day," she said with a sad shake of her head. "This should have been Lee."

"I couldn't agree more," her patient muttered without opening his eyes. "And who is Lee that you would have preferred knocking him into the next time-and-space continuum instead of me?"

Gen's laughter was adrenaline fueled and breathy. "No. I didn't want to *hurt* Lee.... I mean, I didn't want to hurt *you,* either."

"Something for which I should probably be profoundly grateful, I'm sure."

Another laugh, all around this time, as others realized that the man on the ground was not only alive but coherent.

"No," Gen continued. "Lee's my sister. It's just that she's the one who's usually in the middle of disaster. I'm the one who usually cleans up the mess."

One eye opened, a bit murky and pain clouded, but deadly gorgeous beneath layers of long black lashes. "So now I'm a mess."

Gen couldn't help but smile. "I know it's going to cost me to say this, but yeah. I'm afraid so."

The eye closed, and the doctor sighed. "I'm going to look like a raccoon tomorrow, aren't I?"

"Actually," Gen countered with a slight scowl, "I'd give it about another hour or so."

"I'd heard you people play softball for keeps in Chicago. I should have listened."

"We just wanted to get your attention."

One eye opened with baleful light, and Gen grinned.

"A memo would have sufficed," he informed her dryly.

Gen couldn't help it. All her panic was fueling her anxiety-driven humor. When other people had panic attacks, they hyperventilated. Gen cracked jokes. "You could have thrown a memo away."

"I'll certainly remember not to throw away one of yours."

Out on the street, a siren could be heard approaching.

"That for me?" her patient-cum-boss asked.

"I hope so."

His frown deepened. "I'm sure you'll understand when I say I really wish it weren't."

Gen patted at his shoulder, as if that could make up for what she'd done. "You probably shouldn't argue about it."

His grin was weak at best. "No, I don't think I will. I still feel as if my head is disconnected. And if I'm not mistaken, lunch should be making a return appearance anytime now.''

Gen flushed with new fear. She'd concentrated on the head part and forgotten the rest. ''Can you, uh…''

Both eyes opened this time, smiling. ''Yes, young doctor. I can move all my very stunned limbs. No tingling in hands or feet. I can remember who I am, where I am and why, unfortunately, I was here in the first place. What I don't know is, who are you? Or did those weaselly losers throw in a ringer? That was a hell of a hit.''

Gen offered another smile, this one not in the least bashful. ''Yes, it was, wasn't it? Wyoming all-state pitcher and clean-up hitter two years in a row, thank you.''

The siren stopped, no more than feet away. Gen could hear people melting away from the edge of the crowd to guide the paramedics in. Probably going to drown them in an avalanche of advice and orders, too, she thought. She stayed where she was.

''Which makes you now…?'' Dr. O'Neill was asking her.

Gen flinched. ''Your rotating fellow. Genevieve Kendall.''

It was O'Neill's turn to flinch. ''You do know how to introduce yourself, Doctor.''

''I meant it,'' she apologized. ''This usually doesn't happen to me. It's usually my—''

''Sister. I know.''

The crowd was parting like the Red Sea, which meant the paramedics were there. Gen prepared to give up her spot so her new boss could get off the hot, dusty field.

''Dr. Kendall?'' he said.

She turned back to him. ''Yes, sir.''

His grin was a little weak. ''I don't believe I'll be insisting on prompt attendance in the morning.''

Gen winced. ''Yes, sir.''

She'd just made it to her feet when the afternoon suffered its second shock. From the edge of the field Gen heard a sudden, almost eerie wail.

''Daddy!''

Everyone turned that way. On the ground, Dr. O'Neill suddenly twitched to attention.

"Oh, damn," he muttered, trying unsuccessfully to get his arms and legs to move in a recognizable direction. "Somebody get me up."

Gen caught sight of a girl running across the diamond. "No," she said, pushing Dr. O'Neill back down. "Not yet."

Even the paramedics turned. Everyone stopped as if waiting for the next actor to enter, stage right. The girl was young, maybe twelve and pretty, with dark, flying hair and wide blue eyes. Tear-streaked, freckled features. Layers of baggy clothes and cross-trainers in this heat.

"Please," O'Neill begged.

Gen looked down at him to see a matching distress on his features. She patted his shoulder, more to remind him to stay where he was, and jumped to her feet.

"I'll get her," she promised and hurried away.

She intercepted the young girl at the edge of the crowd. "He's all right," Gen greeted her, gathering her in like a runaway horse.

The girl stalled, froze, looked up at Gen in distressed surprise. Gen gave the girl her best big sister smile.

"I mean it, really. He's fine. But if you keep running that fast, you won't be able to stop till you're halfway up his chest. Wanna see for yourself?"

The girl shuddered, seemed to shrink in Gen's arms. "Really?"

"I may do many things I shouldn't," Gen assured her, "but I never lie. You can ask anybody in my family. And if anybody's going to rat out a person, it's her family. Now, come on and smile. You're scaring him worse than he's scaring you."

The smile she got was watery and weak, the skin even pastier than the girl's father, but Gen saw the same instinctive dignity. The same composure that would grow to look so much like her father's. And something else. Something Gen felt through those layers of baggy clothes. Something that made her uncomfortable.

But now wasn't the time to think of it.

"Dr. O'Neill?" she said, pushing back through the enthralled audience of her peers and superiors. "Got a minute for a cute girl?"

The girl gasped when she saw her sweaty, dust-covered father lying on the ground. But then he smiled. She sobbed and fell to her knees, and he wrapped his arms around her.

"Oh, honey, I'm so sorry," he said in his quiet way. "I'm fine. I didn't mean to scare you."

"That should probably be my line," Gen said to herself.

"I have a feeling," a voice suggested beside her, "that for the next month your line will be more like, 'Another shift, Dr. O'Neill? Why, of course, Dr. O'Neill. I'd be delighted, Dr. O'Neill.'"

Gen turned to see Abbie Viviano grinning at her. The short-stop on the attending team, Abbie was one of the trauma docs who had befriended Gen during her stint at Memorial Medical Center.

"You have to admit, it was a hell of a hit, Ab," she said with a matching grin.

"Remind your boss of that when he's got you taking his call for the rest of your life."

Alongside her, the paramedics moved in to wrap Dr. O'Neill in a c-collar and backboard, and recheck his vitals around the trembling child who refused to leave his side.

Gen looked down at the now-disheveled man and the frantic girl at his side and sighed. "Might as well start tonight. And I just left that damn place."

Abbie wrapped an arm around Gen's shoulders. "It's not your fault."

Gen rubbed shaking hands across her too-tired face. "Of course it isn't. That doesn't mean I don't feel responsible."

Abbie patted Gen like the mother she was. "I'll drive."

Gen wasn't exactly sure how it happened. She had a feeling that Abbie had a hand in it. She knew for certain that guilt played a large part, not to mention the natural maternal instincts of an oldest sister. Whatever it was, no more than three hours later she was promising to baby-sit a twelve-year-old girl whose father had taken up temporary residence in the surgical intensive care unit.

"I don't mind," she said, putting a hand briefly to the girl's slumped shoulder. "Really."

The girl, rigid and silent, pulled away so carefully that the movement didn't seem an insult. Gen figured that it was because she was so focused on her father.

Her father, the newest chief of pediatric critical care, who lay disheveled and pasty and discolored amid a frightening collection of technology that threatened to make his daughter even more pale than he.

"We have a housekeeper," he was saying, his voice less assured than it had been out on the field. "But the nanny isn't supposed to start till next week. I'm just not sure…"

Gen jumped right in. "Don't worry about it. Elizabeth and I will camp out at my place for a few days. My family's coming in for a big party we're having, so there'll be plenty of people around if she gets bored."

"Big party, huh? You celebrating your escape from residency?"

"Oh, yeah," she said with a too-bright grin. "Free at last, free at last. I'll be counting down those last few days while you're in here wasting your time."

Wasting his time, Gen thought with a halfhearted sigh. The man had a fractured skull. Only a linear fracture. Nothing serious enough for surgery, she told herself repeatedly when she thought about it.

The neurosurgeon had insisted on throwing Dr. O'Neill into ICU only because of his status at the hospital, but it still looked too grim for a child to see. Elizabeth O'Neill's father was being fed intravenously, his vital signs were blinking above his head like a stock market ticker, and he wouldn't be able to successfully count fingers for at least three days.

Gen had spent twenty-eight years on this good earth, and in all that time she'd never precipitated a disaster of this dimension. The least she could do was follow the oft-repeated lesson she'd inflicted on her sister, Lee, every time she'd perpetrated such a fiasco: take responsibility for your actions.

Okay, it had been an accident. To an older sister like Gen, born and raised to be responsible, that didn't make any difference.

"But I want to stay here," Elizabeth protested, voice hushed, eyes red from silent tears. "Please, Daddy."

Father and daughter shared a look that spoke of terrible history and worse need. Gen knew those looks well. She'd shared them with her own family. Knowing from Abbie that John Parker O'Neill was a widower, she figured she didn't have to go far for explanations. So she waited until father and daughter had shared their grief and guilt and fear, and then she laid her arm around Elizabeth's shoulders once again. Just that. Just the kind of contact a girl needs who sees her father hooked up to so much equipment.

And again, very carefully, the girl slid away from her grasp.

"You have French camp to worry about, Mouse," Elizabeth's father said, taking her hand. "You can't study in here, and I can't think straight enough to speak English, much less French."

Tears welled up in the pretty blue eyes. "But—"

"Your dad needs to sleep, honey," Gen whispered quietly enough in her ear that Dr. O'Neill couldn't hear. "He can't when he's worrying about you."

Guilt, Gen thought, silently begging her siblings' forgiveness for every time she'd wielded it on them. It worked just as well on Elizabeth, though. Gen felt Elizabeth stiffen and straighten, as if marshaling her discipline. She saw those beautiful blue eyes of hers go dry, as if by will alone. She saw the girl pull a smile out of she knew not where, and do it so well she convinced her dad she was sincere.

"The Ecole," Elizabeth said, her voice trembling only a little. "I almost forgot. Silly, isn't it? Do you mind, Daddy? I haven't finished the book I'm supposed to do that report on."

She got another faint squeeze of her hand. "Of course I don't, Mouse. And I'll only be here a day or so. Consider it a vacation from the old man."

"Yes, sir," Elizabeth responded, as if he were her new boss, too. Then she bent to kiss him good-night, and Gen saw the tears that glittered in a father's eyes.

She turned away, checking oxygen levels and cardiac monitoring and blood pressures, because she knew too well how precious a commodity privacy was in an ICU. She knew, too, how terrible it was to try to tough out a visit like this. And she'd only had to do it for her baby sister. Not her only surviving parent.

"I assume my vital signs are all terribly fascinating," Dr. O'Neill said a moment later.

Gen heard Elizabeth giggle. Gen flushed and returned her attention to the man who held the end of her fellowship in the palm of his pale hand.

"Riveting," she said, answering his grin with one of her own. "I'd lay five-to-one odds they mean you're fine, but I'm not very good at numbers as big as these."

"I am a bit larger than your usual patient," he conceded. "What's your schedule like this weekend, Dr. Kendall?"

"Gen," she demurred, unable to keep her eyes from where his hair lay tousled against that poor, bruised forehead. "Please."

"In that case, call me Jack."

Gen's smile this time was a little more reticent. "Oh, no, sir. I don't think so. As for my schedule, I'm supposed to be off till Tuesday. By then my sister, Lee, will be more than happy to have Elizabeth with her."

"The Lee of multiple-disaster fame?"

"Well, yes. But she's gotten much better since she's been married. And she knows French."

He nodded very carefully, as if unsure whether or not his head would simply keep on bobbing and end up rolling across the floor. "My car's in the doctors' parking lot. Why don't you guys use it this weekend? If you're anything like me when I was a fellow, a set of wheels can come in handy."

Gen all but twitched with discomfort. "Oh, I don't think—"

"You do drive, don't you, young doctor?" he asked, his eyes wry.

Gen blushed. *Blushed,* as if she were fifteen and being visited by the football captain. Genevieve Anastasia Kendall did not blush.

So she stammered instead. "Well, I mean, of course I do, sir. It's just such an imposition."

Dr. O'Neill didn't exactly shake his head. With all that equipment, he couldn't very well. "The car keys are in the doctors' lounge. Mouse, you know the combination."

"Sure, Dad," Gen heard from the door.

"Then it's set. Thank you, Dr. Kendall."

Gen offered one last, faint smile. "My pleasure, sir."

His smile, though only a shade of what she'd seen moments after the injury, was magnetic. Good Lord, Gen thought, what was this guy like on full power?

It wasn't the teeth, although they were straight, white and strong. It wasn't exactly the lips, although they were just the right size and shape, soft enough to distract a person with thoughts of kissing—*if* said person were interested in that kind of thing.

It wasn't even the dimple that teased the corner of his mouth.

It was his eyes, even dim and taut with pain. Even half-closed against the lethargy she knew he was fighting. Those eyes, that could suck a girl straight in and spin her faster than a good knuckleball.

Not that it could happen to Gen.

She was the sensible one. She was the caretaker. She was the one so focused on her goals she'd shut out everything else but her family, and sometimes even them.

So no, it couldn't happen to Gen.

Even so, it would have been impolite not to smile back. Even though she suddenly wasn't sure what she was smiling about.

"I'll be back on my feet in a day or so," her new boss promised.

"Lay you five-to-one on it," she answered automatically, knowing damn well they were both lying.

So they both smiled again, and Gen felt even more foolish. Much more uncertain. So uncertain, in fact, that she almost forgot the young girl waiting at the door.

But she didn't forget for long. Gen Kendall was not a dreamer. She wasn't a chance taker. She'd spent her entire life working hard for the next month when she would finally graduate from her residency, and she wasn't going to let a touch of sunstroke set her back.

Especially if the sunstroke made her blush. So she smiled one last time, turned toward Dr. O'Neill's daughter and ran like hell.

John Parker O'Neill did not have flights of fancy. He was a dedicated surgeon, a genius at hospital organization, not a bad hand with the shaping of young doctors' dreams. But he did not feel delighted. He didn't feel light-headed in that stupid, fuzzy kind of way he once had as a young man. He didn't have hormones for the simple reason that he didn't have the time. He didn't have the need. And he certainly didn't have the inclination. Not since his Meggie had died.

So he closed his eyes—right after he saw that thick, shiny braid sway its way out the unit door—and focused his thoughts on getting better. On getting his motor functions back, on regaining his focus and his direction. Because all he could think about now—when he wasn't thinking about how nauseated and dizzy he was—was the surprise of opening his eyes onto a pair of soft hazel ones. Of sun-kissed, freckled skin that had glowed with the sheen of humidity. Of soft lips that could twist into the most wry, delightful smile he'd ever seen. Of sense and serendipity, when he'd sworn he could never find the two in the same place again as long as he lived.

But John Parker O'Neill didn't take time for wry smiles or serendipity anymore. And certainly not when they belonged to someone dependent on his calm, objective judgment for the benefit of her future.

So he lay there as quietly as possible in his cold, empty little cubicle, comforted only by the whisper of machinery and the beeping of monitors, and did his best to think about nothing. And managed to convince himself that he was just being a good head of service when he asked the nurse who was taking care of him if she knew Dr. Genevieve Kendall.

"Gen?" she asked as she punched buttons and checked settings. "Oh, don't worry about leaving your daughter with her. She's absolutely great with kids. She all but raised her sister and younger brother after her parents died, and they turned out just fine. No, don't worry about a thing. She'll be so good to your little girl, she probably won't even remember you're not home.''

And he'd thanked her, without ever admitting that the last thing he really cared about was how responsible Gen Kendall was.

## Chapter 2

A Volvo.

Gen wasn't sure what she'd expected. Okay, maybe she'd fantasized a little. The last car she'd had the privilege of driving had been her sister Lee's Volkswagen, and she'd spent most of that trip replacing popped spark plugs. The idea of getting behind the wheel of a real car, the kind of car a chief of service might drive, tickled her fancy.

A Mercedes, she'd thought. Maybe, God help her, a Porsche. Fast and low and reeking of pretension.

But it seemed Dr. O'Neill didn't need pretension. He needed a Volvo.

And not just a Volvo. A Volvo station wagon.

"He's real safety conscious," Elizabeth O'Neill apologized again as she followed Gen up the stairs to Gen's apartment. "See, my mom died in an accident, and he, well, like…he…"

Pulling out her key, Gen smiled. "Wouldn't want to see you hurt, too. He's perfectly right, Elizabeth."

Elizabeth, Gen thought a bit sadly. Not Beth or Liz or any of a hundred diminutives that might denote lightness or fun. Elizabeth. As formal as a wedding invitation, as polite as a debutante. As quiet as a...well, at least Gen understood where the nickname had come from.

But Gen knew she was being unfair. Heck, she would be quiet, too, if she'd just seen somebody she loved laid out in the dirt like a bowling pin at the end of the alley. But when Gen had taken Elizabeth by the O'Neill house to get her things, the girl had maintained the same careful, quiet attitude. Even with the housekeeper, a small, plump little Nicaraguan lady named Estela of hesitant English and fluttery hands. Elizabeth had soothed the woman as if it had been the housekeeper's father who'd been injured instead of her own, then seen to her own needs with dispatch and ease.

And Gen had stood in the echoing, quiet living room of that impressive home in Lincoln Park and thought how tomblike the whole place felt. Stark Scandinavian furniture and sleek white walls. Echoing flagstone-and-wood floors, and a smell of pine cleaner and wax and emptiness. As if the life of this family went on somewhere else.

It had been that way in her own home back in Wyoming when her brother Jake had lived there alone. The front rooms had been for company and ranch business. It had been his bedroom that had contained all the crayon drawings, the class photos and framed awards that had represented the lives of his three siblings.

But now that Jake had a family, it all spilled over every room as untidily as everyday life did.

Elizabeth's home was as sterile as a surgical suite.

As opposed, of course, to Gen's home. At least, her current one.

*"Voilà,"* she announced thirty minutes later as she threw open the door to her own apartment.

For a moment Elizabeth just stood there staring.

"How'd you get it up here?" she demanded.

Gen grinned. Her apartment was on the third floor of a Victorian brownstone on Barton in the Lincoln Park West neighborhood. Lots of windows, high ceilings, wood floors and enough crown molding to encircle a ship. Only last summer, the rooms had been stuffed with color and kitsch and some twenty years of personal memorabilia. Early eclectic, her sister, Lee, had called it. Early, middle and late Lee, Gen had always thought. The decor had been a perfect fit for Lee, the actress and playwright. But then Lee had married and taken her circus along to share with her husband, Rock, and Gen had decided a change was needed.

Lee thrived on stimulation. Gen was stimulated enough in the pediatric ICU. What she needed from her home was solace and simplicity. So she'd spent a week transforming her rooms from a Turkish bazaar into a Tuscan villa.

Ochre plaster walls and distressed wood shutters and white gauze curtains that fluttered in the summer breezes. Yellow and blue ceramicware, sunflowers and a dozen different fabrics and patterns, from rugs to pillows tossed over muslin-covered couches. A few Renaissance sketches and a street scene she'd found in Italy to brighten the walls. Clean lines and bright sunlight and the illusion of warmth, even in a Chicago winter.

Especially in a Chicago winter.

And, to add the perfect finishing touch to it all, a black baby grand piano tucked into the bay window.

Gen's baby, her pacifier, her motivator. The worse her day on the halls, the longer the hours she spent at the keyboard. In the last month alone, Gen had become really proficient.

"She's a beauty, isn't she?" she asked, walking over to stroke the gleaming instrument like a pet. "Do you play?"

It took Gen a second to notice the silence. When she turned, it was to surprise an odd glint in Elizabeth's eyes.

"A little," she said.

"Well, feel free. Emily is used to abuse of all kinds."

Elizabeth quirked an eyebrow. "Emily?"

Gen shrugged. "Most people name ships or cars. I name musical instruments. Emily replaced her sister, Anne, who was lost in a fire last year. Anne was my Chicago substitute for her auntie Charlotte in Wyoming."

This time she almost got a smile. So Gen opened her arms to take in the rooms and smiled her best welcome. "*Mi casa,* et cetera. Your bedroom is that one. It used to be my sister's before she went off and got married and I redecorated it into something coherent. It is now a lovely replica of a room I stayed in while in Pisa last year. Including the view I could see out the window, which is painted on the wall.''

Gen walked as she talked, leading the girl into Lee's old room, where jewel-toned pillows lay scattered across a wrought iron double bed, and a pair of wing chairs upholstered in cinnamon-and-gold-silk stripes bracketed the gauze-curtained windows.

"It's beautiful," Elizabeth admitted, then eyed the mural on the far wall, of the Tuscan hills through a stone archway. "Did you paint this?''

"I paint stick figures and fence posts. The set designer from my sister's theater company did it for free beer and brats.''

Elizabeth turned toward her. "Your sister's in theater?''

Gen puffed up like a mother. "She's at Fandango over on Halsted. Quite the little star, if a proud sister may say so. Do you like theater?''

For a second Elizabeth seemed only able to blink. Then, her eyes growing impossibly wide, she sucked in air as if she were drowning.

"Fandango?'' she demanded, actually excited. "Oh, my God. Kendall. Your sister's Lee Kendall!''

It was Gen's turn to blink. "You know who Lee is?''

Lee was definitely a star on the rise, but as far as Gen knew, she hadn't yet risen much higher than the Chicago horizon. Evidently Gen had been mistaken.

"Lee Kendall wrote the play *Some Men's Dreams,*'' Elizabeth intoned, as if she'd meant to say *Hamlet.* "Oh, do you know how wonderful it is?''

Gen forbore the obvious answer to that. "You've seen it?'' she asked. "I didn't think anybody'd seen that but her fellow students at Harvard.''

"One of her classmates taught at my school in Boston last year. He got Ms. Kendall's permission for us to put it on for the school. Oh, to be able to do something that…that true. That poignant.''

*Poignant* was a good term for the play, Gen thought. A lovely, insightful, painful look into family and need and loss.

It had basically been the story of their own family, of the

price paid by four orphaned siblings left to fend for themselves on a poor ranch where nothing went right. Where sacrifice seemed the only coin of the realm, and loyalty and love the only forces that held fear at bay.

And Lee had immortalized it.

Sometimes Gen loved the play. Mostly, she couldn't make it past the first act.

"Well," she said, as if that weren't important, "you'll be running into her while you're here. She lives downstairs."

For the first time, Gen caught real interest in Elizabeth O'Neill's eyes. More than interest, actually. Breathless awe.

"'Some men's dreams don't come true,'" the girl quoted from the play, her eyes going distant and soft. "'Some men, I guess, don't deserve them to.'"

Even hearing that line hurt Gen in old, sad ways. She smiled, though, and kept smiling, because this little girl didn't need her history.

"The good news," she said gently, "is that the real Luke did see his dreams come true. You'll get to meet him, too, if you like. Lee's new play is premiering in a couple of weeks, and he's coming into town for it."

Elizabeth's eyes seemed to grow even larger. "Then *Some Men's Dreams* really *was* written about your family?"

"Uh huh. Luke is based on my big brother, Jake."

Elizabeth tilted her head, considering. "Then you're Emma?"

"Oh, no," Gen disagreed with a grin. "I'm much prettier."

Elizabeth just shook her head, as if clearing it of impossibilities. "My family's so dull."

Gen couldn't help laughing. "Sometimes dull is a much preferable state, Elizabeth. Now, do you want something to eat? I'm starved."

"Oh, no, thanks," Elizabeth muttered, still distracted. "I ate just before I got to the field."

"Well, I do need food. I think the last time I ate was Thursday. And that was the popcorn I stole from X-ray. But first, unless you desperately need the bathroom, I'm going to soak three days of dirt off me."

"Oh, no," Elizabeth said, starting as if she were coming back to life. "I'm fine. Really. Uh, is there someplace nearby where I can run?"

"Like exercise?" Gen asked with a slight grimace. "If you insist. Dr. Viviano and I run a couple times a week. Come along."

"Oh, I need to run more than that. I really do."

Zealot, Gen thought with another grimace. Those runners were all alike. Which was why she ran with Abbie Viviano. Abbie knew that one ran just to be able to eat another box of Girl Scout cookies.

"I'll show you tomorrow, okay?"

Elizabeth looked out the window with a certain longing. "Okay. Thanks."

So Gen left Elizabeth opening her overnight case and headed for her own endorphin-booster. A little Debussy, maybe, or some Nat King Cole, a glass of lovely white Burgundy, and at least forty minutes in a hot, steamy bath to ease away every ache and cramp that had accumulated in the past three days.

Gen knew she should be thinking about how she was going to cover shifts tomorrow. About the 1012 questions she was going to have to answer while the boss remained in a state of injury-induced nonparticipation.

She should think about that girl in her bedroom. Something about the piquant little face tugged at old pains. Old struggles that even Lee hadn't brought to the stage.

But, Gen thought, those were all problems she could put off for a little while. For now she was bound and determined to enjoy a very selfish pleasure and worship at her personal altar of peace.

It had always been her way. Her escape. The sanctuary within which she dreamed. When Gen had been a teenager, she'd horded a transistor radio and Silhouette romances in the linen closet to read late at night in the tub when her responsibilities had been safely abed. During med school, she'd soaked in hot water and rock and roll and painted pictures of far places behind her eyelids. Now she didn't have to close her eyes at all. Peter Simpson, who had painted her mural, had done another for her bath.

And this one was a masterpiece.

It wasn't rolling Tuscan hills, though. Not stone archways or bright Italian sun. It was better. It was certainly more personal.

There on the wall at the foot of her tub, in perfect and realistic technicolor, rose a perfect replica of Michelangelo's *David* to smile down on her.

David, at least Peter's David, had lovely black hair and liquid brown eyes. Perfect pecs and the steeliest thighs a wall could hold. A big girl's fantasy, Lee had giggled when she'd seen it. A tired doctor's secret whimsy.

As strains of Verdi wafted through the room, Gen perused the David, her head cocked, and smiled. Always have a gay man paint the male anatomy, she thought. Not only was it beautiful, but it was so anatomically correct that she could use it to study for boards. Grandly, deliciously anatomically correct. More anatomically correct, Peter had insisted, than the original David, who he insisted fell woefully short of expectations.

Gen lifted her glass in a toast. To David. To friends. To whatever struck her fancy while she lay in her secret haven.

She closed her eyes and got her answer.

Oh, dear.

Usually Gen saw scenes. Places she'd been. Places she dreamed of going. Home, where the Wind River Mountains crowded the sky across a Wyoming sunset and winter was as harsh as the hospital. Italy, where the sun was a blessing and the colors seemed to swell before her eyes. The middle of Lake Michigan, where everything that mattered lay caught between wind and water, and the rest of the world simply disappeared.

Not this time.

This time she saw eyes.

Sea-blue eyes. Incandescent eyes. Eyes that could make a woman give thanks just to know they existed. Gen saw again those eyes like a perfect mirage. She saw the angles and shadows of the handsome face that carried them. The patrician nose with just that one small dent to keep it from being perfect. The dimple just to the left of his mouth when he smiled that belied the hard angles of his jaw.

His mouth.

She saw his mouth.

Dr. John Parker O'Neill's mouth.

He had a mouth like poetry. Like music. He had a mouth to which symphonies should be written. He had a mouth that carried a voice that could command in the quietest of words and bear humor like a stealth weapon. A voice that crept along a woman's nerves and set her scalp to tingling. A voice that was meant to be heard in the dark, whispering.

He had a voice that, with wit and whimsy, could diminish a disaster with a few well-chosen words and a chuckle.

Gen took another sip of wine and sighed.

Not because of the picture of her new boss that had taken shape in her mind. She would have had to be dead not to enjoy something that striking. What bothered her was her reaction to it.

An instinctive reaction, albeit rusty. A more sincere reaction than any she'd ever had to her personal David.

Her breasts felt suddenly full, her belly warm. She wanted to rub her bottom against the tub and arch herself against an imaginary hand. Gen wanted to know what those talented artisan's hands would feel like against her skin. What his skin would feel like uncovered, what mysteries he might lay bare if given the right provocation.

Heck, he had looked sexy even wearing that saggy, faded hospital gown. What would he look like without it?

Well, Gen decided with a chuckle as she took another sip of wine, if she was going to fantasize about a handsome man, it might as well be here in her tub where nobody could catch her. Especially a certain doctor.

She surely couldn't afford to do it anywhere else, no matter how much her pulse jumped when she actually saw him. Not only didn't she have the time or attention, with less than a month to go before finally graduating into the real world, she didn't have the right. She was, after all, drooling after the man in charge of her professional life for the next month.

But that was okay. Because she knew perfectly well that the brand-new head of pediatric critical-care medicine in one of the major medical centers of the Midwest sure as hell wasn't going to waste his time fantasizing about *her.*

But, oh, wouldn't it be nice, just for once, to be able to have the time, the attention span, the optimism, to begin and to nurture a new relationship? To meet in odd corners and exchange entire conversations with just looks and smiles? To savor the flare of an unexpected attraction without regret? To want without frustration? To flirt and tease and attract without hesitation?

What she would give to remember that shock of electricity at the touch of a man's fingers, the serendipity of a smile, the simple comfort of an embrace. To rediscover the fact that scent could mean something more than symptomology.

John O'Neill smelled like soap and subtle cologne. The expensive kind, a little citrus, a little something else. He didn't smell like hospitals or sickness or antiseptic. Gen thought she could fall in love with nothing more than his scent.

Taking another sip of wine, she stretched just to feel the shudder of steamy water over her suddenly sensitive skin. Was this a symptom of imminent freedom? Gen wondered. She hadn't taken the time for this kind of active fantasy in so long. But she was less than a month away from liberation. She was so close to the end of a very hard road that she could taste it.

Gen had so long trained herself not to react. Not to waste time with distraction. She had a goal to reach. A mission to accomplish. A dream to realize that had been paid for not only by her hard work but her brother's sacrifice.

Ah, that word.

*Sacrifice.*

Such a hard word. Such a sad word. Gen knew that John O'Neill understood that word. She knew it from the relationship he had with his daughter. From the shadows that weighted both their eyes, the subtext of their words. The silent, secret burdens they shared without so much as an utterance.

Gen recognized those things because her family had its own language. Its own history.

But it made her sad somehow to see it on John O'Neill's handsome face. In his daughter's soft eyes.

It made her want, for just that moment in her solitary haven, to share the whimsy of flirtation with him and know they could enjoy it like normal people.

But then, they weren't normal people, with normal people's burdens or dreams.

And Gen's dream had been bought at too high a price for her to sacrifice it now to whimsy.

Another month and she would be a real doctor. With a real schedule, not some marathon torture session. With real money to help her pay back her family and her loans. With real control over her life.

A future. The kind she hadn't actually ever envisioned. Not really. Not one of her very own that didn't owe itself to anyone else or bear anyone else's burdens. Gen had never really believed she would be lucky enough to make it that far.

But she had. And for the first time in her life, she could think about pleasing only herself.

Only, she kept seeing John Parker O'Neill and his too-quiet daughter stepping into her dream.

His daughter.

That quickly, Gen opened her eyes and sat up. She had a guest to see to. Not only that, she thought with another appreciative glance to old David, she'd better warn Elizabeth about the bathroom wall. Frescoes were all well and good, but Elizabeth was only twelve.

Reluctantly standing up, Gen yanked the plug, grabbed her towel and patted David on the belly for good luck. Then, just to make sure Dr. O'Neill's daughter didn't fall over in a faint the first time she walked into the bathroom, Gen practiced a little judicious censorship and draped her towel across the two towel hooks that bracketed David's hips.

Which would stay there only until Elizabeth decided to salve her pubescent curiosity and peek.

Wait till her father found out what he'd let his little girl in for.

# Chapter 3

What the hell had he let himself in for?

Jack O'Neill closed his eyes, saw the same damn thing he'd seen the last time he'd closed them and considered the ceiling instead. Acoustic tiles and instrument arms and the snaking linear art of multiple IV bags.

It was the ICU that was making him nuts. He knew that. He'd only been stuck there for a matter of hours, and already he was stir-crazy. Tied to a bed in a room that was never silent. Plagued by nausea and dizziness and the memory of a sweet, whimsical face leaning over his that gleamed with the summer heat and crinkled with concern.

He'd dreamed about her. Dropped off to sleep for no more than moments and seen her there, outlined by the sky, her hair on fire from the sun and her eyes wide and beguiling. He recognized her, as if he'd known her before. As if he'd known her always.

And he'd never felt that way about another soul on earth except his Meggie.

Why didn't he dream about Meggie? he wondered in frustration. He always had. She always settled him to sleep and then haunted the lonely hours of night.

Every night since she'd died.

Every damn night.

She laughed at him, confided in him, chastised him. She claimed him with her eyes, those huge blue eyes he'd fallen head over heels for when he'd been no more than fifteen, those eyes that now always seemed so gently reproachful.

And sad.

So sad.

But here, in this hospital where the noise was constant, like the chirp of insects, he hadn't been able to see those beloved blue eyes.

He'd seen hazel ones. Great, soft, intelligent hazel eyes.

And that simply wasn't something he would allow.

He'd made a promise to his Meggie. Eye to eye, hand to hand, as she lay dying in his arms. He'd promised to take care of their little girl. He'd promised that he would devote himself to it, to her, to being the best man and doctor he could.

He was doing that. And it took up all his time. Which meant that he didn't have time for fantasies or unruly hormones.

And yet he had woken to find himself not just dizzy but hard.

Hard.

Lord, he hoped nobody came in and noticed. He hoped if they did they would chalk it up to the head injury, which he knew could produce inconvenient symptomology like that.

He hoped like hell they didn't recognize the much more immediate reason. He hadn't had sex in probably a hundred years, and he'd dreamed about hazel eyes and the glisten of sweat on a long upper lip.

And that upper lip was spending time with his twelve-year-old daughter. His much-too-perceptive twelve-year-old daughter, who didn't need another complication in her life.

As if he did.

What the hell *had* he let himself in for?

"So, you enjoy theater?" Gen asked her young guest in desperation.

Elizabeth had sat at her table in silence while Gen had thrown

together her special chicken fried rice. The girl had played with
her plastic tumbler of ice water and tapped her feet on the floor.
She'd accepted a little rice and then proceeded to do no more
than make geometric patterns on her plate with it. She'd watched
her handiwork as if it were divination and then rearranged it
again.

And then she sat there.

Gen wished Lee were here. Lee could talk to rocks. Lee was
the people person. Gen was the big sister.

Big sisters organized. They ordered. They herded like collies.
They didn't, evidently, converse.

Elizabeth took so long to respond to Gen's question that she
almost forgot what it was she'd asked.

"Yes, ma'am. I do."

Theater, Gen thought, her sleep-deprived brain catching up.
"Have you seen any since you've been here? Chicago's a great
theater town."

A shake of Elizabeth's bent head. "No. We've been busy
settling in."

"I heard you lived in Boston before?"

A nod.

"I imagine you miss your friends."

A shrug.

This kid should be a mime, Gen thought, scooping up her last
spoonful of rice and dispatching it.

"I get homesick, too," Gen admitted, settling her cutlery.
"My family's from Wyoming. Wind River Mountains." Gen
saw, even as she said it, the high, whistling grass of the mead-
ows, the jagged sculpture of the mountains. Glossy, sleek horses
circling the pastures. She ached, just as she always did.

"But then, if you saw *Some Men's Dreams,* you know that."

"Are you going back?" Elizabeth asked in so quiet a voice
that Gen almost missed it.

"In about a year or so. I'm going to work the ED here long
enough to get some experience under my belt, sit for boards,
and pay off some of my student loans. Then I'm going to set
up practice in my old town."

"But you're in critical care."

"I'm doing a stint in critical care. We're isolated enough up in the mountains that I want to have a well-rounded base to last us till the helicopters come."

"*I'm* going home," Elizabeth blurted, then blushed and hung her head.

Gen heard echoes and layers in that young voice, and wanted to ask. She wanted to hold the girl in her lap and give her some comfort. Elizabeth O'Neill was much too self-contained for that, though.

"Must have been tough to move," Gen gently prodded.

Elizabeth shrugged. Kept her attention on her plate. "Daddy just couldn't live there anymore. He tried. He really did. But after my mom was killed by that drunk driver...." She stopped again, her attention on her plate, her eyes distant and brittle. Gen stayed silent, knowing there was more. Wondering if this angry child would share it with her.

She did.

"The funny thing?" Elizabeth said, looking up with those brittle, superior teenage eyes Gen recognized so easily from Lee's stint at the same age. "He used to talk about going somewhere like Wyoming. Someplace smaller, where they needed him. Where we'd ditch the rat race, and we'd..." For a second she struggled with the memories, with words that could seem such a betrayal. "After reading your sister's play, I thought it would be totally cool."

"After *Some Men's Dreams?*" Gen demanded, thinking of how bleak most of the scenery for that play was. A broken-down barn, a patched-up house, a weed-choked yard.

But Elizabeth didn't seem to hear her. "Daddy was offered the chance to be the chief here, though. He's the youngest head in the Midwest, you know. It's an honor."

Gen was getting whiplash. She so desperately wanted to answer one thing. An accusation, a question, a plea. She was so tired, though, and she had the strangest feeling that what she said would make a terrific difference. Briefly closing her eyes to marshall her acutely flagging energy, Gen picked a point with the science of tossing a dart and waded in.

"I've been gone from Wyoming for six years," she said. "It's really hard sometimes. But a lot more times I find that there are great things here. Great people, who've become my friends. And I know that I can go home again. You will, too, when you and your dad are ready."

Elizabeth didn't answer. She didn't make eye contact.

"Are your grandparents in Boston?" she asked, another random dart.

"No," Elizabeth said, still not making eye contact. "Florida."

Evidently not a favorite, either.

"Ah. Well, maybe if you'd like, while you're here, we could see some of the sights."

This time all she got was a shrug, as if Elizabeth suddenly realized how much she'd said and regretted it. Or as if she were running out of steam as quickly as Gen.

I should never have taken that bath, Gen thought. Somewhere during that time, I seem to have lost my ability to make sense of teenage conversation. Which meant that it was going to be a long few days. Sighing in defeat, Gen got to her feet and began cleaning up.

She was rinsing her dishes with so much purpose that she almost missed Elizabeth's voice entirely.

"He *is* going to be okay, isn't he?"

A little girl's voice. A daughter's voice.

Gen dropped the plate she'd been holding and spun around. In three steps she reached Elizabeth and crouched down onto her knees before the girl could raise her head. And then, whether Elizabeth wanted it or not, Gen took hold of her hands where they rested on her knees.

What an idiot she was, Gen thought. Of course Elizabeth was a little preoccupied.

"I'd love to say I could give you a guarantee like an infomercial," she said quietly. "But I'm afraid your dad's a little out of my league. He's at least a hundred pounds heavier than anybody I'm used to taking care of."

That at least got Elizabeth's eyes up so Gen could smile for her.

"But I talked to the people who do know. He's fine, Elizabeth. Well, not fine. His head's probably ringing like a cathedral bell, and his stomach thinks he's on the space shuttle. But the only reason he's even in the hospital instead of lounging around your house is because he's a bigwig. Hospitals take it badly if it looks like they're not taking care of their own bigwigs. Especially the youngest bigwig in the Midwest."

"I can see him tomorrow?"

"Of course. Right after we practice French."

Finally Gen got a true reaction from her guest. A universal, schoolwork-induced grimace.

Gen grinned and patted a knee. "I'll teach you all the French curse words I know. Just don't tell your dad. Oh, and, Elizabeth? I think I'd better tell you about my bathroom.…"

Gen should have been more surprised an hour later when Elizabeth asked to take a long bath.

It was six in the morning, and the only thing Gen was sure of was that she was way too tired. Way too tired, however, was not one of the acceptable excuses for not showing up at the hospital for an emergency. Especially when she'd been the one to put the man who should have handled the emergency on the adult side of the hospital.

So she rubbed her eyes, yawned and tiptoed to the doorway of his ICU room to check on said man before heading back home.

"Gorgeous, isn't he?" asked the night nurse, who stopped next to her.

Gen took a second to consider the swollen face, the grossly blackened eyes, the underlying skin color that still bore a close resemblance to wallpaper paste, and fought a smile.

"Oh, yeah," she said with a wry nod. "Deadly."

The nurse laughed. "He can't fool us with all that camouflage. Under that raccoon is a very handsome man."

Hard to argue with that.

"I hear you're the one who put him on the ICU bus. You must feel very secure about your career."

"I did before I went to that damn game."

"Aw, don't worry. You still have a leg up on the rest of us. You get to make friends with his daughter. A man can't deny a woman who comforts his kids, ya know."

Gen turned to see that the nurse had never taken her gaze from the shadowy aspect of the sleeping pediatric chief. "A leg up?" she asked. "For what?"

The nurse just turned and gave her that age-old woman smile. Donna, her name tag said. Gen didn't know her, since Gen didn't often visit this side of the hospital, but what she saw was humor and common sense, not salacious interest. Donna wasn't asking inappropriate questions. She was just participating in the oldest game in hospitals, sexual banter.

"If it means I can finally get some sleep," Gen assured her, "you can have the daughter *and* the leg."

Donna just snorted. "I knew there was something unnatural about you."

Gen didn't get her chance to answer, because just then one of the other room alarms went off. Donna was gone like a flash, and Gen was left to look into a shadowy room, wondering why she didn't just go home.

She wanted to make sure he was really okay, she thought. It had been a helluva hit.

She wasn't sure, though, why she stepped in for a closer look. It wasn't as if the numbers on his monitors would make any more sense than they had that morning. She made it as far as the foot of his bed before she realized that she wasn't the only one awake in the room.

"What are you doing here?" Dr. O'Neill demanded, his voice gravelly with early-morning weariness.

Gen jumped a foot.

"What are you doing awake?" she demanded right back.

Suddenly he was struggling to sit up. "Is it Elizabeth? Is something wrong with Elizabeth?"

Gen got to him just before he went over on his nose. "No," she assured him, her hands on his shoulders. "Elizabeth, if the gods are with us, is sound asleep in my guest room. She's fine."

"Then what are you doing here?"

Gen settled him back against his pillow and grinned. "I work here. And neither rain nor sleet nor preteen daughter of the department head will keep me from my unappointed rounds.''

He squinted at her. "You look like hell.''

Gen couldn't help but laugh. "I hope you don't expect me to say you look any better.''

She was glad when he closed his eyes. He wouldn't see her rub her hands along her pants to wipe off the sudden perspiration. He wouldn't be close enough to hear the sudden staccato of her heart.

Good grief, she thought. He looks like day-old hamburger, and I'm about to swoon. Her hands were tingling all the way to her elbows, and she'd done nothing more than push him back into bed.

At least she hadn't imagined her reaction to him.

But was that a good thing?

"Elizabeth isn't used to being alone," he insisted, his voice a little fainter, his color waxing and waning.

"She isn't. I got my sister to stay there till I got back. She lives downstairs.''

One eye opened. "My, you are an all-purpose doctor, aren't you?''

"It's the least I could do to impress my chief," she assured him.

"What kind of rounds?'' he asked, eye closing again.

Gen wanted to tell him to open it again. She wanted his teasing. She wanted, ridiculously enough, to settle herself on the side of his bed and just enjoy his company.

A man who was recovering from a head injury in the ICU. The man she'd singlehandedly put there.

She needed to stay out of that bathtub.

*Rounds.* Oh, yeah. What had brought her in, he wanted to know, at six in the morning?

"Newborn with a hypoplastic left ventricle," she said. "It's a toss-up if he's going to make it long enough to get a Norwood shunt put in. They're trying to get the cardiac team ready while we keep him out of congestive failure.''

A beautiful mite of a thing with wide blue eyes, downy black hair and a critically defective heart. A baby with the same name as Gen's big brother. Jake. Jacob Edward. Too big a name for such a tiny, fragile thing. Gen had been able to hold him in one hand, like a baby bird fallen from his nest.

"Looks like it's been a long pull," Dr. O'Neill observed.

Gen could do no more than nod. For a few minutes they tossed treatment and drug choices back and forth, but Gen had done everything she could to give the baby his best chance, and they both knew it.

Or, Gen thought a second later, maybe she was the only one who knew it. Because suddenly there was Dr. O'Neill swinging his legs over the side of the bed again.

"If you'll give me a hand, maybe I can be of some…" He stopped even before he attempted to sit up. "What's so funny?"

Gen couldn't keep the amusement from her eyes. "I'm just trying to figure out how the family's going to react to you."

Dr. O'Neill grimaced manfully. "Because I'm in a patient gown?"

"No. Because you have the trademark Rawlings imprinted backward on your forehead." Gen tilted her own head a little to better consider the phenomenon even as she ignored her boss's massive scowl.

"It's very impressive," she said. "I can read every letter."

She got another grimace, this one with a wry twinkle in those wonderful sea-blue eyes, the eyes she saw when she closed her own, those eyes that—

Gen had to pull herself together. She almost missed what he said.

"…little more respect for your betters, if not your elders, Dr. Kendall."

Gen chuckled. "You were certainly in a better mood yesterday afternoon."

"You said you were sorry yesterday afternoon."

"And I was," she assured him with a broad smile. "That hit should have easily gone for extra bases."

Dr. O'Neill's laugh seemed to surprise him. It certainly must have surprised his head, if the quick wince was any indication.

"Another line like that, young doctor, and I'll have you pulling shifts till you reach menopause."

"Ah," Gen responded, the delight of sparring with him bubbling in her. "But you only have control over me for another month, older doctor. And unless I'm a medical miracle, I should be able to retain my childbearing capabilities at least a month or two beyond that."

"Not if I get my hands on you…" he muttered, struggling to keep the grin from his face.

Gen waited a moment, knowing she should leave. Catching that faint scent of citrus and something else and wondering how it had survived amidst the hospital miasma.

She cleared her throat and kept her hands to herself. She turned for the door. "Elizabeth will be by later today. She'll be very reassured you're okay."

She almost made it out to safety where she could hide herself among the staff. Where she could distract herself from Jack O'Neill long enough to get home. Safely past that door and beyond the radius of Dr. O'Neill's personal force field.

"Wait…"

It was no more than instinct and the peculiar sound of his voice that spun Gen around.

"What the hell do you think you're doing?" she demanded, already on the run.

Dr. O'Neill had almost reached his feet.

She caught him just as his knees buckled. Just as his eyes rolled up and his face lost the rest of its color. Relying on instincts and training, Gen spun far enough around so that his heavier weight didn't pull them both flat to the floor. Instead she landed flat on her back on the bed with an unconscious doctor on top of her.

A gorgeous unconscious doctor.

The gorgeous unconscious doctor of her dreams.

Oh, hell, what else could go wrong?

"You have to let me up," she insisted in his ear, where his face rested against her throat. Gen could feel his breath against her damp skin, and chills raced all the way down to her toes. Her heart raced from more than exertion. Her nipples pebbled. She could smell that citrus cologne and man sweat, which seemed to be a powerful aphrodisiac.

She tried her damnedest to unwrap her arms from around him and couldn't. "Please," she begged, too frantic to worry about sounding...well, frantic. "If I get caught in bed with you right now, my fellowship goes right out the window, and a lot of kids are depending on me."

"Yours or somebody else's?" he asked right against the sensitive skin of her throat.

That did it. Gen all but melted onto the bed.

"What? Mine?" she demanded instead as she gave him a good push so that he began to roll off her. "Dear God, no. I have enough on my plate right now, thank you. I'm talking about the kids in my hometown who are waiting for me to finish my training."

He reached his back, where he landed with arms outflung like a particularly handsome rag doll. Her legs still tangled with his, Gen leaned over him, knowing she should do something. She was a doctor, after all, and his skin was the color of putty.

But just as she reached out to check something, his pulse, his skin tone, something, his eyes opened, and all Gen could manage was a stunned stare.

"Okay," he said with a distracted nod, his gaze locked onto hers. "Then I'll just have to wait till you're out to get you into bed."

Gen froze. She caught the flare of surprise in his eyes and realized that he'd just said something he hadn't intended. Something, she thought suddenly, he just might have meant.

Oh, hell.

# Chapter 4

"**W**ow!" a by-now familiar voice caroled with great delight from the doorway. "I need a camera! The hospital newsletter's gonna *love* this."

Still only halfway off the bed, Gen closed her eyes in mortification.

"Only if the story is that the new chief of pediatric critical care is an idiot," Dr. O'Neill said with perfect, precise meaning.

Donna didn't lose an ounce of bravado. "You guys are always ruining my fun," she whined as she marched into the room. "He was trying to get up again, wasn't he?"

"He was," Gen assured her as she finally managed to untangle herself and make it the rest of the way to her feet. "I don't suppose you could have warned me. I caught him right before he took out two monitors and an IVAC."

Donna shook her head briskly. "If I warned you, you would have lost points in the game. Besides, the more equipment he takes out, the more points *I* get. And the more new equipment the hospital can charge to his account. So far he's good for an IV pump, two electric thermometers and an EKG machine from the last time he tried to get up."

"I think you left that EKG machine there on purpose," Dr. O'Neill groused.

"Of course I did," Donna assured him, finally heading over to the bed. "We've needed a new one for months. I'm just not sure where he thinks he's going."

"He's right here," Dr. O'Neill reminded her as he struggled to yank the blanket up over his bare legs and too-revealing patient gown and into a more decorous arrangement. "And can probably answer for himself."

"I doubt he can make sense, though," Gen grumbled, brushing at her terminally crumpled scrubs. "Since there isn't any good reason to get out of bed when you can't stand up in the first place."

"It's the delusions of grandeur that come with a new position," Donna assured her. "I've seen it happen before."

With two very economical moves, Donna got Dr. O'Neill straightened up, comfortable and well-covered. She even patted the top of his head like a two-year-old. "Would you mind waiting till day shift before you do this again? We don't have anybody else here right now who can manage another save like slugger's over here."

"Did ya like it?" Gen asked, trying very hard to hide the trembling in her hands. "I'm quite proud of that little move."

"One of the lessons the pediatric fellows learn here?" Dr. O'Neill grumbled.

"Dear heavens, no," Gen said with a too-big grin, as if her heart weren't still thundering in her chest. "I used to have a real job. I worked my way through premed as a nurse's aide."

"And aren't you just glad she did?" Donna asked the disgruntled physician. "I sure as heck wasn't going to catch you."

Dr. O'Neill growled at her. She laughed right back. Gen edged toward the door, hoping the furious blush that had scorched her Irish/Scots skin had paled a little.

"And I'm not doing it again," Gen said, keeping her gaze just to the left of Dr. O'Neill's eyes, as if that would keep her safe. "I'm going home."

Safe.

Stupid her. She was still breathing hard, and she wanted to fall right back onto that bed.

He had legs. Well, of course he had legs. But he had *great* legs. Strong and hairy and manly, just begging for her touch. Legs she somehow hadn't really noticed out on that softball field. Well, she noticed them now.

Not only that, but she'd been plastered up against him like a wet sheet. Gen didn't know what he looked like beneath that atrocious patient gown, but she knew what he felt like. Michelangelo's David was a nerd with a pocket protector.

David had also never, at least in her bathroom, reacted quite so strongly to the close proximity of a woman.

The effects of concussion, Gen thought frantically, the memory of that surprise still shaking her. Nothing more than an embarrassing side effect of a skull fracture. After all, she'd seen it before.

"If this is the way you're going to be, young doctor," Dr. O'Neill spoke up, "don't feel obligated to show up when Elizabeth stops by."

Gen grinned, still not actually facing him. "Wouldn't miss it. By then, who knows what other secret messages we'll be able to read on your face?"

"Probably Medtronics," Donna suggested, rechecking the IV machine of the same name.

"I'm going back to sleep now," Dr. O'Neill announced, as if it would forestall more abuse.

"I'm going home," Gen said.

But just before she left, for a nanosecond no one else would notice, she looked back. Just to check, as if she could convince herself with another look that she'd really seen that sharp, sudden hunger in his eyes a moment ago. Or, better yet for everybody involved, that she hadn't.

Unfortunately, she couldn't. He'd been watching for her to turn. He smiled. Only a little, as if he were just as bemused by what had happened as she was.

Gen felt that wry little smile to the very tips of her toenails.

Oh, hell, and here she'd thought her life was going to get simpler when she graduated her fellowship.

Suddenly she wasn't at all sure she was ever going to get that far.

\* \* \*

One foot in front of the other.

That's a girl. You can do it.

Three more steps.

Gen was so exhausted she didn't trust herself not to just curl up on the apartment stairs and fall asleep. She shouldn't have taken the extra time to see Dr. O'Neill. She shouldn't have inhaled the scent of him. She shouldn't...

She just wished she understood it. She wished she could still laugh about it, but she couldn't.

She simply didn't comprehend her reaction to Jack O'Neill.

She'd had boyfriends. She'd had two lovers, impulsive, exciting young men she'd succumbed to in premed, in those first heady years of her freedom from drudgery. From sickness and death and a struggling ranch that had seemed, for so long, to be made up of nothing but dust and overdue notices.

She'd enjoyed her experiences. She wouldn't say she hadn't. But she'd never conjured a man's eyes in the steam of a solitary bath. She'd never felt as if she were tumbling face first off a cliff when she met him, no matter how tired or traumatized she was.

She'd never let herself.

She shouldn't now.

She *couldn't* now.

It didn't seem to matter. She was still trembling, and no matter how much she wanted to tell herself it was exhaustion, she knew better. And no matter how hard she tried, she couldn't manage to forget the intriguing feel of the very distinctive pressure she'd felt against her thigh.

Gen shook off that last thought just about the moment she realized that she'd come to a stop about halfway up the last flight of stairs. For a second she just blinked. Then she saw what had made its way through the haze to bring her to a halt.

Gen looked up to find her sister, Lee, standing perfectly still by her apartment door, her expression just as stunned as Gen's. But before Gen could ask why, she finally realized what had stopped them both in their tracks.

Music.

Piano music.

The most beautiful piano music Gen had ever heard issue forth from her lovely Emily's ivory keys.

"What are you doing out here?" Gen asked her sister, her attention still on the door, rather than the perky blonde standing before it.

She always thought of Lee as perky because it so annoyed her sister. But perky she was. Perky and pretty and unquestionably brilliant.

But then, Gen was prejudiced.

Lee never turned her attention from the doorway. "I went down to get Rock off to school. You know we never miss that time together, since I'm gone so many evenings. I told Elizabeth I was going. I figured she'd still be in bed when I got back. But when I got here, I heard the music, and I thought you'd gotten home." Lee tilted her head a moment, listening. "But then I got this far and realized it couldn't be you. You're not that good."

Gen managed a scowl. "Thanks."

But she wasn't. Nobody Gen knew was. She could manage Bach. Some Beethoven. Show tunes. She couldn't wrap her fingers anywhere near Schopenhauer, which was what she thought she heard coming out of her apartment.

"You get a new CD?" Lee asked.

"If I did it wouldn't be that. It'd be…uh, not that."

Lee shot her a sly look. "Then what *would* it be?"

Gen damn near blushed again. "Not that. Wanna see what's going on in there?"

Lee swung her attention back to the door. "I think I'm afraid to."

Gen just nodded and finished climbing the stairs. "Yeah. Me, too."

But she opened her front door anyway.

After hearing that waterfall of music spilling across her wood floor, she shouldn't have been surprised at what she found. She was anyway.

Emily the piano should have been smiling. Purring in delight.

Finally fingers that did her justice. An artistic soul that matched her craftsmanship. And from a twelve-year-old girl with braids.

For a long time Gen and Lee just stood watching. Elizabeth didn't notice them. She was one with that piano, like a samurai with his sword. Bent over, swaying and grimacing and flowing right along with her music. Caught in the morning sun that filled that front window, her movements sending the dust motes dancing.

It was a moment of magic, and Gen was loath to stop it. She was afraid that if she moved, it would all vanish, like soap bubbles.

She was hesitant to come between that surprising child and her music.

Because Gen saw something that a thousand other people wouldn't see. But then, she was privileged. She was surrounded by gifted people.

Not just talented people. People with that rare, precious something that set them so far apart from the rest of the humdrum, unaware world that sometimes they couldn't even communicate what they knew to others. People who lived on a different plane entirely than most of the sorry human race.

Gen didn't live on that plane. She was a worker bee. A doer, a facilitator. She was a good doctor. But she didn't create magic. She didn't live and breathe and die for something as ephemeral as the notes that sparkled and spun around her in the morning sun.

Lee was one of those rare people, a purveyor of truth and sorcery in the elusive moments of stagework. Gen's sister-in-law, Amanda, who wove words into miracles that became award-winning books. Gen's brother Jake, whose gift lay in his hands and feet and his communion with horses.

Gen wasn't one of them, but she recognized them. She recognized the look that came over them when they were caught in the compulsion of their art. The otherworldly glow that took a witness's breath and made a normally sane person jealous, like Salieri hearing Mozart. Because not that many people were invited to that place. That realm.

That realm that Elizabeth O'Neill now ruled.

And Gen, who loved the piano, who loved people who carried the kind of genius that could make such an instrument a thing of wonder, was jealous, because she knew she would never experience it herself.

Elizabeth brought her piece to a close with the lightest of fairy touches, and Gen could almost feel her piano sigh like a woman after orgasm. For a long moment the room held nothing more than the fading echo of the last notes. Neither Gen nor Lee moved. Both knew better than to profane that perfect moment with applause. They simply waited for Elizabeth to come back and notice them.

"Oh…"

Gen smiled at the confusion in Elizabeth's eyes when she finally spotted them. Halfway off the bench, the girl froze like a deer in a scope. Embarrassment fled across her gamine face, hesitation, just a breath of defiance.

"If that's a little," Gen said quietly, "I'd be terrified to hear what you could do if you played a lot."

"I'm sorry," Elizabeth apologized, reaching her feet. Scooting away from the bench, as if caught in an illicit act.

"For what? Giving me the only really lovely moments I've had in the last four days?"

"I shouldn't…I mean…"

"Please," Lee begged, walking closer. "Don't apologize. You've made our Emily happy. And us, come to think of it. Thank you."

Elizabeth's head came up in surprise. "I was afraid I bothered you."

"Oh, you bothered me a lot," Gen admitted with a grin.

"You reminded her how much better a doctor she is than a pianist," Lee giggled.

"I envy you," Gen told the little girl. "To have a talent that wonderful to pursue. I have no talent but differentiating heart sounds. Not the same. God knows, the tunes certainly aren't nearly as nice."

"Rhythm's better," Lee retorted.

"Well, you hope so."

"Pursue?" Elizabeth echoed, stiffening to some kind of attention. "Oh, no, it's not like that. It's just…you know, like, a hobby. But the more proficient I am, the better it looks on a med school application. It's been documented that science and music have, like, a definite correlation. Med schools like to see musical ability."

Both Gen and Lee stood there stunned into momentary silence.

"Med school?" Lee laughed. "*Med* school? You're twelve."

Elizabeth blinked as if she'd missed something. "Yes?"

For a second Lee just stared at her, as if she couldn't figure out how to ask an obvious question. Gen just watched. When she'd been playing, Elizabeth had as much been the music as played it, lithe and supple and sweet. Suddenly she was stiff, severe.

It was as if she'd donned some kind of protective clothing. A cloaking device of some kind.

Gen recognized it. She didn't know what it hid, but it was certainly more than the fact that Elizabeth O'Neill ached for the music she played.

"You'd really rather be a doctor?" Lee finally asked, frowning.

Elizabeth took another step away from the piano, as if declaring her loyalties. "Of course," she said in a grave little voice that sounded almost coached. "I want to help people."

What Gen didn't hear was, *I want to be a doctor.*

Lee flashed Gen a look of pure frustration and then shrugged. Lee, Gen knew, had thought she'd found another one of "them." Another artist she could trade rarified insight with, exchange arcane and complicated theories or share the simple joy of the perfect moment in art. When she'd heard that piano from out in the hallway, Lee had actually glowed herself.

But now wasn't the moment to solve that particular conundrum. Gen was weaving on her feet, and Lee refused to acknowledge that any brain function was possible before noon.

Gen saw her shrug away the mystery like a pesky insect.

"Well," Lee said blithely, "if you're right about that music thing on a med school application, you should be a shoo-in. Until then, we'll just enjoy your practicing. If you don't mind.''

''No...'' Again Elizabeth looked bemused, her head ducking in discomfort. ''I guess not.''

Gen just wished she'd gotten a little more sleep. She felt unsettled, unhappy with the course of this conversation. But she was too tired to pull the pertinent facts together.

''You're getting that glazed 'I've been on call for a month' look, big sister,'' Lee said, giving her a little shove. ''How 'bout if I take the baby bird off your hands?'' Without waiting for confirmation, she turned to Elizabeth. ''Wanna see a play rehearsal? Ian Griffin's going to be there.''

Ian Griffin, the latest hot young star who had taken on Lee's play to prepare it for a possible Broadway run as his claim to legitimacy. Gen saw the information sink into that pubescent brain and grinned.

''What a great idea,'' she said. ''I'll meet you both at Fandango at three, and we'll have a late lunch at Juan Ton's so we can finish up plans for your opening-night party.''

Gen had collected some five uninterrupted hours of sleep in the past seventy-six. Even so, it took her a while to settle in that morning. She couldn't get those notes out of her head. The vision of that intense, shining face caught amid sunshine and genius.

Genius.

The gift so few had.

The gift so few understood.

And young Elizabeth O'Neill, who *did* have it, was going to sacrifice it to be the doctor she didn't want to be.

And she knew this at twelve.

Why can't I ever find myself in an easy situation? Gen wondered bleakly. All I set out to do was help my softball team hold its head up, and suddenly I'm hip deep in shocking hormones and sudden perplexities. And all she wanted to do was finish her fellowship and feel free for the first time in her life of other people's problems and expectations.

But it was never that easy, was it?

* * *

Jack woke at noon. He knew that because there was a big clock on the wall across from his bed. Something they didn't worry about in the land of pediatrics. Six-month-olds were never quite as concerned with how much of their lives they were wasting in a hospital bed.

For once, the need to focus on the business at hand failed to rule Jack's thoughts, though. No, what ruled his thoughts was the all-too-vivid memory of him lying atop Gen Kendall that morning. Of the sweet softness of her beneath him, and his instinctive, potentially embarrassing reaction to her scent.

She'd smelled like peaches. Peaches in a hospital ICU. Probably the hand soap in the bathrooms, he tried to tell himself.

It didn't matter. She'd brought peaches and soft, full breasts into his room, and he'd reacted like a high school jock behind the bleachers.

Maybe she hadn't noticed. Maybe she'd been so distracted by what he'd said that she hadn't felt how hard he'd gotten in no more than fifteen seconds.

What he'd said.

Jack closed his eyes, completely mortified.

He couldn't have said what he thought he had. He simply couldn't have.

He couldn't even have thought it, much less said it. Not to his critical-care fellow. Not to the woman to whom he'd entrusted his daughter.

But he had. And he'd meant it.

He still did, as evidenced by the fact that the sheet didn't lie quite flat over his hips. He wanted Genevieve Kendall.

Jack shook his head at his own folly and was almost disappointed that it no longer felt as if it would fall off. He deserved a little punishment.

No, a lot of punishment.

He had been reprehensible with her. Unforgivable.

He never would have talked that way to Meggie. Well, not until they'd been married awhile, anyway. Meggie hadn't been somebody who took to casual sex talk. Meggie had believed that sex was something too precious for that. And with Meggie, it *had* been. Which, maybe, was why he had reacted so strongly to Gen Kendall.

Jack had the feeling, whether he wanted to or not, that it could be the same with her. Bright and funny and sweet, and dark as smoke at the same time. He didn't think Gen Kendall brought less than all of herself to anything she did. But, he thought, she wouldn't offer that unique gift lightly or freely.

She certainly wouldn't with him.

He couldn't afford to consider it. He simply wasn't in a position to handle any more than casual sex. He had promises to keep that precluded anything more. He also knew without any question that he would never be able to offer her more, or accept less. At least from her.

She deserved more.

And he couldn't give it.

Not now. Not ever.

It didn't make the ache for her ease.

It did, however, give him a sense of purpose. From this moment on, he would simply avoid Gen in any fashion except at work. He would thank her for her care of Elizabeth, treat her like a trusted colleague, and hope this month with her on his service flew by.

By about four o'clock and after two more naps, he'd firmly convinced himself of the rightness of his actions. He'd made himself believe that Gen probably hadn't really heard him that morning. That if she had, she wouldn't place any significance on it. Even though he'd seen the heat in her eyes when she'd turned back to him in that final moment.

It didn't matter. He was strong. He was, for God's sake, the youngest head of service in the history of the med center. He could do this.

He would have been a lot happier about his conviction had Elizabeth not run into his room no more than fifteen minutes later to rhapsodize about meeting Ian Griffin at rehearsal for a play.

"And Lee said she could score us two tickets for the premiere," she said, her beautiful blue eyes more alive than he'd seen in weeks. "We can go with her family, Dad. Won't that be wonderful?"

At which point Jack O'Neill knew he was doomed. Because no matter how strong he was, he couldn't refuse his baby girl anything.

Even an entire evening spent with Gen Kendall and her whole family.

Damn.

Gen was tired again. Well, all right, she'd been tired since she started med school. No, probably since her twelfth birthday. But it seemed that she hadn't had a full two hours' sleep since beginning her last month's rotation in critical care. And today was no different.

She'd meant to get back at 7:00 a.m., after her thirty-six-hour on-call shift, so she could accompany Elizabeth to get her father from the hospital. But she'd been held up by, of course, an emergency.

Tiny Jacob Edward again. Jacob Edward Christian, who'd had a bleeding crisis after surviving his first-stage Norwood shunt surgery for his defective heart. Jacob Edward who had claimed five hours from her, and another round of tears and anxiety from his parents, a couple who had almost become Gen's personal family. It was she they called with questions, she they asked for advice. She they simply cried on when it all became too much.

As it had again this morning.

But Jacob had survived, and Gen had trudged home.

"We're gonna be late," Elizabeth fretted as Gen pulled fresh underwear and socks from her drawer in preparation for the quick shower she refused to miss.

"We have the car," Gen retorted, catching a look at herself in the gilt-framed mirror she'd found at a flea market and flinching. She really had to figure a way not to look so…tired when she was tired. The ringed-eye look really only worked for lemurs. And she wasn't in the mood for attracting any randy lemurs today. In the mood she was in, the silent and studly David was probably just about all she could handle.

Sighing, she shut the drawer and headed back out of her room.

"He can't go anywhere without his Volvo, Elizabeth. Play some scales while I shower."

"I don't really need to play any scales," the girl said from where she was bouncing back and forth on her feet by the front window.

"*I* need you to play," Gen said without elaborating.

Elizabeth looked abashed, but she sat down.

She'd just slammed into a discordant opening key when somebody knocked on Gen's door. Gen seriously thought about ignoring it and just heading for the bathroom. But Elizabeth was climbing to her feet, and the knock came again.

Gen retraced her steps to the front door and opened it.

And stopped dead in her tracks.

"What are *you* doing here?" she demanded instinctively.

Jack O'Neill grinned, even as he gently panted and sweated on her doorstep. Even so, he looked better. After a week, the bruising had faded to a lovely pastel yellow, and the swelling was down. He was dressed and pressed and groomed as if he were on his way to work, not home from a stint in his own hospital.

"Daddy?" Elizabeth gasped, and all but shoved Gen out of the way. "Are you okay? Why didn't you wait for us? Oh, I told her we'd be late, but she just got here, and she wouldn't let me go without her."

"We have the car" was all Gen could think to say as she watched Elizabeth guide her father over to one of the overstuffed couches.

Before Gen closed the door, she took another look outside, just to be sure he hadn't brought somebody else with him. Like Elvis.

"I knew you wouldn't get there before they dismissed me," Jack said, plopping onto the couch as if his legs had given out. "The Christian baby, wasn't it?"

Gen didn't answer him. She really didn't know what to say. He was sitting there in her living room, when all she could think of was that early-morning romp in the ICU no more than a week earlier. Heck, she'd seen him since, ensconced in his hospital room like a potentate with all the other residents there asking advice and blessings. She'd gone in alone, and she'd been in with Elizabeth, and she'd been able to act like a perfectly rational human being without letting any hint escape that she had been caught almost in flagrante with him in his room.

He hadn't even betrayed embarrassment, which made Gen wonder if he even remembered what had happened. It reinforced her belief that what had happened had been an aftereffect of his head injury, that his reaction had been completely inadvertent and meant nothing.

She wished she could say the same for herself.

This was her home. Her sanctuary. And she wasn't sure she wanted him here with his great legs and beautiful eyes and unbearable chemistry to disrupt it.

So she did what she always did in a crisis. She turned into a big sister.

"Elizabeth," she said, in her best physician voice, "get your dad some water."

He was still smiling, but his skin was the color of putty, and there were droplets of sweat on his temples. The last thing Gen needed was her chief—her sexy, handsome chief—upchucking on her good Italian silk pillows.

"I'm fine," he insisted.

Gen made to wave off his statement, when she realized that her hand was still full. Of her bra and panties.

Well, there went her sangfroid. Blushing like a teenager, she shoved them into the pocket of her lab coat and ignored Dr. O'Neill's chuckle. Then, straightening back into competence mode, she followed Elizabeth to the kitchen.

"I'll get the whiskey."

"For you or me?" Dr. O'Neill asked.

"For the man who's about to land face first on my floor," Gen retorted.

He chuckled. "That's okay. Water's quite enough."

"Daddy doesn't drink," Elizabeth whispered loudly enough that Mrs. Moffitt on the first floor should have been in on the secret. "Not since…"

"Yeah," Gen whispered right back as she shoved the whiskey bottle back into the cabinet. "I get it."

So she got a cold washcloth instead.

"Dr. O'Neill…"

He raised a hand in objection. "You know, I think it's about time we overcame that burden. My friends call me Jack. And anybody who can put up with Elizabeth for a week without simply dumping her at my feet is my friend."

"Oh, Daddy," Elizabeth protested in classic little-girl fashion.

"Elizabeth isn't the one who persists in bad behavior," Gen said without thinking.

For just a second she thought she saw a flash of mortification in the doctor's eyes. She was suddenly plagued by another of her fiery blushes. She ignored them both.

"I'm sure that as the youngest chief of pediatric critical care medicine in the Midwest, you gave considerable thought to the fact that a man who's just been discharged from the hospital should not climb three flights of stairs," she archly informed him as she stalked back into the living room. "Especially when he's eventually going to have to get back down again."

"Oh," Jack O'Neill said. "*That* bad behavior."

Gen ignored that, too. Elizabeth ran back in with the glass of water. Gen slapped her rag against the back of Jack's neck. He just grinned and sipped and waited as the color slowly seeped back into his face.

"I was impatient," he admitted. "I wanted to see my mouse."

His mouse collapsed at his feet like a pet spaniel, her big eyes focused on him as if waiting for him to die right in front of her.

"We were late," Elizabeth said again, as if apologizing.

Jack reached a hand over to cup her cheek. "Honey, it's not your fault. And I'm fine. Just a little…out of shape. This apartment was farther away than I thought."

"The bathroom in your house is going to be farther away than you thought for a few days," Gen retorted, not knowing how to make it better. Not knowing what to do with this man in her living room.

He filled the empty places with his smile. His laughter echoed like music. Gen wondered if she would still get all tingly just from being in the room with him after she finally got a good night's sleep.

Maybe it was just exhaustion that kept doing this to her.

She thought of trying to make another run for that hot shower and gave up. Sighing with as much drama as she could, she settled herself onto the couch next to him.

And regretted it right away.

There was still that something. Lightning. Quicksilver. Static electricity.

She was tingling again, and breathless, and she wanted to move.

She wanted to stay.

She wanted to bang her head against the wall in frustration.

"How did you get here?" Elizabeth asked her dad.

He kept his hand on her head as if grounding himself with her. "One of the residents gave me a lift."

"One of the residents would probably have given you his *kidney*," Gen retorted.

Jack laughed. "Undoubtedly. Fortunately for him, I only needed a ride. I thought I'd save you some time."

"Not if you'd fallen down three flights of stairs."

His grin was bright and challenging. "Mighty feisty for a woman who still needs a positive evaluation from me at the end of the month."

"That's okay," she said with a blithe wave of her hand. "The way you're going, you're not going to be alive at the end of the month."

She'd no sooner gotten the words out of her mouth than she realized how ill-advised that kind of statement was. "Oh, Elizabeth…"

"He won't listen to me, either," the girl said with a scowl at her father, completely unaffected.

Her father, now laughing, let them both off the hook. "I promise I won't sue either of you for negligence. I just couldn't spend another minute in a hospital bed, all right?"

Elizabeth patted him on the knee as if he were the child. "We'll let you get away with it this time."

For just a second Jack looked surprised. Then he ruffled Elizabeth's hair and took a sip of water.

"This is really a nice place," he said, looking around.

"You should see the bathroom," Elizabeth chortled.

Jack looked surprised again. He looked even more surprised when Gen nudged Elizabeth in the ribs with her foot.

"What does she mean?"

"She means it's pretty," Gen said.

Elizabeth giggled.

Jack took another look at both of them. "Maybe I should take a look myself."

Gen refused to make eye contact. Elizabeth couldn't stop giggling. Jack looked as if he were about to get to his feet.

Just then the front door swung open and Lee came strolling in.

"Oh, hi," she said. "You must be the famous, youngest-chief-in-the-Midwest dad," she greeted him. "I'm Lee, Gen's about-to-be-famous-playwright sister."

Gen darn near hung her head in mortification. She didn't. That came when Lee walked on up to them and grinned.

"Has he seen the bathroom yet?"

# Chapter 5

He saw the bathroom.

He saw it and walked out looking pale again.

"I didn't expect to be entertaining a twelve-year-old anytime soon when I had it painted," Gen said, defending herself.

Now Lee was giggling.

"Oh, Daddy," Elizabeth objected. "I see worse things on TV."

He gave his daughter a long, assessing look. "Well, it looks like I'll be locking out some channels."

Elizabeth gave him the classic teen eye roll.

Fortunately, Gen saw the twinkle in his eye. She hungered for that damn twinkle in his eye.

"Well, don't expect me to paint pants on him," she challenged.

"Certainly not shorts," Lee muttered.

"I appreciate art as much as anybody else," Jack offered before Gen blithely interrupted him.

"Elizabeth and I had a *very* productive lesson in muscle identification for the science camp she's going to next week," she said.

"Except we didn't get to see my favorite," Elizabeth said.

Jack simply plopped back onto the couch, as if it were all too much for him. "Gluteus maximus?" he asked in a very long-suffering manner.

Elizabeth's smile was almost piratical. "Lee said she'd take me to a Cubs game so I could evaluate the ball players' glutes."

"Glutes?" her father retorted, sounding outraged.

Elizabeth looked very superior. "It's what women in the know call buns. Don't they, Gen?"

"Ask Lee," Gen suggested. "I haven't been in the know for years."

"She hasn't," Lee mourned dramatically. "No matter how hard I work on her. The family has a bet going that David's the only naked male over the age of fifteen she's seen since she started her residency."

"*That* was probably more than anybody needed to hear," Gen protested.

"It's probably true," Elizabeth giggled.

Gen gave her a mock cuffing, and the girl giggled all over again.

Jack seemed to need to hold his head up with his hands about then. "I've lost control over my child."

Elizabeth settled at his feet again. "Don't be silly, Daddy."

Lee laughed. "You never had control of her."

Jack just shook his head. Gen was once again fighting the feeling of unreality. It seemed so comfortable here, so whole and bright and happy with Jack and Elizabeth in her home, as if they belonged there. As if their laughter had already been woven tightly through the fabric of her life.

"You want to get your stuff, honey?" Jack asked his daughter with another pat and kiss.

"You're not leaving yet," Gen informed him quite severely. "I don't have enough liability insurance to let you try those stairs again yet. Besides, I bet you haven't eaten lunch, and nobody in their right mind considers hospital food nutritious. Why don't you guys hang around for a little while?"

Why don't I just drive a nail through my eye? she thought in distress. In the long run, it would probably bother her less.

"Yeah," Lee countered, yanking Elizabeth to her feet and guiding her toward the bedroom that had once been hers. "If you're *really* lucky, Elizabeth will throw together something positively *yummy,* like roots and berries."

"Salad's good for you," Elizabeth protested halfheartedly from the doorway.

"So's protein," Lee could be heard retorting. "And I just happen to like mine medium rare and slathered in cheese."

Gen was already turning back to Jack when she heard the very distinctive "Eeeew" that comprised Elizabeth's editorial comment on Lee's diet. Rock's diet, actually. Lee actually ate much the way Elizabeth did, a lot of fresh vegetables and whole wheat products. She just loved getting a teenage reaction from the girl.

Jack was looking bemused again.

"Problem?" Gen asked, itching to touch him. To nestle against him like a favorite pet.

Oh, God, she thought immediately. Now I'm so tired I'm thinking in terms that are completely politically incorrect.

It still didn't mean she didn't want a snuggle.

Jack turned back to her and smiled, and Gen thought people would gladly die for that smile. "I think you've been a good influence on Elizabeth."

Gen raised an eyebrow. "You've just been waiting for permission to put a naked man on your bathroom wall, too?"

He gave her a great scowl. "You might have let me know about that."

"Before or after I was making sure your pupils reacted to light?"

Jack laughed, and Gen fought a fresh wave of exhilaration.

"What I meant," he said, "is that Elizabeth is laughing more."

"You can blame Lee and Emily for that," Gen assured him. "My only contribution to the week was as running partner and salad tosser. And may I say that it is a particularly brutal form of humiliation to find oneself run into the dust by a twelve-year-old. Might I suggest you sew some weights to that child's rear end?"

Jack smiled. "That's my fault. We got started running together back in Boston. I think I created a monster."

"I *know* it. My hamstrings will never be the same."

"Well, I'm just glad she's been comfortable with you. She's been so quiet since we got here. I don't think this has been an easy move for her."

That brought Gen almost to a halt. Okay, she thought, truth or platitude? Jack was too smart for platitude but still a little too pale for truth. At least the margin of truth Elizabeth had afforded her that first day in the kitchen. Since then, she had offered not a word more.

But Gen had heard the yearning in the notes of the piano when Elizabeth thought no one was listening. She heard all the angst and anger a confused teenage girl could put into her music.

"Yeah," she said finally. "I think you're right. But she talks about friends she's making at camp. And she has the Kendall family to hang around if she wants. We like her a lot."

"I'm glad. Speaking of which, is Emily another sister?"

Gen laughed. "More like a cherished child." Before Jack could react, she turned and pointed. "Meet Emily."

He followed her motion and frowned. "A piano."

"*Emily* the piano. Please don't insult her. She's going to feel slighted enough in the coming days when she only has me to play her. Your daughter has spoiled her for all time."

His smile was fond and proud. "Elizabeth is accomplished at everything she sets her hand to."

*Accomplished.* Not the word Gen would have used, but then, she had Lee and Amanda to guide her.

"Well, as long as either Lee or I are around to let her in, Elizabeth is welcome any time she wants to make my piano happy."

"You're sure about that?"

"I told you. She's always welcome."

Jack gave her a wry smile. "And you wouldn't think anything of taking on another responsibility?"

"Elizabeth isn't a responsibility. She's a delight."

"She's a teenage girl who's often mad at her dad."

That at least got a laugh out of Gen. "Teenage girls have to be mad at somebody. It's in their contract. You want a little time off, let me know. I'll let her be mad at me for a while.''

''You sound as if you have a wealth of experience, young doctor.''

''Oh, I do,'' she said. ''My experience is in there right now helping your daughter pack. I was the oldest sister, you know.''

Which was all she gave most people, even on a good day. Which was all they needed. The rest was tucked away among her family, where it belonged. There and a stage play that one day would surely be seen by more people than Gen ever wanted.

She hadn't realized that the silence had lengthened in the living room until she caught Jack frowning at her again.

''What?'' she asked.

''You feeling better?'' he asked, his attention now solely on her.

Gen straightened a little, almost backed away. ''Better?''

His smile was so gentle. ''It's one of the reasons I came over. I heard from the unit that you had a hell of a morning. Two codes *and* the Christian baby. I figured you didn't need to run right back just to pick me up.''

That fast, the comfort was gone. ''Yeah, well, all in a day's work.''

''Your scrub shirt's still wet.''

From the tears of Jacob's mother. And he wasn't out of the woods yet. Heck, he was barely alive enough to be *in* the woods. Gen felt it weigh on her like a stone. She knew that burden, knew it like an old friend, rock upon rock of it until it seemed to bow your back.

But somehow, sitting in her bright living room with Jack O'Neill, the weight wasn't so bad. His smile lifted it, along with Lee's laughter and the whimsy of a mural on the bathroom wall. Even though she wanted the laughter back, the banter, she didn't mind so much the rest.

So she nodded. ''Yeah, thanks. I do feel better.''

''Not really your specialty, is it?''

Gen could smile at that. ''Critical care? No. It isn't. I hope you're not insulted.''

"As long as it's *my* favorite specialty, I figure that's all that counts."

"I'm eternally grateful for the experience, but I think I'm going to enjoy spending most of my day thumping healthy kids' chests and pulling peas out of their noses."

"Back in Wyoming?"

Gen looked up, stunned.

"Elizabeth told me. Right before she reminded me that we'd once talked about doing much the same thing. I think it sounds romantic to her right now."

"I'm sure it does. But just in case you want to try it on for size, you're welcome out anytime. There's always a crying need for specialists in the smaller towns of America."

"Thanks, no," he said with a smile. "This is where I need to be."

Gen nodded, knowing that this line of questioning was over. She should have been thankful for that gentle reminder of why physical reactions should be ignored, but darn it if she didn't feel sudden disappointment.

He was staying in Chicago. She was going home. As simple as that.

For just a moment, though, deep where hopeless fantasies lived, Gen wished it weren't.

She really, really wanted that shower now. Instead, she climbed to her feet.

"Time to find out what kind of nutrition is lurking amid the penicillin mold and sour milk," she said, doing her best to ignore the fresh ache the simple act of standing incited in her legs.

She was just passing Jack when he made a move to follow her. Gen stopped in her tracks.

"Sit down," she snapped. "I still don't trust you around sharp objects or hot surfaces. You could go out on me any minute."

Sagging back into the couch, he harrumphed like an old man. "You make me sound feeble."

"Only as feeble as a person needs to be who tries to—"

"Climb three stories with a fractured skull. Yeah, I know."

He looked up at a burst of laughter from Elizabeth's room and smiled. "You win, though. I think I'll just sit here and listen to that for a while."

Gen turned back toward the kitchen.

Okay, she thought. I can do this. I can be around him without melting into an untidy puddle from just his proximity. I can distract myself with any number of things, buffer myself with other people. I don't have to worry that I'll do something stupid before I finish my residency.

And after that, heck, she only had another year before she could blow this pop stand and run like a coward for the hills.

Even so, even tired and scratchy and stressed from the attraction that never waned, she felt better. Calmer. Better able move past the awful morning she'd had than if she'd just come home to face the empty apartment.

Even if she had Emily there to soothe her.

If Emily had any sense in her piano soul, after being treated to the artistry of Elizabeth O'Neill, she'd figure out a way to slam the lid on Gen's hands the next time she even tried to start a scale.

But she felt better.

She just wished she didn't feel better because Jack O'Neill was sitting in her living room.


"It's really too bad," Lee said later that day when they returned home from dropping Jack and Elizabeth off at that handsome, echoing house nearby.

"What's that?" Gen asked, thinking only of the shower she'd been promising herself for the past ten hours.

Lee shrugged. "Oh, that Elizabeth's mother died. That Jack hasn't gotten over it."

Gen cast her sister a bemused look. "And you know this how?"

Lee smiled. "Elizabeth and I talked a bit."

"Of course you did. What did she tell you?"

"Not much, really. I get the feeling, though, that they have formed this inviolate little circle. Just the two of them against the world. Reminds me a little of how we became after Mom and Dad died."

Gen nodded. "I feel sorry for the nanny, if that's the case. She'll fit like a sixth finger on a glove."

"Nannies don't need to fit. But it would be nice if there were some room left for more family. I think they need it."

Gen sighed. "Not our problem, sister mine. Our job was to temporarily baby-sit and then send the fledgling back to her nest."

"You're mixing metaphors," Lee protested.

"I am not."

"He calls her a mouse. Not a bird."

That was true, Gen thought. For some reason, after hearing Elizabeth play the piano, the imagery bothered her.

But as she'd said, it wasn't her problem to solve.

"Well," she said as she dropped Lee off at the Moroccan-blue doorway on the second floor behind which her sister lived, "considering all the money we spent on your college education, I'm just glad you at least know how a metaphor is mixed."

"And that's all you have to say?"

Gen stopped one step up and turned. "Okay, how's this? Stirred, not shaken."

"What?"

"How to mix a metaphor. How'd I do?"

But Lee wouldn't be distracted.

"About Jack O'Neill." Her eyes sparkling with pure Lee comprehension, she tilted her head like an editorial comment. "He's beautiful, you know."

Now Gen knew for sure she wanted her shower. Anything but a family interrogation about what was probably painfully obvious. Gen was lusting after a man who'd only responded briefly because of a head injury. Story of her life, really.

She especially didn't need that kind of introspection from the sister who had, for an entire two years, named herself Gen's personal matchmaker.

"He's mostly yellow and green right now."

"That's all you have to say?"

Gen tilted her own head. "Let me think, Lee. Is it? Why, yes, come to think of it. It is. Now, good night. I'm about fifteen hours past my bedtime."

She'd made it almost all the way to her door when she heard Lee's parting shot.

"You may go to bed, but you won't get to sleep," she called softly up the stairwell. "You can still smell him in there."

And damned if Lee wasn't right.

Citrus. Citrus and something very male and compelling, clinging to her Italian silk cushions and crowding the air. Which made it all so much worse, because the only thing Gen could think about as she paced those hardwood floors through the afternoon was that for the first time since she'd gained her hardwon isolation, she felt…isolated.

She felt alone. And she hadn't before Jack O'Neill had walked into her apartment.

Her days evened out after that. Gen got on with her final month of fellowship, and at home she tried to help keep Lee calm as the premiere of her play approached. Gen helped organize the opening-night party and cleaned her house for the company that was coming and laughed about her new nickname of Slugger. Suddenly everybody at work was giving her names of other attending physicians to hospitalize for them. And for five days she thought she was doing just fine. She thought she was happy and active and thundering through the home stretch of her residency without any problems.

Then, on the sixth day, Jack O'Neill returned with all the fanfare of a conquering hero.

Gen wasn't there to see it. She'd spent another night putting out fires in the unit and was now closing in on the end of her regular shift. She'd heard the nurses rhapsodizing about the new chief as she did her rounds. She'd shared enthusiasm with the other pediatric residents. And then she disappeared into her routine, as she always did. And, as always, she made the most of it.

This morning she did it singing. Crooning, actually. Rocking and smiling and listening through her one earpiece to the flutter of a tiny heart. The rasp of quick breaths into miniature lungs. As she followed her personal checklist of a daily assessment, Gen made faces to the wide eyes of tiny Amanda McCauley.

"See how much better you feel without that tube in your throat?" she asked the baby and then swung into the next verse of "Mandy."

The baby seemed delighted, even though she couldn't move much. She was pretty restrained, with her two IVs and chest tube and oxygen. But Gen was an old hand at this and knew just how to juggle ICU paraphernalia. Besides, it wasn't as if the tubes were that big. Amanda weighed eight pounds soaking wet.

Gen was so busy with her work that she didn't hear the footsteps stop beyond the other side of the high crib.

"I don't suppose you'd like to tell me where my patient is?" a very familiar voice demanded out toward the desk.

Gen almost fell off her footstool. "Uh-oh," she said to the wide-eyed little girl in her lap. "I think we've been busted."

"Slugger Kendall has her," one of the nurses called back.

Calm down, Gen instructed herself. No tachycardia, no sweaty palms, no heat to sear every one of my nerve endings. I have to learn how to deal with the man on a day-to-day basis. I might as well start doing it now.

"Slugger Kendall has her *where?*" Jack O'Neill demanded, already sounding tense only five hours into his first shift back.

Gen pulled the stethoscope from her ear. "Right here."

Jack's scowling face appeared over the top of the crib.

"You're sitting on a footstool," he accused.

Oh, God. He was in scrubs, and that just wasn't fair. Tailored, crisp clothing was bad enough. Heck, even a rumpled, nondescript patient gown was bad. But a scrub shirt was the stuff of medical fantasies, with its V-neck that betrayed just enough of a man's throat and chest to prove that he had the most lovely dark hair curling at the hollow of his throat.

Just enough to make a person fantasize about what else he had.

About how a person's fingers could suddenly just *itch* to touch it all.

Oh, God.

Though what she wanted to do was melt all over the floor, Gen did the only thing that was acceptable. She grinned. "I think one of the mothers absconded with the chair. They always know when family isn't going to be using the furniture. You're looking much less…colorful this morning. Welcome back.''

''Thank you. What are you doing on a stool?''

''The floor's too far down. How's Elizabeth?''

For a second Gen got a flash of that O'Neill whimsy, a telltale spark in his beautiful, now unswollen eyes. For a minute she almost forgot the patient in her lap.

''I'm just glad you told me who Emily was,'' Jack said. ''Otherwise I would have thought one of Elizabeth's friends at school had moved away.''

''I told you to send her back to the apartment if she started suffering withdrawal. Emily misses her almost as much as I do.''

His eyebrows went up. ''You miss a twelve-year-old in hormone overload?''

''I *was* a twelve-year-old in hormone overload. Very little can frighten me after that.''

His grin was bright and fleeting. ''What *are* you doing on a footstool?'' he asked, a furrow growing on his brow.

His faded brow. There was a bit of rainbow color down his cheeks, leftover green and yellow. But his forehead looked better, and the word SGNILWAR was no more than a smudge of mauve. It had been five days since Gen had seen him. Since Elizabeth had deserted Emily to Gen's heavy hand. Gen had really thought she'd succeeded in steeling herself against seeing him again.

Not so.

Her heart was redlining, her hands were starting to sweat, and her chest was puddling in a heat that had no business flaring in an ICU in front of an innocent baby.

Gen did miss Elizabeth. She missed the music and the magic. She even missed the regular jogging sessions that had worked her legs far better than usual. She missed the company in her suddenly too-still apartment.

But mostly, she had to admit, she missed the sight of Jack in it. Even though she knew better than to think she would ever see that again.

Even though she knew the physical reaction was just that and should disappear when she did from his life.

In about a year or so.

"I'm doing Amanda's assessment," she informed him with what she considered to be remarkable aplomb. "I find we both enjoy it more when I can hold her. Amanda's doing much better, by the way. Extubated last night and holding her own quite nicely. Chest tube's next on the agenda, don't you think?"

Amanda gurgled and waved a free hand up toward Jack.

Gen laughed. "Amanda says she would appreciate that very much, thank you."

Jack gave the baby a quick, comprehensive look and nodded. Then, inexplicably, frowned again. "Were you singing just now?"

That made Gen blush. "Well, uh, yes. You see, her nickname's Mandy, and…"

"And so you were inflicting Barry Manilow on a critically ill child?" He shook his head now. "I should probably question your judgment, not to mention your compassion."

"*This* child likes it," Gen defended herself a bit too sharply. "I was thinking of putting it in her orders. Prescribe first verse 'Mandy' every hour while awake. If baby smiles, sing second verse."

"Babies don't smile. They get gas."

There it was. That sly sparkle she so loved to see in his Caribbean eyes. Gen wanted to laugh out loud in triumph. She merely shook her head.

"Typical medical cliché. Amanda smiles at *me*. But that's because I sing to her."

"No," he said, resting against the crib side and leaning toward her. "I think she smiled when you stopped."

Gen smiled down at the blinking baby. "Everybody's a critic."

"This critic is in charge of your career."

"For another fifteen days, older doctor. Only another fifteen days. Then I will be free to sing whatever song I wish."

She shouldn't have looked up at him just then. If she hadn't, she wouldn't have caught the flare of something in his eyes, that same heat that lit in her chest, in her belly. She wouldn't have seen him smile and known that there was real regret in it, real wonder and surprise.

For a very long moment she just froze. Just counted heartbeats and wondered that they kept on coming.

Do it again, she wanted to beg. Let me know you meant it.

That smile. That odd, almost embarrassed smile that betrayed the fact that he was as surprised as she by the chemistry that seemed to spark between them.

Good God. She'd so completely convinced herself that she'd imagined it. That he'd only experienced it as a symptom of a bruised brain. She'd thought she'd begun to come to grips with a perfectly commonplace, one-sided sexual attraction.

But things had just become way more complicated.

He felt it, too. She could swear to it. For her. For plain, practical Gen Kendall, who spent her life helping to keep her small family together and had no talents but first aid and people herding.

Gen wanted to reach up, to touch that smile. To catch the light in those eyes like quicksilver in a bottle. She wanted to test the lightning that seemed to spark between them and see just how strong it could be.

Instead, she bent her head, confused. Exhilarated. More than a little frightened.

"Oh," she said in an unforgivably breathy voice, reaching a finger to stroke the cheek of her tiny patient. "We've bored Amanda right to sleep. I guess it's time to put her back, huh?"

She didn't look up to see his expression. She heard his hesitation, though. Closed her eyes, only briefly, against the walls she could almost hear him erecting against that surprising attraction.

"You really do this with all your patients?" he asked in a perfectly pleasant voice.

Gen nodded, her attention still on Amanda. "Until they reach a certain age. Fifteen-year-olds get entirely the wrong impression when you try and pull them into your lap."

Then she heard it. His laughter. Soft, satisfied, surprised. Gen betrayed a quick smile of relief and rose to her feet, Amanda still nestled against her chest. ''I just don't want to get away from the habit of holding the babies. Sometimes they need that more than medicine, I think.''

''Another lesson from your real job?''

This time Gen faced him, even as she resettled the baby and her equipment in the oversize crib. ''Too many doctors never learn that, you know. And they miss so much of what's going on with their patients if they don't touch them.''

''You can't do an assessment without touch,'' he challenged.

Gen smiled again, this time with a real challenge. ''I mean *touch*, older doctor. Patting and calming and just holding a hand. Best sedative in the world is just having human contact.''

For a second she thought she'd gone too far. She thought she saw the flashing memory of their own contact at the back of his eyes, the residue that still lingered in them both, like coals waiting to flare at the slightest breeze. But professional that he was, Jack applied his chief-of-staff smile like a uniform, and Gen was left breathless with distress.

''I imagine that philosophy put you quite at odds with Elizabeth, then. She's not the most tactile child on earth.''

Gen should have smiled back. She couldn't. ''I know,'' she said, and knew she sounded too troubled for the jest he'd meant.

Jack had been just about to straighten, but he stopped.

Gen saw the sudden question in his eyes. She knew she'd said more than she'd meant. That she'd meant more than she knew. A feeling, a disturbance, that had plagued her. Another entire problem that she didn't want to face.

Uncomfortable with what she still couldn't define, she shrugged. ''But then, she's twelve and in the middle of that great preteen hormone rage. I didn't want to be touched much then, either.''

It wasn't enough. She knew it. She didn't know why. But Jack was going to ask, and she didn't blame him. Again that taut silence fell that isolated them and yet connected them in ways neither could define.

Gen held her breath, not knowing why. Jack looked at her with bemused, curious eyes. Gen thought he meant to speak.

He never got the chance. Gen had just stood up from resettling

Amanda when she heard a thud and a curse from one of the other rooms.

"Call a code!" somebody yelled out in the work area. A chair tipped over, and somebody else yelled, "Oh, hell!" Without another word, Dr. O'Neill ran for the door, Gen behind him.

And that fast, the bubble of connection, the friable bond that had begun to form between them, snapped.

# *Chapter 6*

Gen couldn't believe how fast a person could fall in love.

Not lust. She'd acknowledged that days ago. Weeks, it seemed, with that first bolt of lightning that had hit her out on a hot softball field.

No, not lust. Love. I-want-to-spend-the-rest-of-my-life-sharing-toothbrushes-and-morning-conversation love. The kind of love that inspired poets and wrecked friendships. The kind that made strong women weep and weak ones succumb to insanity.

That kind of love.

And for the most stupid reason.

Not because Jack O'Neill was brilliant, although he was. Not because he was funny, although Gen couldn't pretend she didn't feed off his wit as if it were spring water in a desert. Not because he was about the best-looking thing on two legs to reside within the city limits, though she had left David's towel on for the past three days and not even noticed.

She knew she'd been leaning toward an unforgivable infatuation. She'd been sniffing her Italian silk pillows, after all, just to feel that sweet kick of heat in her belly. She'd stuttered and stammered in front of him like a teenager at the prom when he'd bent over Amanda's crib.

But not fifteen minutes later she did the unforgivable.

Gen Kendall fell in love with Jack O'Neill because of the way he ran a code.

Gen had worked in the world of medicine since she'd been about twenty. She'd seen a lot of codes, those frantic efforts by a specialized team to restart failing hearts or drag a person back from the brink of traumatic death. She'd never once fallen in love with anybody over one before.

She sure did now. And she made sure she did it when it wouldn't do her a damn bit of good.

The baby whose heart they had to restart was about three, a little boy who had suffered chest and pelvic injuries in a car accident. He had been on a respirator for three days to support his bruised lungs. He'd been to surgery twice to repair damaged organs. He'd been sedated and cared for and prayed over. And then, while Gen and Jack had been chatting over little Amanda, that little boy had thrown an embolus to his already insulted lung and shocked his already overloaded system straight into shutdown.

Gen and Jack had skidded into the room no more than seconds after the monitors had gone haywire. No more than nanoseconds before the rest of the team, who usually resided in the unit for events just like this. And no more than five-point-five minutes later, Gen did what she'd never done before. What she'd sworn she would never do, certainly not while performing critical tasks over a child.

While monitoring blood flow and fluid replacement and medication usage, she fell in love.

It wasn't simply that Jack O'Neill orchestrated the initial chaos of that little boy's cardiac arrest into cohesion, that he stood aside to let his residents and nurses and techs handle the situation with only a few quiet suggestions to guide them along so that the residents gained strength in their judgment and the nurses knew they weren't being deserted to students.

It wasn't that he then personally walked in with Gen to speak to the terrified young parents, or that he'd crouched down on his haunches to hold that mother's hands as he'd explained how they meant to treat this latest threat to their son's young life. It wasn't even the fact that when Gen began singing Barry Manilow to settle the team back into an easier, less panicked rhythm, Jack had just smiled and sung along.

It was the fact that, as the team had worked so frantically to save that little life, eyes to monitors, hands to equipment, attention on numbers and iridescent green patterns, Jack O'Neill had kept his big, square hand on that little boy's head.

Just resting there, sometimes stroking the matted blond hair. Sometimes patting the minute expanse of sweaty forehead beneath. Touching. Standing just to the left of the respiratory therapist while she patiently pumped air into those stricken little lungs, his eyes on all that happened, his attention quiet and sure, his hand never losing contact with his patient, as if he could imbue a little encouragement, a little comfort, to that hurt little boy as he fought for his life.

It was a gesture Jack O'Neill didn't even seem to notice. A gesture no one else noticed.

Except Gen.

Who not five minutes earlier had suffered his ribbing about her own tendencies to do the same.

And when she saw him crouch down, never taking his eyes off the action, and whisper encouragement into that little boy's ear, she lost every other option she had.

She had no choice at all in the matter.

She fell instantly in love.

And regretted it almost as quickly.


"He's such a good man, your new super," Abbie Viviano said two days later as she and Gen finished their twice-weekly run down by the lake. "It's just too bad."

Gen swiped at her sweaty forehead with her towel and bent over, hands on thighs, to reclaim her breath.

"Why is it too bad?"

Abbie was looking out toward the water, where an early-afternoon regatta fought the wind. Bright triangles against sharp blue water. High, puffy clouds in a pale sky. A perfect summer day in Chicago.

"Well, don't you think it's too bad he lost his wife so young? She died in his arms, ya know. Right at the scene. Every woman at the hospital is just aching to be the one to help him forget."

Gen hid her distress behind a scowl. "We as a sex can be such a cliché sometimes. Besides, nobody dies in anybody's arms these days. They die in trauma centers on respirators."

Chuckling, Abbie turned her attention from the lake. She didn't sweat, darn her. She glowed. Even after three kids and a career as a trauma doc. Well, Gen admitted, a part-time trauma doc, now that the youngest had been born. But that didn't make any difference. No one who had given birth to three children should still look that good.

"You're such a cynic for a baby doc," Abbie said with a grin. "O'Neill's wife never made it as far as a trauma center. Torn aortic arch. She bled out right there on the side of the highway. And after watching his wife die without being able to save her, O'Neill ended up with nothing but a broken ankle. Which, of course, isn't fair in the cosmic sense."

"After working in a trauma center for this long, you expect fair?" Gen asked.

"No. But I guess I'm an optimist. I keep hoping."

"Yeah," Gen sighed, thinking of the realization she'd come to no more than two days ago, and what today's revelation would mean to it. "Me, too."

She didn't notice the glint in her friend's eye or the lift of that intelligent eyebrow. "Does this mean you want to comfort him, too?"

Gen stuttered to a stop as if she'd been slapped.

"No."

She knew she sounded too abrupt. She knew she shouldn't have let Abbie drag her anywhere near this conversation. She already couldn't get the image out of her mind of that big man holding on to that little boy as he struggled to live. She couldn't get those laughing blue eyes out of her head. She couldn't wait to see him again.

But she sure as heck didn't want anybody else to know that.

Especially now that she'd been forced to add the picture of that big man holding his dying wife in his arms.

"Good thing you don't," Abbie said, wiping at her own shiny face. "From what I've heard, he hasn't so much as lusted in his heart since his wife died. I think anybody who wanted to comfort that man would be ending up in a threesome with a dead woman."

Gen didn't realize she sighed again. "I think you're probably right."

But he *had* looked at her with lust. He'd talked with lust, that first morning. But he had never followed up on it. And the brief times she'd caught that surprised, hot look in his eyes, he'd warded it off with humor like a wizard banishing demons.

He had done nothing to make her think he would allow more than that surprising chemistry. That chemistry he seemed to control with much more ruthless ease than she could.

He'd done nothing to encourage her.

He'd just made her fall in love with him. Without ever knowing he'd done it.

Undoubtedly without ever meaning to.

Because he still loved his wife who'd died in his arms on the side of a deserted highway. The wife who had undoubtedly given Elizabeth those sweet blue eyes and left shadows that still lived in both the O'Neills' hearts.

But oh, Gen thought, as she followed Abbie across the street toward home, wouldn't it have been nice to have a dream for just a little while before somebody shattered it?

"Was Elizabeth there?" she asked.

Abbie looked over at her, startled. "Where?"

"When her mother died."

"No. The doc and his lady were on their way home from a wedding. Drunk driver, typical story."

Gen found that she'd stopped forward momentum again. Standing there in the park, beneath the lush foliage of a maple with the lake breeze winnowing her damp hair. "Poor little girl," she said.

"Elizabeth?"

She nodded. "She's…"

But Gen could only shrug when it came to exactly what Elizabeth was. A little girl too soon grown. A survivor who hadn't come to terms. A penitent without reason.

Maybe that was why she hadn't been able to follow up on her statement about Elizabeth the other day. She sensed something in the little girl, something that lived beneath her music and her laughter and her sullen silences.

Something that was propelling her toward med school instead of Juilliard.

Something that surely wasn't Gen's problem.

"Is she still coming to Lee's show with you?" Abbie asked. Gen nodded and started walking again.

"Yep. Family's coming in today. Premiere tomorrow, followed by party at Juan Ton's. Lee is hysterical, her husband, Rock, is…a rock, and I'm giving over my bedrooms to my brother Jake's family. I'm thinking of moving to a Holiday Inn."

"Don't be silly. You love having your family here."

"I love having my family here," Gen parroted and earned herself a chuckle.

Abbie patted her like an infant. "And you get to go to a brand-new play, mix with the likes of Ian Griffin and be escorted to the chi-chi premiere party by the best-looking doctor in Cook County. I, on the other hand, get to go see *Disney on Ice* with three children and a cranky police captain. I don't know how I'll survive the excitement."

"Just don't let him threaten to shoot Cinderella again," Gen suggested.

Abbie rolled her eyes. "Are you sure *you* wouldn't rather watch ice-skating mice?"

Gen grimaced. "Thank you, no."

Abbie stopped, stretched one more time and looked up to where the white tower of the hospital broke through the trees not two blocks away. "Okay then, back to work."

Gen followed her gaze. "We really want to do this, huh?"

Abbie shrugged. "A little late to do anything else."

Abbie never saw the startled look of dismay Gen sent her way. She was already halfway across the street to complete her shift.

* * *

Gen was late getting home. She hadn't meant to be. She'd meant to hand off her cases on the dot of five and then run the four blocks home so she could swing her niece and nephew in her arms and coo over the new baby and let her brothers crush her ribs. She'd meant to get there in time to double-check with Seamus Schmidt—also known as the Juan of Juan Ton's—about the last-minute requirements for Lee's party the next night. She'd meant to sit calmly with Lee, who, as Gen knew, would be completely un-Lee-like and having a panic attack right in her living room.

But she was late, and that threw every good intention into the toilet.

She was late because Jacob Edward Christian, her blue-eyed baby with the malformed heart, the one who had been given the Norwood shunt, the one with the same name as her brother, had died. Suddenly. Inexplicably. Irreversibly.

It happened sometimes with shunts. Nobody knew why, and nobody seemed to be able to stop it. One minute the baby looked fine, and then he was just gone, and no bag of medical tricks could bring them back.

And God knows, they'd pulled everything they could out of that bag. They'd worked on him for two hours, praying and pleading and cursing in turn. They'd called in the cardiothoracic surgeon, and they'd called in the critical care specialist, and they'd called in the priest. And finally they'd called in Jacob's parents to hold him and say goodbye.

Gen wasn't sure why this one hurt so much. Maybe because she'd gotten close to the parents, who had waited so long for their son whom they'd named after his grandparents. Jacob Edward. Maybe because she superstitiously thought that nothing bad could happen if one were in the throes of love, not to mention that the one she loved was at the front lines of this particular battle. Maybe because, for any number of reasons, she just felt that the burden was hers alone to bear.

When he found out that his son had died, Jacob's father put his hand through the wall, right by Gen's head. Silently, as if words were too small for the grief that consumed him. He broke his hand and then walked out of the hospital, his accusing glare reserved for Gen, who had been the one to finally talk him into attempting the potentially lifesaving shunt in the first place.

The shunt that had failed.

The shunt he blamed for his son's death.

It was human nature. Someone or something had to be blamed for the inexplicable. Jacob's father blamed Gen, and she felt it to her toes. It had been her responsibility, and the shunt had failed. She walked out of the hospital feeling battered and sore and tired in a way that had nothing to do with sleep.

And then she walked into her apartment to find herself surrounded by chaos.

"Gen," Lee pounced, at the head of the pack. "Seamus isn't answering the phone at the restaurant. Can't you get him to answer? You said you'd make sure everything was ready. How the hell are we supposed to know if everything's ready, and do you know that I have three Broadway producers coming? What the hell are they going to eat if there aren't any pot stickers?"

"Hey, sis!" Gen's younger brother, Zeke, called from the open refrigerator in the tiny kitchen. "You don't have any beer. I just got off a dig in the desert, and all I've been able to think of is a cold beer."

"I think Sienna is running a fever," her sister-in-law, Amanda, said of her five-month-old daughter. "You'll look at it, won't you?"

"In a minute," Gen said to them all without really seeing them, without so much as hugging them hello. "I'm going to take a shower first."

"As to that," her older brother, Jake, announced in high dudgeon from where he stood at the window with his youngest in his arms, "I saw what you have on your bathroom wall. You're not somebody unacquainted with responsibility, Gen. You knew perfectly well we'd be bringing the kids. You should have known better."

Not someone unacquainted with responsibility? Well, Gen guessed, blinking in exhaustion, *I guess that sums it up. I've been acquainted with responsibility since the age of six. Since I began to take over the care of my siblings from my ill mother.*

Since the moment I saw the bathroom as the only refuge in a world of responsibilities.

She'd been so looking forward to seeing her family. To wallowing in the comfort of their chatter and stability and wholeness. To sating herself on their health and happiness. But she'd forgotten that she wouldn't only see her family. She would assume the family role. The girl in charge. The one who'd held the house together while Jake battled for the ranch. The one who had grown up to take responsibility first for the children in her own family and finally every sick child in Chicago.

But sometimes, she thought, as she turned away from where her family all waited for her to solve things the way she always did, where they wouldn't understand if she told them that she'd just faced one responsibility too many today, she didn't want to be in charge.

Not now.

Not later.

Maybe never again.

She was going to be free in a few days. As free as a pediatrician would be. It was hard to remember that right now.

So she walked into the bathroom, locked the door and pulled the towel off David's censorship hooks. And then she did her best to ignore the voices that demanded her return while she stood in her shower and wished she could cry.

It got worse.

Of course it did. Baby Sienna did have a fever. Baby Sienna had a middle-ear infection and screamed like a banshee for the two hours it took Gen to get her medicated and asleep.

Juan of Juan Ton's—Seamus—was having a crisis of pork, that being that the pork and ginger pot stickers that were one of his signature dishes had gone, somehow, bad, and he wasn't sure if he had time to fix them.

Zeke whined at the thought that he might have to go find beer all by himself on the Gold Coast and demanded that Gen go along to direct him.

Jake called Gen to account for some of the expenditures she'd made on the house she and Lee inhabited. The one the family had bought from its old owner right after the fire that had almost destroyed it last fall. Which made Gen the new landlord and Jake her overseer.

And the next morning Gen had to go back into the hospital and survive another shift before she could take off for the theater with her family and the most handsome thing on two legs in Cook County.

That was what kept her going. Jack O'Neill was going to be there. Even Elizabeth, to whom Gen hadn't had a chance to talk since going home, would be there. Gen's family would be there, and it would be fun.

It would be fun if it killed them all.

It had to be.

Because at ten the next morning, while Gen was doing grand rounds, baby Jacob's grieving father called.

"My son is dead," he said without greeting.

Gen stood where she was, her chief and her fellow residents no more than ten feet away, and she fought a chill of apprehension.

"I know, Mr. Christian. I'm so sorry. You know that."

"You murdered him. You with your degree and your superior science and your patronizing bitch attitude, you murdered him."

Gen couldn't even answer.

"And don't tell me you're sorry," he continued, not even noticing. "You don't hurt, and you're not sorry, damn it! You're a cold, calculating bitch who's just making money for your hospital. Well, it's time you were hurt, too, isn't it? Isn't it!"

Gen just hung up, as if the conversation were finished. She knew perfectly well that she should call the police. At least security. Instead, she set down the receiver and simply walked away, and nobody noticed. Not her fellow residents, and not Jack O'Neill, who was presenting a new case.

He didn't notice that her hands shook and her skin grew ashen. He didn't notice that she couldn't quite keep her mind on what he was saying, because what she kept hearing was that anguished voice calling her a murderer. She kept wondering if that voice was right.

But Gen was an old hand at hiding problems. She wasn't

about to change now. So she smiled and nodded and answered questions and got on with the rest of her shift, sometimes singing off-key Manilow songs to her babies so she could make it to the end of the day.

Because at the end of the day, she was going to be escorted to Lee's play—even if there wouldn't be pork-and-ginger pot stickers afterward to celebrate—by Jack O'Neill of the smiling Caribbean eyes.

In his Volvo.

In good clothes Gen had never seen, but could easily fantasize about. With not even the rest of her family to dilute his presence, with no work to distract them, with only Gen and Elizabeth to share his scent.

Gen made it through those long hours on that simple fact.

And then, thirty minutes before she was supposed to be picked up for the theater that evening, Jack called.

"Don't worry," he assured her before saying hello. "I'm not calling you back in. But there's a situation here, and I'm not going to get out in time to pick you up. In fact…"

"You want us to get Elizabeth?" Gen asked, fighting the jagged shard of disappointment that suddenly lodged in her chest.

"I know it's an imposition…."

Gen just closed her eyes against the feeling that she couldn't breathe.

She'd asked for so little.

Not that he love her, but that she simply get a chance to enjoy his off-duty company for a little while, if only to balance out what her day had been. Her week. Her life.

She should have known better. After all, her entire family was here to remind her just how her life had been.

"We'd be happy to pick her up," Gen said, proud that she sounded sincere. "I don't want her to miss this if you can't get away at all."

"Oh, I'll get away," he promised. "I'm just waiting for the surgeons to get this kid ready. But if you don't mind picking her up, I'd really appreciate it."

"Of course not," Gen agreed, just as she'd agreed with every request made of her in the past two days. She was the girl in charge, after all.

But she thought she was finally tired of it.

"Thanks, young doctor. I'll call her and let her know."

Zeke drove her over in his rental car and waited for Gen to walk into the O'Neill house without him, since he seemed immersed in the play-by-play of the Cubs game on the radio.

"I don't get to hear this stuff much in the Four Corners," he said, dropping a kiss on her forehead.

"Don't think about it," she said, and climbed out in her new dress.

But Elizabeth wasn't waiting for her. The housekeeper greeted Gen with a spate of such fast Spanish that Gen just followed the general hand signals toward what she figured was Elizabeth's room.

She knocked.

At first there wasn't an answer.

Gen's stomach slid. Suddenly she wasn't sure she wanted to stay. Maybe Jack had picked his daughter up already. Maybe Elizabeth didn't want to go.

Maybe there was another problem to put on Gen's plate.

Why not? Everybody else was loading it up.

"Elizabeth? It's Gen."

Silence.

Gen knocked again.

Nothing.

She tried the door. Amazingly enough for the room of a preteen girl, it opened easily. Gen figured there was nothing to do but go on in.

"Elizabeth…?"

The first thing Gen realized was that the room was a revelation. Considering how sterile the rest of the house was, it was a comfort to see some life in this room. All right, a lot of life.

Elizabeth's room bore more resemblance to a storage attic than a girl's bedroom. There were walls full of baby art and shelves full of beautiful dolls, a bed full of stuffed animals and a desk overflowing with books. There was a bouquet of instrument cases in the corner and a map of Gettysburg on an easel in another corner. A Save the Whales sign and a World Trade Center photo that simply had Remember printed at the bottom.

Most amazing, over by the Gettysburg map stood a dress form clad in what looked like a child's dress from the Civil War, all hoops and ruffles and big, coal bucket bonnet. And in the most lovely shade of magenta.

Gen almost walked over to it. Then she saw Elizabeth and stopped.

The little girl was dressed to go in a cute striped tank and skirt, with wedge sandals. Her hair was pulled back by rhine-stone combs and then fell below her shoulders in lovely sable curls.

But Elizabeth was so focused on what she was doing that she didn't even notice Gen's arrival. Elizabeth was standing before a window in which hung some kind of sun catcher. She was watching it as if it were a devotional picture, her hands tight against her sides, her eyes wide and glistening.

Gen knew right then that she should just back out the door. She knew that Elizabeth, the Elizabeth who had so challenged Emily the piano, had faded, or had maybe hidden herself away again. This Elizabeth was the first Elizabeth she'd seen, quiet and controlled and too adult.

This Elizabeth set Gen's stomach to churning, because Gen smelled something wrong, something she should have seen be-fore, something she still couldn't put a name to.

"My dad says I shouldn't leave it here," Elizabeth said con-versationally as if she'd known all along Gen had arrived.

Gen felt the hairs go up on her arms. She stepped closer so she could see what Elizabeth was contemplating.

"What is it?" she asked gently, careful not to come too close.

Elizabeth's smile was at once sad and whimsical. "A picture of us."

Gen saw now. Her own mouth opened in surprise. It was a photo, but on glass, so that it could be seen through, so that it seemed more mystical than real. Magic suspended midair. Three people were posed grouped around a chair, where a lovely woman sat in Civil War period attire. A lovely, sweet-faced woman who held a little girl wearing the very magenta dress that waited in the corner.

And there, standing behind them, his hand on the woman's shoulder, dressed in full Union officer uniform, complete with the plumed hat he cradled in his arm, stood a smiling Jack O'Neill.

"Oh, my," Gen couldn't help but breathe.

Elizabeth's smile grew as she reached a finger out toward the faces on the glass. "We used to go all the time when I was little. Daddy would be a cavalry colonel, and my mother would crochet doilies with the other women. We lived in a tent and had dances in the evening."

Gen couldn't take her eyes off those spectral people.

"Your dad is a Civil War reenactor?" she asked.

Elizabeth's finger reached the glass and brushed against what must have been her mother's face. "Was."

"Oh."

"At night, around the campfire—if there wasn't a dance, of course—he would join the men in singing old camp songs. I can still remember hearing them as I fell asleep. My mother would rock me to sleep by the fire. And there was Daddy, playing the banjo and singing."

Farther and farther down the rabbit hole, Alice. Gen simply couldn't breathe, because his eyes, those ghostly, translucent eyes, were so happy. The picture was so perfectly complete.

"Your dad plays—played the banjo."

Gen felt stupid just parroting Elizabeth's words. But she felt so at sea. So disconnected from the man she thought she knew.

A Civil War reenactor.

A deliberate separation from his real world that involved quixotic behavior and whimsical music. A land of serious and silly fantasy in which he'd immersed his family.

Gen saw the bright smile, the sly humor of the moment in that photo in which they all sat to perfect attention, and she knew what Jack looked like without the shadows that always lurked. She saw him happy.

Which hurt worse than just about anything she'd seen that day.

"I think I'm losing her," Elizabeth murmured, her hand still hovering near the picture. "She's fading."

Gen kept her silence. She gathered in her own distress and listened to Elizabeth's. She recognized it so easily. Looking at that sweet, calm face of Elizabeth's mother that seemed to hover in the air between sunset and reality, she felt the loss herself.

"Daddy says I shouldn't keep her in the window," Elizabeth said, "but in the window she's more alive. There's light in her."

Silence.

"But she's fading."

It took Gen a long moment more to summon the courage it took to call up her own pain. To share it with this little girl who needed to know it.

"When my mother died," she said, her eyes still on that soft, spectral picture, "we didn't have pictures of her. We didn't really ever have the money or time for cameras. And Mom never really felt well enough to think she was pretty…although she was." Frail pretty, the kind that comes with terminal disease, paper-white skin and the delicate shadows and angles of decay. "And then, after she died, I was afraid that if I didn't remember her face, I would lose her, too. I was so afraid, I'd draw pictures myself and hang them on my wall."

"Did it help?"

Gen chuckled. "I told you before. I'm a terrible artist. It didn't help at all. My mother's been gone more than fifteen years, and I really can't remember her face that much at all. But I remember *her*. The way she smelled of peaches. Her voice, her hands. Oh, her hands were wonderful. They were always patting us and stroking our cheeks and holding our hands. And when I see the ice begin to melt in the mountain stream behind our house, I know my mother's close, because she used to take us up there, walking through the snow sometimes, so we could know that spring was coming at last and we'd made it through the winter."

Gen reached out, very gently, her attention still on Elizabeth's mother, as if asking her blessing, and laid her hand on Elizabeth's shoulder. "The important things never go away. When I smell peaches, I feel safe and warm and loved."

"I can smell peaches on you."

Gen nodded, her image an even softer ghost in the window that lay behind the photo. "I know. Nothing wrong with feeling loved all the time."

And so they stood there before Elizabeth's mother, as the sun settled a little farther beyond the trees and the photo took on a golden tint.

"Am I too young to wear Oil of Olay?"

Gen chuckled again and squeezed Elizabeth's shoulder. "Get a bottle and uncap it by your bed."

Elizabeth nodded. Sighed. Settled a little, as if she'd been fighting this battle alone for a long time. And then, with the sun behind her, she turned to Gen and offered a rather watery smile.

"Thank you."

Gen folded the girl into her arms. "Nobody understands losing a mother like somebody who's lost her own. I kinda think we all need to stick together."

Elizabeth nestled just a moment against Gen's shoulder before pulling away. Gen let her go, but the feel of those shoulders and arms and ribs was still imprinted in her memory.

"Just so you know," she warned, brushing a stray curl off the high forehead that was so like her young mother's, "Lee likes to use that theme a lot in her work."

Elizabeth nodded. "She did in *Some Men's Dreams,* too. That's okay. She understands."

Gen nodded. She let Elizabeth go, so the girl could pick up her purse. She saw the angle of her cheek in the slanting rays of the setting sun as Elizabeth turned, and suddenly Gen stopped cold.

There was something wrong. Something more than Elizabeth's moment of insecurity and anxiety. Something that had been bothering Gen for days.

Gen's stomach slid south and her hands went cold.

She couldn't be right.

She didn't *want* to be right.

She should have recognized it right away. She would have, sooner or later. But it was the discussion of mothers and loss that had crystallized it.

As if her day hadn't been going badly enough. As if Elizabeth's confidences weren't hard enough.

As if falling in love wasn't hard enough.

Just a minute ago Gen had thought she had chipped away a little at a big problem Elizabeth hadn't wanted to admit to. Suddenly she realized that that big problem was only part of an even bigger problem.

A huge problem that had the capability of sending not just Elizabeth but Gen and Jack, as well, into free fall.

And Gen, who had just promised herself that she was going to stop being the girl in charge, the one who bore all the responsibilities, knew that if she were right, this was a responsibility she couldn't hand away.

She had to figure out what to do.

Reaching out as if simply seeking to guide Elizabeth on her way, Gen laid her hand back on the girl's shoulder.

"Hey, there's a guy outside in a rental car who seems to think he's lost his sister."

Startled out of a year's growth, Gen whipped around to find Jack leaning in the doorway.

Elizabeth tautened like a bowstring, but she stayed right where she was, beneath Gen's hand. "Hi, Daddy."

His smile was soft for his daughter. "You ready to go, Mouse?"

"Sure."

"Why don't you go with Gen, and I'll meet you there after I shower and all that stuff?"

The shoulders sagged, just a fraction. Less than a person could see. "Okay. See you there."

Gen wasn't sure how she got out the door. She wasn't sure how she managed the rest of what was supposed to be a perfect evening. She did know, though, that she'd just caught her foot in the biggest trap of her life, and she didn't know how to get out of it.

# Chapter 7

Barry Manilow had a lot to answer for.

It was the only thing Jack O'Neill could think of as he mingled with all the theater people who had crowded into Juan Ton's restaurant to congratulate Lee Kendall O'Connor on her new play.

It had been a good play. A hell of a good play. A play Jack hoped like hell he never had to see again, especially sitting next to his daughter, who'd been tight as a bowstring through the whole thing. Who'd held his hand when the three men who fought for their piece of Lee Kendall's mythical mountain had mourned their mother. Their mother who had died too early. Their mother who had died out of their sight so they couldn't properly grieve for her.

As if Elizabeth needed that kind of thing.

Gen should have warned him.

Hell, Gen should have warned him about a lot of things.

Like how she sang sappy Manilow jingles to babies. She'd even done it during the code a few days ago when everything had gotten too tense. Coaxed everybody into singing along to "Copacabana" until they settled back into their rhythm.

"Oh, don't stop her," one of the nurses had begged when she'd seen his eyebrows shoot up. "There's something about Barry Manilow that lightens things up just enough."

"This is a code," he'd snapped. "Not *Oklahoma*."

But the nurse had been right. A little sashaying, a little off-key singing, a little laughter, had, oddly enough, snapped the terrible tension that could so interfere with calm action and intelligent decision making when it was needed the most.

From that moment on, the team had worked like a machine and yanked that little boy right back from the brink, so that not twenty-four hours later, he'd been able to smile for his frantic young parents.

Gen Kendall had done that with her bad music.

And she'd sung to that baby. Mandy. A sight Jack thought he would never forget, wide eyes open to wide eyes, smile to smile, so that that tiny scrap of life had seemed to dance in her arms while she'd done her very professional assessment.

God, what a stupid reason to fall…

Ah, but he was not about to do something that reckless. Not him. He had responsibilities, and he had expectations. And not a one of them was named Gen Kendall.

Even if she sang to babies. Even if she kept her head and turned her interns into a show chorus to settle them and danced the salsa with her big brother at her sister's premiere party, where the room was decorated with Navajo pots and Indian saris and a world-famous movie star was simpering at her sister like a prom date.

Even if she looked more alive than anything he could imagine as she did all those things, with that mass of gleaming mahogany hair and that smattering of freckles on her nose and that surprisingly decadent figure exhibited to perfection in a long slinky-something blue dress.

Blue.

No, not just blue.

Really blue. Strapless blue.

And slinky.

So slinky his hands were sweating and he couldn't quite catch his breath.

Like that really made a difference, he thought grimly. She hadn't been wearing a slinky blue number when he'd come upon her singing to that baby. She'd been wearing Winnie the Pooh scrubs and a stuffed elf wrapped around her stethoscope.

She'd looked like a teenager in a Disney movie, and he'd gone as hard as a stone just at the sight of her. He'd had to bend over that damn bed just to hide the fact that he was being completely and inexcusably unprofessional.

But he could have handled that. He really had to believe that. After all, he'd done it before. He'd done it for the four years since Meggie's death, because a randy dick didn't mean anything more than enforced abstinence.

But then he'd heard her singing "Mandy" and somehow everything had changed. Everything he knew for certain wasn't nearly so certain anymore.

Except for the fact that simple lust wasn't anything approaching simple anymore.

And for some reason, it made him furious.

So he stood there in the middle of that laughing, eclectic crowd, and all he could think about was that he wanted to walk up to Gen Kendall and dip his face right up against her neck so he could smell those peaches again. So he could test the texture of her pale Irish skin. So he could kiss at least one freckle.

So she would sing to him in that breathy, off-key voice and make him smile, too.

"She's something, isn't she?" one of the patrons asked him, as if he knew him.

"Oh, yeah," Jack agreed. "She's something."

Which was just about the moment he realized that the guy had been talking about the wrong Kendall. A blue-blazer-and-tasseled-loafer kind of guy, he was beaming at Lee like a proud papa.

Jack, on the other hand, hadn't so much as noticed Lee Kendall in the crowd.

He didn't have time for this. He didn't have the patience for sweaty palms and an itchy groin. For unexpected flushes of delight and the surprising ache of loneliness. He was too old to succumb to infatuation, too controlled to fantasize about a pretty woman. Especially a pretty woman under his auspices.

At least under his auspices for another ten days or so.

And here he'd been hoping it had been no more than a head injury.

Downing his bottled water like a shot of whiskey, Jack searched out his daughter. His daughter who had been last seen blinking up at Ian Griffin, of all people.

It was *definitely* time to go home.

"Before I start singing Barry Manilow, too," he muttered to himself.

"What's that about Barry Manilow?" asked one of Gen's brothers.

The not-so-tall and not-so-granite-looking one. The one who looked more like Gen. The anthropologist or geologist or some other -ist, Jack thought.

Zeke? Pete? He wasn't sure. They'd all been introduced en masse.

"Pardon?" Jack asked.

The brother grinned. "You mentioned Barry Manilow for no apparent reason. Just wondering."

"Your sister."

"What about her?"

"She sings Barry Manilow."

The brother's eyebrows rose almost to the roofline. "She does?"

"All the time."

"Really? Are you sure?"

The guy was already grabbing hold of Gen's sister, Lee, who had been talking to some dignitary.

Jack watched, a bit bemused. "Tough to mistake it for anything else."

"You owe me ten!" the brother crowed at Gen's sister. "Tell Jake. You all owe me money. Manilow! I knew it!"

"Not even Gen would be so lost to sense," Lee protested. Then she turned a smile on Jack as if he were one of the family. "Gen would never admit it…well, for good reason. Gen's taste in music has always been…questionable. BeeGees, B52s. Milli

Vanilli, for heaven's sake. Anyway, she's been hiding CDs again lately. We had a bet going who it was." She shook her head, grinning, effervescent with the success of the evening. "Barry Manilow, though. I bet on John Tesh."

"What about John Tesh?" Elizabeth asked, stepping up.

She looked so beautiful tonight, Jack thought. She also looked more comfortable than she had earlier tonight when he'd walked into her room. More comfortable than she had since she'd been back home, come to think of it. Brighter and more lively.

It must be something about these Kendalls, Jack decided as he reached over to wrap an arm around her to keep her close. He just wasn't sure it was a good thing.

"Unsubstantiated rumors," Lee said with a wicked grin. "So, brat, how'd you like my play?"

Jack stiffened. He tightened his hold on Elizabeth, but she didn't seem to mind. In fact, she didn't seem anything more than suddenly shy.

"I had an idea," she offered, eyes down.

Lee smiled. "And?"

Her eyes came up, and Jack saw the sharp edge of uncertainty there. "Have you thought of putting it to music?"

"Music?" Lee echoed, bemused.

Elizabeth straightened, leaned forward a little. "Like, oh, bluegrass?" she asked. "Old country music? Like an opera or something. I could really see it…I mean, like, I could hear the music in my head. Especially when they bury James. The preacher's words about James's place on the earth are a perfect lament."

Jack held his breath. Not only Lee had stopped, but Gen, and Gen's sister-in-law, the writer. And the big brother. The one who looked as if he'd been hewn from the mountains. Jake. All watching his daughter as if she'd just changed colors or something. Hell, even Ian Griffin was watching her, his too-perfect young face suspiciously blank.

And Jack could do nothing to protect her.

And then he heard it. An intake of breath. He saw the birth of a smile. Delight, when he'd expected disdain.

"You're right," Lee said, her eyes already unfocused with ideas. "I can hear it, too."

Somehow, at that moment, Elizabeth looked taller, older. "And his mama, who's a powwow woman? You know, the healer? Oh, maybe a song for her about her wise ways. Their mother should have a song."

Jack wanted to step in then, to shield her. He heard that plaintive note in her voice. Didn't they? Didn't they understand what that damn play could do to a little girl who was still grieving over her own mother?

"Some old Irish music," Lee countered quickly, her hand now on Elizabeth's arm. "You know, the kind that came over and morphed into our folk music."

And before anybody could do anything else, the two of them wandered off, talking music and voice and meaning.

Jack watched in stunned silence. He'd never seen Elizabeth's eyes light up like that. Never. And he was the one she brought all her exciting ideas to.

He needed to go home. He needed to be back at work, where everything made sense. Suddenly, in no more than two weeks, his world was spinning out of control, and he wasn't sure he could handle it.

"I'm sorry about those two," Gen said with a smile. "I hope you don't need to leave soon. When they get started, they talk for hours."

Jack spun around to smell peaches. "They do?"

Gen nodded. "Those creative types are like that."

Creative? Elizabeth? Jack looked after her, unsure what to think. Elizabeth was a good student, a dutiful daughter, a keeper of her mother's memory.

But creative?

"I think she's just trying to get over her mom" was all he could say, feeling even more uncertain.

Gen's smile wasn't quite as bright as it could have been. "I think she wants to write music for her."

For what seemed like an eternity, Jack could only stand there staring at her, then at Elizabeth. He could hear the clink of glasses, the sophisticated murmur of well-lubricated throats, occasionally a laugh. He could smell roasted meat and garlic and expensive perfume, and he could see the swirl of bright colors and flashy smiles at the periphery. But he couldn't quite answer Gen Kendall's assertion.

He couldn't even tell her that he had no idea what she was talking about.

Then he noticed that she wasn't paying attention to him anymore. Her attention was on Elizabeth, where she stood with Lee by the buffet table. And where she'd been bright and open with Elizabeth, suddenly she looked concerned.

Jack took another look at Elizabeth, just to be sure, to find her nodding and listening as Lee expounded on something. Elizabeth looked interested; she looked animated. She certainly wasn't getting into any trouble.

"Anything the matter?" Jack asked.

Gen started, as if she'd forgotten he was standing there. This time her smile was almost too bright. Brittle. "No, of course not. You haven't told me yet. Did you like the play?"

He looked down at her, struggling to keep up with her sudden mood change. "It was brilliant."

That quickly, Gen was back with him, bright and uninhibited and proud. "It wore me away," she said honestly. "All her work does. But I'm hearing wonderful things."

She glowed, he thought. Fresh skin and vitality and intelligence, even with the circles beneath her eyes that betrayed what kind of day they'd had at work. What kind of a two weeks she'd so far survived in a service she didn't like.

"I saw the other play, too," he said, struggling for control. For something to say besides *Let me kiss you.* "You know, the one Elizabeth's school put on."

*"Some Men's Dreams,"* she said. "Yes."

"Elizabeth said it was based on your family."

"Loosely."

He shook his head, remembering the bare, weather-beaten look of the play. He remembered the struggle and the pain and the sacrifices of four children who just wanted to stay together. He looked down at Gen and wondered at the strength of a girl who could survive that to become one of the best doctors he knew.

She had done everything but offer her own life for little Jacob Edward yesterday. She'd held his mother in her arms and faced his father's rage with gentle understanding, and comforted her team when they'd failed.

He'd never met anyone like her.

And he could still smell those peaches.

"The plan for *Fire on the Mountain* is for it to end up on Broadway next season," she was saying, her attention now on her sister. She shook her head in amazement. "Imagine that."

Jack caught a quick glimpse of her sister, too, where she was evidently introducing Elizabeth to some more friends. "Your sister has an amazing insight," he admitted. "I'm amazed that somebody so young shows so much depth."

Gen didn't look away from her sister. "Lee's very special. I'm really glad her party is turning out so well. She deserves it."

Jack looked at her closely. "Isn't this your party, too?" he couldn't help but ask.

Gen turned back to him, bemused.

"For your graduation from slavery," he said. "You said you were celebrating both Lee's play and your freedom from people like me."

Gen laughed. "Oh, that. No. This is Lee's night. She worked awfully hard for it, and she deserves every pat on the back. Jake will take us all out someplace nice for my night."

For a second Jack could do no more than just stare at her. *Did Lee work as hard as you?* he wanted to ask. *Did she save lives or sing to babies?*

It occurred to him in that moment, as he watched Gen fondly watch her family, that he was angry. For her. For his bright, dedicated resident, who had raised that brother and sister to adulthood. He was angry because that brother and the other one, the older one, and the sister, as well, didn't realize how special their sister was.

He'd watched her all evening, settling disputes, solving problems, providing calm and coherence in the midst of the party, and not one of her siblings had noticed. Not one had thanked her or praised her or taken any of the burden off her shoulders.

Not one had any idea what kind of doctor she was or the impact she made.

Not one seemed to think that her triumph was as important as her little sister's.

More importantly, neither did she.

"It's not enough," he insisted.

Gen turned back to him, her hair swirling against her shoulders. Her bare shoulders. Jack's mouth went dry. He could smell those peaches again. And he couldn't quite take his eyes from all that hair, where it curled along her bare arms. Along her full, high breasts.

Oh, God.

And then he saw her eyes. Really looked. Looked more than her family or her friends or her chief attending ever had. And he saw that there was something way at the back, some detritus that wasn't happy and proud. Something anxious and dark and heavy.

"I'm sorry," he immediately said, sure he'd insulted her. "It's just that I know better than they do what it takes to get where you are right now. And they should be celebrating."

For a second Gen just stood there, wine in hand, gaze soft and considering. Then it seemed as if she shook off her pensive mood. She gave him a big smile and clinked glasses. "I take that as the finest compliment I've heard, older doctor. Thank you. And my family doesn't have to understand. They helped me get through it."

"Not when they've been in Wyoming and you've been in Chicago," he insisted a bit more gently.

Gen's smile was a little tighter. "Oh, I've only been in Chicago since Lee went to college. I couldn't leave before then. I commuted to Bozeman, Wyoming."

Jack couldn't think of a thing to say. Nor, he realized, did he have a right to. He was caught next to a surprisingly lovely Gen Kendall in her blue, blue dress and her long, thick hair, and his brain went completely dead, because the only things he wanted to say, he couldn't.

"Oh, dear, now Lee has Elizabeth talking to her producer," Gen said. "You could be here all night."

Jack looked vaguely in that direction, seeing how animated his daughter suddenly seemed and not understanding it.

"I wish she'd eat more," Gen said softly. "She's too thin for her age."

"Her mother was thin," he said automatically.

Gen turned to him, and Jack saw that anxious look again. He saw her straighten, her glass of wine trembling just that much, as if she were holding it more tightly.

She was going to say something, and Jack realized suddenly it was something she didn't think he would like. She was bracing herself.

"Barry Manilow, huh?" a voice suddenly chortled behind them. "You've made your brother Zeke a lot of money."

Gen started like an animal in the headlights. She turned to stare up at her brother. The mountain. The one who clapped her on the shoulder as if she were a bowling buddy.

Jack saw the almost comical dismay on her features and wanted to laugh.

"Barry Manilow what?" she retorted, head high.

Jake Kendall flicked her nose and laughed back, a rumbling, satisfied sound. "Nowhere to hide, Mom. Your boss gave you away. You sing Barry Manilow. All the time."

Gen swung to Jack in high dudgeon. "You had to tell them?"

"You didn't tell me not to."

That quickly, the chance for quiet conversation fled. The family was back, all noisy and challenging and close. Jack didn't mind, really. He needed to distance himself. He needed to distance his daughter, who had school tomorrow.

He needed to run like hell before he made a stupid mistake.

So he edged his way out of the conversation, gave Lee a wave goodbye while she argued with one of her brothers about musical taste, and headed off to grab Elizabeth from the clutches of those theater people and get her out the door.

"Do we *have* to go?" she asked.

Not in that spoiled, whiny kind of way most kids did. Sincerely, almost anxiously.

"I'm afraid I work for a living, Mouse."

At which point she nodded. She said goodbye, she took his hand, and she walked out the door with him. And Jack couldn't shake the feeling that she left her sparkle behind in that still-crowded room.

"Did you enjoy your big evening?" he asked.

She barely saw him next to her, even with her hand in his as they crossed Halsted. "I think I'm going to write a few tunes" was all she said.

Jack couldn't help staring at her. It was the Kendalls, he decided. All of them. Tumbling into his life like clowns from a Volkswagen and upending everything he knew.

It was Gen.

But it couldn't be.

So he walked across the street with his daughter and tucked her back in his safe Volvo so he could take her home, where they both belonged.

He dreamed of her that night. Sweaty, hot, twisted-in-the-sheets dreams that left him painfully hard and agonizingly embarrassed. He'd seen her in his dream in that dress. That blue, soft dress that hugged her curves like a second skin. He'd seen her out of it, in nothing but that long, lush hair. He'd seen her smile up at him in delight, and then in satiation. He'd almost lost the ultimate control right there in his silent bed in the empty hours of early morning, touching nothing more than his pillow.

And not once had he thought at all of his wife, whom he had loved so much.

He didn't get back to sleep.

She dreamed of him. Anxious, restless dreams of his hands, his eyes, his mouth. Urgent dreams of his laughter and his sighs, caught at the edge of the shadows in the deepest of nights. She woke frustrated and panting, knowing perfectly well that those wonderful surgeon's hands had been on her, had stroked and kissed and incited her.

And not once did she think of Elizabeth, who she thought might need her help.

She didn't get back to sleep, either.


She had to tell him.

It wasn't enough that she had to fall in lust with him, it seemed. It wasn't even enough that she fall head over her bloody heels in love with him, even though she knew better than anyone on the planet what kind of doomed project that would turn out to be.

No, evidently she also had to find herself in the position of hurting him.

Hurting him? Hell, she wasn't going to hurt him. She was going to shatter him.

Gen had begun to suspect the truth that moment in Elizabeth's room as the sun set to create sudden, sharp shadows on a young girl's face where there should have been none. When for the first time she'd seen the girl in something other than oversized T's and baggy jeans or sweats. She'd worried over it like a sore tooth all through the play when she'd sat next to that quiet child as she relived the pain of watching a mother die, and then during the premiere party, when she'd watched Elizabeth skirt the edges of the buffet table without ever really lighting. She'd all but closed her eyes to keep from watching the inevitable when Jack had handed his little girl a full plate with the choicest delicacies Juan Ton's had to offer.

Jack had placed that plate in Elizabeth's hands with a whimsical grin and a kiss to the forehead. Elizabeth waited until she thought no one could see her and then surreptitiously dumped every crumb of that food in the trash.

Even then, Gen had wanted to ignore it. Deny it like Cleopatra so that she would end up with another big dollop of guilt and responsibility to pile on her overloaded life plate. She'd pretended she could hint her way to the truth with Elizabeth's father, and that after that he would simply take care of the problem.

She'd tried that little stalling tactic for two days. But then, as if God had been ashamed of her, he sent her a little reminder.

A tiny, sweet fourteen-year-old who had collapsed in the middle of a gymnastics event. A girl who reminded Gen painfully of the earnest, intense Elizabeth. A little girl whose best friend, thinking that her friend was dying, finally admitted what all her friends knew but her parents didn't, that her friend had been subsisting on nothing more than laxatives and lettuce for the last three months to keep her weight down.

Gen couldn't avoid the problem anymore.

She knew what was wrong with Elizabeth, but she couldn't prove it.

She knew, but she couldn't approach Elizabeth until she talked to her father.

Her father whom Gen saw every day but never for a moment in private.

She knew, though, that she had to act. She knew with the instincts forged in a harsh furnace what had been bothering her from the moment she'd caught Elizabeth in that headlong flight onto the softball diamond.

Elizabeth O'Neill wasn't eating.

That bright, intense, painfully confused girl who missed her mother and adored her father was starving herself.

And her father didn't realize it.

Gen had to tell him. She had to break his father's heart in the hope she could help him save his daughter.

And she'd thought falling in love was going to have to be the most painful thing she faced in her life.

On each of the final six days of her residency, Gen tried to tell him. It was all she could think of. Well, that and the fact that she swore she could smell that citrus scent on her pillows at night. But in the grand scheme, that wasn't important. It wasn't, after all, anything that would make a difference. She might dream of Jack O'Neill late at night when her own defenses were down; she might stammer at the sound of his voice and blush at the sight of him. She might suddenly find her home in an intolerable disarray simply because the man in charge of her life for the last six days of her residency made her go weak in the knees.

But that didn't mean he would ever feel the same about her.

After all, she'd seen the picture of his wife, with the sun shining right through her pale-blue eyes. Gen knew what she was. More importantly, she knew what she herself wasn't.

But she could make a difference with Elizabeth. She had to.

Gen knew exactly how this situation was going to play out, though. She knew what it would cost. It would cost her any chance that Jack would even remain her friend. It would cost her sleep and sympathy and Elizabeth's smiles.

There was nothing she could do, though. She thought Elizabeth was in trouble, and she had to help.

No, she didn't think so. She *knew* so.

Deep in her gut, where her best instincts lived. Where the truth belied her family's memory of her own unmemorable childhood. The more Gen thought about it, the more she knew that Elizabeth desperately needed someone to help her.

But she wouldn't get that help without her father being told.

Gen tried every one of the last six days of her residency without success. It was summer, and in the summer pediatric hospitals were disaster zones. Every time she had a second, sitting in the cafeteria over mystery food or crashing for a nanosecond in the softly lit, overstuffed doctor's lounge, she was interrupted.

Gen helped save three children with meningococcal meningitis. She worked with Jack to pull four separate organ recipients through bleeding crises. She sat overnight by numerous cribs and cots and emergency room carts, monitoring and treating and interceding. She did much of it alongside Jack O'Neill.

What she wasn't able to do was tell her chief of service that his own little girl was in trouble.

The last day of Gen's residency did not begin well. She reached the hospital to find one of her kids in crisis, and then spent the morning fighting a losing battle to save her. And then, after she'd soaked the shoulder of her scrubs with another young mother's tears, Gen answered a page to find yet one more crisis on her hands.

"You murdered him."

A slurred voice. A grieving father's voice that brimmed with the poison of unrelieved grief.

Little Jacob Edward's father.

Again.

"Mr. Christian…" Gen pleaded, just as she had the last eight mornings and four afternoons when he'd called.

"Don't," he snapped. "Just don't. I only want you to know…to know. But you can't, can you? You don't have any kids."

"Please," she begged. "I don't want to have to call the police. But I will. You have to stop this."

"I will. When you're dead. And you're going to be dead. I've been watching, you know. Every day when you walk out of the hospital, and I know where you go. I know where you live, and I'll set fire to it. I'll lock you in, and maybe everybody else in there, so you'll know that you've murdered those people, too, and I'll watch you burn and scream and—"

Gen hung up. She sat there, right in the middle of the workplace, staring at the phone as if she could somehow change what had happened. What was going to happen.

Then, with shaking hands, she called the police. She called Mr. Christian's wife where she worked and warned her what was happening. She called social services and tried yet again to set up some kind of therapy for the family. At least a contact with one of the support groups that helped parents who had lost children.

"Dr. Kendall, line two," the operator droned overhead.

Gen picked up the phone, already knowing she wasn't going to like what she heard.

"The police are here, you bitch!" he screamed at her. "What have you done? What have you *done?*"

Gen dropped into a chair, her head in her hands. She wanted to cry. She wanted to scream. She wanted to run away. "Yes, Mr. Christian, I'm sure they are. You need help, and they're going to make sure you get it."

By the time she actually spoke to one of the answering officers, who assured her that they were taking a screaming Mr. Christian into custody, Gen decided that she had had enough. She just sat there in the ICU lounge and stared at the wall.

She wanted to cry. Somewhere in her residency, she'd forgotten how. Actually, she hadn't cried since the day her father had dropped dead in the barn, leaving a failing farm in the hands of an invalid wife and four young children.

It didn't make the hot ache ease in the back of her throat.

"You're looking a mite peaked, young doctor," she heard from above her.

Gen didn't bother lifting her gaze. "Jacob Edward Christian," she said.

"The baby boy with the Norwood shunt? I remember."

Gen nodded, her neck aching from the tension in her shoulders. "I just had his father arrested."

She sensed more than heard Jack O'Neill sit next to her. "He's the one who's been making those threatening phone calls?"

Gen startled. "How did you know?"

Jack's smile was wry. "Ginny, the evening operator. She says that all the hospital operators know. And that they're outraged."

"Me, too."

His eyes were crystalline. He reached over and took her hand, and Gen didn't even flinch at the spark of contact. She squeezed back and held on. She held on as hard as she could.

"I'm sorry, young doctor."

Gen sighed. "Me, too, older doctor."

Hold me, she thought. Put your arm around my shoulder and help me bear this weight. Just be there so I don't have to do this alone.

So I don't always have to do it alone.

"You did the only thing you could," he said. "He needed to get help, and you knew he wasn't going to get it any other way."

"I guess."

There was another silence, punctuated by the shuffle and clatter of the ICU. Gen concentrated on breathing past the distress she'd created. She tried her best to maintain her professional face.

Oddly enough, though, just holding Jack's hand eased her. He didn't move. Didn't touch more than her hand, didn't offer any useless platitudes or bracing encomiums. But he comforted her nonetheless, just like that day in her apartment.

She felt surrounded by him like warmth on a cold, cold night and thought that such a feeling could be addictive. To have another person to lean on, just once. Maybe a few times. To have him understand what you faced each and every day.

She'd always carried her burdens alone. After all, her mother hadn't had the strength, and Jake hadn't had the time. And the kids had been kids. As she'd grown, she'd simply become accustomed to it, like the silence in her apartment.

But for those few minutes in the oddly silent doctors' lounge, she felt as if Jack were holding her to his heart.

Gen closed her eyes against the burning in her throat. For just that little time, she pretended that this was what she could expect. What she deserved.

"It's the last day of your residency, young doctor," Jack said, his voice inexpressibly gentle. "How do you plan to celebrate?"

Gen's laugh was dry and harsh.

"Okay," he said, "I'll rephrase that. How do you plan to work off the stress? You're off in two hours."

Gen shrugged. "Go home. Open a bottle of wine. Torment my piano."

"Wrong."

That actually got Gen to look up. "Pardon?"

His grin was enough to ease a bit of the distress. "You get off at five this afternoon. At precisely seven, I, your last and best chief of service, will pick you up at your apartment and take you out for a celebratory dinner."

Gen straightened, shook her head. "Oh, no, you—"

"I know I don't have to. But I'm going to. It's my final order as your last chief of service. You, young doctor, are going to eat, drink and be merry, for tomorrow you're responsible for your own insurance, and life will never be the same."

Gen actually managed a grin. "Wow, you really have a way with enticements."

Now his smile was pure magic. Teeth and eyes and dimple. "It's one of my finer qualities."

She was so tired. She felt old and achy and washed-out. But she could almost glow in his reflection. She could almost believe that they could have a good time.

"And wear something nice, young doctor. Something that doesn't look like scrubs."

"If you're sure."

An elegant eyebrow lifted. "Oh, yeah. I hate scrubs."

Gen saw the shadow flicker across his eyes. She thought of how much she cherished the idea of an evening alone with Jack O'Neill, uninterrupted hours of his smile and touch and laughter.

Then she thought of the news she should bring to him this evening. News that would ruin that fine dinner he was offering her.

But it might be the only time they would have to talk. It would be her only chance to have his undivided attention.

It would be the only time she could chance reaching out to him, touch his hand, hold on to him while she broke his heart.

"All right, then," she said, losing a little of her borrowed sparkle as she let go of his hand. "Seven."

And he was there at seven. On the dot, knocking on her door. Gen was secretly glad, because she didn't really want to spend that night alone. She'd asked different people to spend it with her, to celebrate somewhere with cheap wine and cheaper food, or take-out movies and popcorn. Anything.

Nobody had been available.

Nobody except the most handsome man in Chicago.

At exactly seven o'clock, Gen opened the door to find Jack O'Neill standing out in the hallway clad in a custom charcoal suit and Marvin the Martian tie, his black hair tousled and his skin smooth from grooming. He was smiling and holding a big bouquet of spring flowers. Gen was glad she'd worn her second-best dress, a long, flowing, flowery number with spaghetti straps and a slit up the side. She was breathless just with the sight of him, the smell of him.

Citrus and something. Something not medicinal. Something sexy and compelling. Something that made her desperately want to dip her nose into his neck. To taste the salt of his skin and nuzzle the sleek silk of his freshly shaved chin.

"Good God," he murmured, eyeing her.

It was then that she saw his eyes. Suddenly dark, his pupils huge. She heard the catch in his breath. She all but shivered at the heat that seared through her just from the intensity of his gaze. She felt the lightning.

She felt it, sharp and sudden, scorching every nerve ending in her body.

"You said no scrubs," she managed, her own voice suddenly throaty and hesitant.

She had important things to discuss with him tonight. She couldn't feel like this.

She couldn't *not* feel like this.

God, she was burning to ashes in her own living room, and she didn't know what to do.

He did it for her. Straightening like a man with his finger caught in a light socket, Jack O'Neill plastered a smile on his beautiful features. "Then I guess it's a good idea I brought you flowers like a real gentleman, huh?"

Gen could smile. "A fine touch of class. You must have studied with a master."

"I got them at the Quick Trip when I put oil in my car."

She surprised herself with a laugh. "The perfect ending to a perfect day."

"Not at all, young doctor. The perfect ending comes at the fine restaurant of my choice when the wait staff sings 'Happy Graduation to You' while putting a silly hat on your head."

Gen shook her head as she accepted the flowers. "I guess I shouldn't expect more from a man who drives a Volvo."

"Hey," she heard as she scrounged for a vase, "that Volvo is *safe!*"

"That's what I hear. Still, a little disappointing in the suave and sophisticated department."

"That was what the flowers were for."

Gen grabbed her purse, locked up with hands that were trembling all over again and followed him down the silent stairs.

Even Lee and Rock weren't home tonight, off doing something with Rock's friends from his time on the police force. Not even her sister to help celebrate the fulfillment of her dream. Oh, they'd had the family dinner at Harry Carey's, all laughter and easy reminiscences of tough-disciplinarian Gen, organizational-fuhrer Gen, everybody-goes-to-church Gen. They'd raised glasses and then left for their own lives, and now she had to rely on her boss to celebrate the day itself.

Her boss who was making her hands sweat and her heart stumble. A good news, bad news joke of the highest order, she decided.

"I hope you don't mind Juan Ton's again," he said as he helped her into the Volvo. "I really got a kick out of that place."

"The Kendalls have their own booth," she assured him.

They drove east on Dickens to Halsted and reached the front door to the restaurant in moments. Gen was busy trying hard not to succumb to the urge to touch Jack O'Neill and didn't pay attention to where she was going. She didn't notice that there weren't any patrons waiting in clusters outside the front door for the next available table. She did notice that Jack rested his hand against the small of her back as he guided her through the door. In fact, she noticed that so strongly that it took her darn near a full minute to realize that he was guiding her in with a purpose.

"Surprise!"

Gen screeched to a halt right in the front door, the sound of Jack's chuckle in her ear.

She gaped. Her heart stopped. She knew it did.

Juan Ton's was packed. There were nurses there, and doctors and med techs and X-ray techs, even several parents of some of her long-term patients. There were residents she'd trained, and Abbie and Michael Viviano. And in the middle, as if it were completely natural, every one of her siblings, back from their homes. And every one of them was lifting a drink to her.

"What's this?" she asked instinctively.

"It's the party to celebrate the end of your slavery, young doctor," Jack told her.

Gen turned to him. She turned back to the crowd.

Then, from the sound system, rose the voice of Barry Manilow, singing, "This One's for You," and all Gen could do was laugh.

# Chapter 8

It was the best party of her life.

It was the most difficult party of her life.

It was the first surprise party anyone had ever thrown for her.

Gen was the one in charge of surprise parties. She always had been, making clandestine calls, sending surreptitious invitations, hiding cars and refreshments, and organizing time schedules like an air traffic controller to ensure the greatest surprise. It had always been her job.

She didn't know how to be the recipient. She didn't know how to handle the fact that all these people had come to celebrate with her.

She especially didn't know how to deal with the fact that it had all been Jack O'Neill's idea.

Especially since it was her big brother who made it a point to tell her.

"I'm not sure I appreciated getting a phone call like that," Jake said, his granite brow lowered as he sipped at his beer.

"He *called* you?" Gen demanded, her voice just a bit weak.

"Got the number from Lee. Suggested that maybe the family

hadn't appreciated just what you'd achieved. That we should know.''

Gen knew she was beet red. She only held on to her place in the room by force of will.

''I didn't know.''

For that she got a grin from her brother, a quick, hard hug. ''He was right, Mom,'' he told her, as ever using the nickname they'd given her all those years ago when she'd taken over the house. ''You're the very best of us, and we forgot to tell you.''

Gen felt that burning of tears at the back of her throat again. Tears adversity wouldn't loosen—maybe sentiment would. She couldn't allow that. Not here. Not now.

''Don't be silly, Jake,'' she insisted. ''I wasn't the one who walked out into the snow and cold every day to hold that ranch together. I wasn't the one who made sure we got our education so we could leave if we wanted to.''

''If we wanted?'' he retorted, eyebrow raised.

''I'm coming home,'' she said simply. ''In another year or so, when I've paid off some of these loans. I'll be going into practice with Doc MacPherson.''

The other eyebrow rose. ''You're sure? You've worked awfully hard to be a fancy big-city doc.''

''I've worked hard to be a doc,'' she amended. ''I miss the mountains.''

Jake didn't betray his emotions much. He'd never had the luxury until his marriage, and since then hadn't had the need, his wife, Amanda, understanding him better than he did. But suddenly there were tears in his pale-gray eyes. He nodded once, hugged her again, and then sent her away to garner the rest of her kudos. But the fact that he'd been happy about her announcement, that he and Amanda had come back eight hundred miles for her, was more than enough.

And Jack O'Neill had been the one to give her that present. Gen saw him standing nearby, laughing at something Abbie Viviano was saying, and her heart skipped a beat. The sweetness of his laugh seemed to seep into her very marrow and soften it. The gleam in those ocean eyes that held such wisdom and mirth and wit enchanted her. The sharp tang of his scent sent her shuddering with a sharp sexual need.

Oh, but she loved him. She loved a man who was so considerate he'd given her the gift of understanding. She wanted him so much she went clammy every time she smelled citrus. She was so attuned to him that she listened for his voice like a mystic seeking revelation.

Gen also saw Elizabeth where she talked with the pale, quiet woman who was her full-time nanny, and the glow of wonder died a little. Because she thought of how she had to repay him.

It was a party, though. Surely she shouldn't have to sully this gift with the truth to come. Surely she could, just for once in her life, enjoy the moment without having to face the consequences.

"I didn't know you could scrape up this many people who'd pretend to be your friends," Zeke said from behind her.

Gen turned to smile up at her little brother, the one who looked like her, but with a chin that could cut glass. "A little money in the right places can scare up anything, Sparky," she said, using the nickname Zeke had had ever since he'd tried to take apart a toaster he'd forgotten to unplug. "Thanks for coming and fooling all of them into thinking I have a family who likes me, too."

Zeke gave her his own hug. "Well, one doesn't ignore a call from Jake, no matter what potsherd one has in one's hands. Or which cute young anthropology major is holding it."

Zeke was their wanderer, an anthropologist who spent much of his time in remote places putting together pieces of dead civilizations.

"Threatened you, did he?"

"Didn't have to. Your doctor was right. We probably would have figured it out if they hadn't delayed Lee's opening until just about the week before you finished. And we were all up here for your med school graduation, ya know."

"No, Jake, Amanda and Lee were at my graduation. You missed it because you and that little—what was it? Flight attendant?—were too distracted to look at a clock in your motel room."

His grin was still brash and bright. "We struck up a cosmic understanding on the flight from Phoenix. I made your graduation dinner, though."

"After you dropped her back off at the airport."

His expression was winsome. "A cosmic understanding doesn't last past the moment when a woman claims that it is her karmic destiny to have your child. Serendipity simply does not extend to parenthood."

Gen shook her head, chuckling. "That'll teach you to listen to a woman from Los Angeles."

Zeke's smile was bright. "I learned never to listen to any woman, honey. It saves time."

Gen scowled. "I'll give you five-to-one odds that you'll be caught in that big 'I do' trap within six months."

"Five-to-one?" Lee demanded from a couple of feet over.

She'd been talking to Elizabeth, probably about music. At least, Elizabeth looked animated in that way she had near music. She looked pretty and bright in her fuchsia print dress.

"Zeke's trying that 'I disparage all women' routine again," Gen said. "I've told him he's heading for the big fall with the next cute girl he stumbles across."

"Not unless she's a dead Celtic warrior," Zeke assured her. "I'm heading to the wilds of Ireland next month to take part in a comparative study of death practices."

"You do have all the fun," Lee told him.

"Zeke, honey," Gen added, "let me be the first to tell you. Ireland has no wilds. You're going to tumble for some fey young redheaded lass, and I'll collect my money."

"I've got ten on that," Lee said.

"Fifty," Jake added, unable, as were any of the Kendalls, to withstand a sure bet.

"And what about you, Mom?" Zeke demanded of his big sister. "Shouldn't we be putting some money on whether you're about to take that big walk yourself?"

"Me?" Gen all but squeaked. "Are you nuts? Now that I'm *finally* free, you want me to tie myself down again? Don't be ridiculous."

"Ten-to-one," Zeke said, never taking his gaze from Gen's.

"I'm on," Jake agreed.

"Me, too," said Lee, her gaze deliberately drifting to just beyond Gen's shoulder.

Gen didn't even have to turn to know what her sister saw. She felt him, just as she had all night long, nothing more than his proximity crawling along her skin like static electricity. She smelled him, sharp and rich and heady. She heard the silky timbre of his laugh as he shared hospital stories with some of the other staff. She knew just what her family was thinking, and she knew with utter humiliation that they thought their assumption was making her blush.

She would be even more humiliated if they knew what she was really blushing about.

Then she saw Elizabeth's eyes track after Lee's and go wide. A little hollow. And Gen knew she had to put an end to this right away. Making the same kind of motion with her own eyes to subtly indicate Elizabeth, she laughed as if her family amused her greatly.

"Excellent," she said blithely. "I'll put fifty on that. Between the money I'm gonna win on Zeke and the ten-to-one winnings I'll score from you guys on me, I'll finally be able to afford that new laptop I've wanted. What about it, Elizabeth? Got any extra money you want to turn into a sure profit?"

Elizabeth just blinked a couple of times.

Over their heads, Barry swung into "Bandstand Boogie." Gen decided that it was providence. Grabbing Elizabeth's hand, she pulled her out onto the floor to distract her with a little swing dancing. It only took another moment for the rest of the crowd to join in and her family to comfortably disperse. Gen laughed and sang in her off-key voice, and laughed again when she saw Elizabeth, with her probably near-perfect-pitch ear, wince in a ladylike fashion.

"Loosen up, Elizabeth," Gen urged, twirling the girl so her hair fanned out. "This is a party."

Elizabeth regained her wobbly balance and attempted a smile. "If you say so."

"You've been hanging around with us Kendalls long enough to expect this."

''That's what worries me.''

Gen laughed. ''David and Emily send their love. They miss you.''

This time Elizabeth laughed. ''I miss them more.''

''Don't tell your father that, okay? The piano's not a problem, but I'm not sure he's gonna get over my wall.''

''I'm not sure I will, either.''

When the song ended, Gen had every intention of working Elizabeth over to the food table, but somebody put an Ellington CD on, and Gen got grabbed for another dance. She danced with two of her fellow residents, one of the pediatric trauma docs she would be working with next week, and the father of one of her patients who had resided in the ICU for the last nine months. She danced with her various brothers. She saw her family dance, and Abbie and Michael. And twice she saw Jack O'Neill dance with his daughter.

Once Elizabeth danced on top of her dad's shoes, as if she were three again, and the entire room smiled. Gen, twirling around in the arms of her brother-in-law, Rock O'Connor, felt her heart constrict at the sight. She saw the tight little world the two of them had formed and inexplicably felt left out. She ached for inclusion.

Her family had moved on without her. They were here for her, yes, but Jake and Lee had found their own worlds, and Zeke had chosen to leave. Gen realized, watching Jack O'Neill smile that bright, happy-daddy smile down on his laughing daughter, that she did want another family. She did want someone to share her bright Tuscan rooms and her friends and her favorite places.

And, damn it, she wanted it to be a doctor who had never recovered from the loss of his wife and his daughter who wanted nothing but him.

It wasn't fair.

She should be looking for a good singles' bar, a health food store, a seat in the bleachers at Wrigley, where she could search out single men. She was free now to enjoy herself. She'd made it. She'd walked her last day as a resident. In another week she would return to the hospital as an attending physician with all

commensurate privileges. She would have a set shift and a pay-
check. She would have security. She should want some fun.

Instead she wanted Jack O'Neill and his fragile daughter, Elizabeth.

She wanted them with a sudden, searing power that took her
breath away.

"Gen?" Rock asked. "You okay?"

Gen looked up at her handsome brother-in-law and smiled.
"How can I not be?" she demanded. "All these people came
to congratulate me on living through my training. What more
could a girl want?"

Gen knew that Rock saw the shadow belying her words. He
wouldn't push, though. He would leave that to Lee. And Gen
was impervious to Lee.

So they finished dancing to "Sophisticated Lady," and Gen
spun to an end to find herself face-to-face with Jack O'Neill.

"My turn," he invited, hand out.

Gen almost wondered if he'd heard her thinking. She almost
balked. Hell, she almost ran. But she hadn't just endured critical
care medicine for nothing. She knew how to survive a crisis.
Her heart was in her throat, and she could feel the first trickle
of perspiration forming between her shoulderblades, but she accepted his hand.

Lightning sparked from his fingertips to send her shivering.
Heat rose in his eyes, and Gen thought she would never be able
to form another coherent thought as long as she lived. She knew
only the need to stay right where she was.

She couldn't breathe.

She couldn't think.

But she had to. There were simply too many people here who
wouldn't understand, chief among them her partner's daughter.
And considering what Gen knew to be in the girl's future, she
didn't need to further tip the apple cart right now by drooling
over Elizabeth's father in public.

Besides, she would never be able to hold her head up at work.

But, oh, how hard it was not to simply sink into his arms,
close her eyes and pretend she was where she belonged.

Instead, she dragged in a breath. She looked away from those mesmerizing eyes. She straightened a little, gathering calm.

"Thank you," she said as they whirled around the room. Glen Miller now, "String of Pearls." Probably Amanda's choice. Amanda loved the standards. Gen kept telling her that Barry Manilow would be a standard one day, but Amanda wasn't buying any of that.

"Thank you for what?" Jack asked, his eyes darker than the smile he showed. "Letting you care for my daughter when I couldn't? Being a hell of a critical-care fellow? Inviting my family to a world-premier play and making my daughter feel special?"

Gen scowled. "Nice try. You upbraided my brother Jake."

"I did."

"Not many people have come through that kind of experience unscathed."

Jack chuckled. "He's something."

Gen actually managed to meet his gaze with a smile of her own. "You have no idea."

"He really couldn't read until he was over thirty?"

Gen sought out her brother, standing foursquare in a linen shirt and tailored slacks. She never thought of Jake in good clothes. She thought of him in worn jeans, battered boots and a flannel shirt. She thought of him out in his mountains where his horses ran. She thought of him as tall and strong as the Wind River Range, and she'd been an adult before she'd realized he was as vulnerable as any human.

"He basically ran the ranch from the time he was twelve. Turned it from a failing cattle concern to one of the finest horse ranches in the country. Pushed the three of us to get college educations so we wouldn't be stuck the way he felt he was."

"That wasn't in the play. That he couldn't read."

"Lee didn't know. None of us did. Amanda saw what none of us did and changed his life."

"Then yours is an entirely amazing family."

Gen looked up to see the warmth in Jack's eyes. Her heart sped up. Her chest tightened until she couldn't breathe. She felt giddy and dizzy and fragile. And suddenly, for the first time in her life, special.

"No more amazing than most," she demurred anyway, wishing she could simply lay her head against his chest. "We just got through."

This time he smiled. But he didn't say any more.

She should tell him, Gen thought to herself as she struggled against the heady delight of his touch, his scent, the brush and nudge of his thighs against hers as they swept across the room. She should ask him if he knew about his daughter. She should finally make the push to keep Elizabeth safe.

She didn't. She hummed to the music and cherished this moment of intimacy. She wallowed in his touch and bathed in his scent, that citrus that tickled her nose so. She savored the sight of his smile, that sly dimple peaking out from his cheek, the sun-kissed water of his eyes. She stoked herself on him like sunlight in a dark world and wished she never had to move away.

She bathed herself in the stirrings of her body, the hummings and sizzlings that were sparked by nothing more than simple contact with his legs, his hands, the whisper of his breath against her hair. She savored his closeness and thought she could manage this much without demanding more.

She wished desperately that that were actually possible, because she knew it was all she would get.

The music ended, and Jack pulled away. Gen was caught by his actions, her hands still up, her eyes wide. Her body protested the separation. Her heart protested his suddenly careful posture. Her brain demanded she act like an adult.

But she didn't want to. She wanted to fold herself back into his arms and forget everything else that needed to be said and done.

She wanted to forget what she'd discovered in the dying light of his daughter's bedroom.

"If I'm not mistaken," she said to him, hoping like hell she didn't sound as breathy as she felt, "there's a whole line of med students waiting to dance with you in the hope they can make a favorable impression on the man who decides their residency."

Jack cocked an eyebrow. "You could at least have left me with my delusions that they think I'm a good dancer."

"You *are* a good dancer," she retorted with a too-bright grin. "We all consider that an added bonus. We'd hate to have to lie when we suck up."

Jack laughed, then lifted his hand, as if he were compelled to touch her. Gen didn't realize she'd held her breath until she saw him stop short and pull back. She got another smile, though, a wry, bemused one, and then he turned away.

So she did the same.

And saw Elizabeth again, as if to remind her of her dereliction of duty.

It was time, Gen thought, breathing slowly to wash away the lingering remnants of Jack's magic. She'd come up with enough excuses. She had to find out for sure if she needed to frighten Jack and further traumatize his daughter.

So she walked over to where Elizabeth was sipping soda with her nanny.

"So, Elizabeth," she asked, "are you going to introduce me to this poor, long-suffering woman who took you off my hands?"

Elizabeth's smile was warmer now that she was with the Kendalls. Gen relished that without giving away the fact that she was measuring the sharpness of the shadows along the girl's face and neck and arms.

"This is Mary McGregor, Gen. Mary, you've heard me talk about Gen, haven't you?"

"I've heard you talk about her bathroom wall," Mary McGregor said with a soft, wise smile.

Gen laughed. "It does go a long way toward encouraging good hygiene. Thanks for bringing the brat along. It wouldn't have been the same without her."

"That's what she says," Elizabeth retorted. "My dad throws a good party, don't you think?"

Gen saw the girl seek out her father and smile. A wistful, yearning kind of smile. The smile of a child who felt she was lacking. Gen wished she knew why. She wished she could make it all better.

"Your dad throws a *great* party," she said. "I'm very honored by it."

"I didn't get a chance to say congrats yet. Dad says that this is the biggest moment of a doctor's life."

"It is," Gen assured her, linking arms with her and stepping down the room. "Because I have so many good friends who came to share it with me. The only thing that could make it more perfect would be if we had a piano. I'd love for you to play for us."

"Oh, no," Elizabeth demurred, cheeks pinkening. "Not an audience."

"Yes, an audience, Elizabeth," Mary McGregor insisted from where she followed right behind.

Gen nodded. "Mary's right, Elizabeth. An audience. You will one day, and you'll be surprised how much you like having them hear you. Why, look what it's done for Barry Manilow."

Who was, just then, singing "I Write the Songs."

Gen grinned. "Prophetic, huh?"

Elizabeth tried very hard not to grimace. "You really like him?"

"Lee listens to Motley Crue. Go figure. Have you come up with some songs for her show?"

Elizabeth nodded, her expression tightening. "I'm afraid to show them to her."

"Didn't I just say she listens to Motley Crue? Trust me, no matter what you write, it'll be better. I'm really looking forward to hearing them."

During their talk, Gen had guided Elizabeth along the length of the brightly decorated room as if they were just watching the party. Her expression considering, Mary McGregor followed along. "Oh, hallelujah!" Gen said, reaching the laden food table. "The famous Juan Ton pot stickers. I can't wait, especially since I didn't get a chance to have any at Lee's party. Have you tried them yet, Elizabeth?"

Elizabeth didn't exactly cringe. She just seemed to shy away a little. "Oh, I had a little something, but I don't eat pork."

"You had exactly two pieces of melon, Elizabeth," Mary objected.

Elizabeth's smile was just a shade too bright. "I'm afraid I was really hungry this afternoon and snacked right before we left. I had a long day at science camp today."

"I can't imagine science making you so hungry," Gen said with a grin as she piled her plate under Elizabeth's critical eye. "But then, I can't imagine going to a camp that doesn't involve horses and handicrafts. What kind of handicrafts do you do at science camp?"

Elizabeth made a moue of distaste. "No handicrafts," she said, looking just like the child she still was. "Physics."

Pronounced *phy*-sics, like *dis*-sentery.

Gen grimaced right back. "Way above my head," she agreed. "It probably would have sent me running for the Chee-tos, too."

Another minimal flinch. "Not if I want to stay in my jeans, it didn't," she said, sounding like every teenage girl in America. "I'm a fruit-and-cheese kind of girl."

Gen handed her a plate. "Well, you're in luck. Juan has plenty of both. And I promise, unless you wear size-four jeans, you'll fit just fine."

"I wear size two," Elizabeth protested, eyeing the table as if it were traitorous.

"Size two," Gen mourned with a shake of her head. "What is the fashion industry doing, trying to make women disappear?"

Elizabeth's gaze snapped up to her. The plate ended up on the table, empty. "You don't understand...."

Gen looked at the plate, and then she deliberately swung her gaze up to Elizabeth.

"Oh," she said softly, taking hold of Elizabeth's hand and facing the little girl with all the empathy she could, "I think I do."

Elizabeth's eyes widened. She seemed to still in Gen's grasp, a small, vulnerable animal fearing a trap. Gen could feel her sudden tension through tendon and muscle. She felt sharp angles beneath her fingers and knew that there wasn't anything else she could do but what she had to.

There was no question in her mind anymore. It was all there in Elizabeth's panicked eyes.

Elizabeth wouldn't understand. This brittle little girl who had withstood so much would blame Gen. Would fight and run and lie.

But Gen had no choice.

She smiled, gave Elizabeth's hand a conspiratorial squeeze before letting go. "I smell Oil of Olay," she said quietly so that even Mary wouldn't hear. "Has it worked?"

Elizabeth relaxed by fractions. "Yeah. It has, some. I smell peaches."

Gen smiled big. "I know."

It was all she could do for the moment. She had her answer, though, in half-truths, evasions and the defense of an obscene pants size. She needed to talk to Jack.

She couldn't do it now. Not during the party he was giving for her.

"Wish *my* last chief of service had been this nice," one of her fellow residents drawled behind her.

"Wish mine had been a recognizable species," another offered.

Gen turned to the group and offered the same bland smile she'd offered everyone.

"You've set a terrible precedent," Gen suggested when Jack joined the group.

Jack's smile was easy. "Not at all. I just found a way to load up on Juan Ton's famous pot stickers once a year for the foreseeable future. He's quite pleased with the idea himself. It seems medical people eat more than the normal human."

"I think you might get mighty tired of those pot stickers after a while, older doctor," Gen said.

"All right, that's enough," he protested. "As of tonight, Dr. Kendall, you can desist from calling me older doctor as if I were in the cast of *Kung Fu*. You are officially an attending physician. You may call me…Dr. O'Neill."

"No, no," Gen demurred. "That is far too generous. I couldn't manage more than, say, Doctor."

"Doc," somebody offered.

"D."

The rest of the group picked up the banter, and the party went on around them, laughing and joking and moving on to other medical oddities and shared stories. Gen, knowing better, looked toward Jack and found him looking back.

She shuddered, stuttered to a halt. She fought the surge of heat that swept her right there on the dance floor in front of her friends.

They hadn't even touched this time. They weren't even close, but it arced hot and sharp between them. The lightning, hot and swift and smelling of citrus and something else, crackling along her skin, setting the hair at the back of her neck to attention. She felt her own body react, softening, anticipating, wanting.

Wanting.

She watched Jack's eyes dilate, saw his nostrils flare just the tiniest bit, as if he would never allow himself even an autonomic reaction. Then, as if pulling himself back from far off, he stiffened. Gave a quick shake of the head, a small, careful shrug. He smiled as if it meant nothing and turned to speak to someone else.

But Gen knew.

It hadn't meant nothing. And she couldn't get it out of her system for the rest of the evening.

Mary McGregor took Elizabeth home early. Jake and Amanda left not long after for the Ambassador East Hotel, where they were making a romantic weekend of it, which prompted Zeke to start laying bets on what their next child's name would be, since it would be too ugly to just name the child Chicago the way they'd named their last child Sienna. Night shift demanded many of the staff, early hours the rest. Lee and Rock refused to offer an excuse when they left, but since Zeke was walking with them, they obviously weren't expecting a romantic anything.

It was after one when Jack and Gen pulled up before Gen's building. Gathering her purse and one of the bright-gold helium balloons that had floated around the restaurant, she climbed out of the car. The pleasure of the evening had morphed into anxiety. This was the time. This was her chance to talk to Jack about his daughter.

It would have been perfect if Gen hadn't been so distracted by her hormones.

Oh, God, but she was distracted.

She was obsessed.

He looked so good. He smelled better. His voice rumbled like velvet in the darkened car, climbing her nerves like a glissando. Nothing more than his proximity had sent her temperature skyward and her brain into meltdown.

She had to think.

Tough to do when one is awash in lust.

She tried anyway.

"Uh, would you like to come up for some coffee?" she asked, mortified by how breathy she sounded. "It just so happens that I don't have to go in for grand rounds tomorrow."

"So I heard." He didn't even look at her as they stood out by the front door to the big Victorian brownstone. Instead, he seemed to gauge the street, the night, the all-but-invisible sky. He seemed to need a deep, slow breath. Then, turning toward her door, he nodded. "Yes," he said, his voice low. "I think I would."

So Gen let them in and led the way up the three flights of steps. She opened the door, surprised that her hand wasn't shaking, and flipped on the lights. She could feel Jack right behind her, crowding the air in her usually airy room. She could hear his breathing, as if all other sound had disappeared.

Or was it her own breathing? She couldn't quite tell anymore.

She knew she could feel her heart. It was suddenly slamming around in her chest as if seeking flight. She could feel the tension in every fiber of every muscle. She couldn't seem to take more than five steps into her high, echoing living room before she stalled to a halt, as if she'd walked to the end of her tether.

She heard Jack stop right behind her.

"Gen..."

Gen turned, for no other reason than the taut edge to his voice. She looked up at him, saw the pain, the harsh need in his eyes. She knew now that it was his breathing she'd heard, because it matched her own, short and sharp and anxious. She saw that perspiration had broken out on his forehead. Above her head, the bright-gold balloon bobbed in the shadows, but Gen didn't notice.

She should move. She should shove him out the door and run and hide under her bed.

She should tell him now what she'd brought him up here to say.

She did none of it.

She stood there, waiting, knowing that he had to make the decision, knowing that he was more torn than she by the sudden, surprising passion that had erupted between them.

"I can't..." His voice was so harsh, his eyes, those sea-green eyes, almost lost to his pupils. He lifted his hand, dragged it through his hair. Straightened and then stopped, as if he, too, were at the end of a tether. Gen could smell his hunger on him, and she couldn't help stepping toward him.

He looked up, startled. Torn. He looked for a second as if he would fend her off. As if he would finally think better of what he wanted to do.

He had no more luck than Gen in doing what he should. In no longer than a heartbeat, he surrendered. Stepping right up to her, he brought up his hands. Held them inches from her face, as if yearning to cup it to him. Sucked in air like a dying man. Shook his head.

"God help me, Gen, I can't walk away."

"He'd better help us both, then, Jack," she answered, tipping her head back a little more, exposing her vulnerable throat. "I can't walk away, either."

His hands came down; they closed on her, around her, and Gen Kendall's life changed forever. Above her, the gold balloon floated away into the shadows and was lost.

# Chapter 9

She was lost before his mouth ever found hers. She was shaking and seeking and awash in sensation. Gen had never wanted anything so much. She had never felt this much, drowning in nothing more than the scent of a man's throat. The sleek texture of his mouth. The hard planes of his athlete's body. She'd never known what it was like to lose control, but lose it she did.

They both did, right there in her living room. She didn't even remember closing the front door, but she must have. She didn't remember how her dress ended up pooled on the floor, or where Jack's clothes went. She just remembered skin and scent and sound, harsh breathing, calloused fingers, soft, soft lips. Sleek, seeking tongues.

She remembered whimpering and sighing and begging, her hands claiming his throat, his chest, his hips, her mouth mating with his with a fury that left them both bruised and tender. She remembered his hands in her hair, his face against her throat, his gaze roaming over her as if memorizing her. She remembered the sweet, hesitant first touch of his hand against her breast. His quick intake of breath, as if he had been holding it until that very moment. She remembered arching against him, allowing him access, aching to have him take her breast in his mouth, to torment her with teeth and tongue and suckling mouth.

She remembered that he did. Oh, he did, until she was keening in the darkened room, her eyes closed, her head thrown back, her skin damp with sweat and her hands anxious against his back.

She remembered that suddenly, somehow, they were on her bed, amid her lush linen covers and soft, downy pillows, trapped in the gauze that fluttered from the four posts, making love in sight of the gardens of Sienna, where they drowsed on her wall. She remembered that he made her want to sing, that he made her want to weep. She remembered that his body fit so well against hers that after a while she lost the feeling of separation entirely. She remembered that he waited long enough, just long enough, to make sure that it was safe for them both.

And then, and then, oh, he was inside her. Full and hard and furious, as furious as she to fuse, to find that perfect place where bodies became something more, something incandescent, something shattering. Gen wrapped around him, she pulled him into her, farther, farther, as deep as she could, as deep as her heart that had been lost hours before, days before, and she welcomed him, she crooned to him and called to him, and he came to her, his arms broad and strong, his words impossibly gentle, his body a furnace that melted and reformed her into something bright and amazing.

And when the lights exploded in that darkened room and her body sang and shattered, she wept, her tears kissed away and her trembling arms easing him as he followed her, his own voice harsh and hoarse and surprised, as if the power of what they'd shared had shocked him, as well.

And then, in the darkness, they simply lay on Gen's Tuscan bed, entwined and sated and silent. The moon peeked in through the flutter of gauze curtains, and down on the street a car crept past. Gen's heart slowly eased, and her body cooled, except where it met his. She felt the stutter of his heart, that great heart that had so endeared her. She heard the rasp of his breath as he calmed. She felt the increasing weight of his body as he relaxed toward sleep. And she claimed him, there in her heart, in the silence of her room, where until now she'd kept only dreams. She held him safely there, knowing how hard it would be to hold him later. She kept her arms quietly about him, cherishing the feel of his weight against her, until, finally, she slept, too.

It was the lightning that woke him. Sharp against closed eyes from a window that lay directly across from the bed. The window in his own bedroom was alongside the bed, not across. It was the first thing that occurred to him. Second, that it was still dark out. There was a storm coming in, the thunder separated by seconds from the shattering, sharp light. The light that limned the sleek limbs that lay atop his.

Jack opened his eyes wider. Funny, the minute he knew he wasn't home, he knew exactly whose limbs those were, even when he'd woken from a deep sleep. He *should* have thought it was Meggie. Meggie had been the only woman he'd ever allowed himself to fall asleep with.

It should have been the familiar weight of Meggie's arm he expected across his chest, Meggie's knee tucked up alongside his. But he'd woken to know that that soft breast that pressed against his chest belonged to Gen Kendall, that the faint breath he could feel against his shoulder was hers.

Maybe it was the scent of peaches. Meggie had always smelled like Oil of Olay, of all things. He still couldn't smell it without expecting to see her when he turned. But what he smelled in the syncopated light of the summer storm was peaches. Peaches and woman. Peaches and woman and sex.

He was already hard again. For the third time that night.

He couldn't believe it. Any of it. Not that he'd followed her home, or that he'd talked himself into following her upstairs. He couldn't believe the flare of need he'd felt when she'd no more than turned to him, those sweet autumn eyes of hers huge and uncertain in the shadows of midnight.

He couldn't really separate one moment from another in those first minutes that followed, just fury and hurry and need. Explosive, all-consuming hunger, as if he wouldn't be able to take another breath if he couldn't touch her, taste her, wrap himself around her as if she were his last lifeline. Drive himself into her as if his very soul depended on it.

Which was ridiculous. He'd forfeited his soul five years ago when he'd watched Meggie's life leak away in his arms. He had nothing left but responsibility and duty. He had Elizabeth to love. He needed nothing else.

He'd sure as hell needed to make love to Gen Kendall twice tonight, though. And now he needed to do it again.

He wouldn't. He would just lie there for a few more minutes, savoring the scent of the shadows in her elegant fairy tale of a room, and then he would go. He'd go before either of them had the chance to believe that what had happened to them had been more than the effect of combustible chemicals and alcohol.

He'd go before he lost himself in her again.

As he had twice already.

Just the thought of being inside her made him sweat all over again. She'd been so tight, so hot and sweet and wild, demanding just as much as she gave. She'd pulled and begged and bucked, driving him to madness. She'd sobbed and sung, and he was sure she'd laughed aloud at least once, as if she couldn't contain the joy of the moment.

God, he wanted to hear her do it again.

He could still taste her on his tongue, hear her soft sighs as they'd woken to each other again, this time to slow explorations and languorous pleasure. He could still feel the weight of her breasts in his hands, the slope of her hip, the silk of her hair.

He had to get home.

Elizabeth couldn't know he'd been gone all night. Except for work, he hadn't been away from her all night since her mother had died.

Thunder rumbled against the windows, and a gust of humid wind ruffled the curtains. Jack thought again about getting up.

"Is that rain?" Gen asked against his chest.

She stretched a little, and he grew harder. Her body was so sleek, so soft. It had been so long since he'd savored the silk of a woman's skin. Since he'd felt the pebbling of a nipple against his hand.

Since he'd wanted to.

He wanted to now.

He gritted his teeth and held still.

"Yeah," he said, knowing he sounded stiff. "I'd better be going."

"Mmm-hmm."

She still sounded half-asleep. It might have been why she was repositioning herself, snuggling closer, her hand slipping to his belly. It might have been, but that wasn't why she was humming, deep in her throat.

"I should go."

"Mmm-hmm."

Her hand moved lower, and Jack was lost all over again.


What exactly did one say to a man you'd made love to three times the night before? Gen wondered. Thank you? Nice job? Come again?

Gen belted her robe and stepped out of the bathroom into a stormy morning that any other day would have sent her right back to bed.

Today, though, she had a man in her apartment. A man she couldn't seem to keep her hands off.

A man who looked as if her touch would send him to hell.

"Gen…"

He was raking his hand back through his hair again, a sure sign that Dr. Jack O'Neill was upset. Gen had seen him in the middle of a triple trauma code, and he'd never touched his hair. His shirt wasn't even buttoned properly, and Gen could swear he'd blushed when he picked his jacket up off the living room floor.

She'd known before she'd fallen asleep the first time the night before that this morning would not be easy. She hadn't been wrong. Her stomach felt as if she'd eaten a stone. Her throat was burning, and her hands were shaking as if she had the ague. She simply did not want to know what he had to say.

And she *still* hadn't told him what she'd needed to when she'd brought him up here in the first place.

"I'm sorry."

She was right. That was absolutely the last thing she wanted to hear from a man she could still smell on her skin.

"You're sorry?" she asked, rigidly controlling her features into calm bemusement as she stuck her hands into her robe pockets to keep them safe. "For what? Being thoughtful enough to give me the celebration my family forgot to? For sharing some of the best hours I've ever spent in this apartment with me? For having a responsibility to a little girl who probably wouldn't understand that her daddy's human, too? Or for knowing perfectly well that this might affect our working relationship? Okay, that one I'm kinda sorry about, too, because I don't want to lose a good friend, mentor and associate, just because we found comfort together."

Comfort. There was a euphemism. Shattering, soul-scorching passion. Desperation, primal need and unspeakable joy.

And comfort.

It was only the comfort that had been lost.

Jack's smile was wry and rueful. "Quite a speech. But that wasn't what I was going to say."

That stopped Gen on the spot. "What, then?"

He reached over to brush a lock of hair from her forehead. "I'm sorry I have to leave. And I'm even sorrier that I can't really see a way of coming back."

Gen looked up and saw all the old pain that lived at the back of Jack O'Neill's eyes. She saw even after what had happened the night before, that it hadn't lessened or left. She realized, suddenly, that she'd hoped very much it had.

She understood that she should have known better. That stone got bigger, the burn tighter.

"I am, too," she said, and meant it.

Jack was all set to lean over and kiss her goodbye, but at the last minute, Gen backed away. Turned her head just enough. Broke eye contact.

"I'm even sorrier, because I still haven't told you what I brought you up here to tell you last night," she said.

This time Jack stopped. "What do you mean?"

Letting loose a small laugh of futility and hoping like hell he didn't hear the near despair in her voice, Gen faced him again. "I wanted to talk to you about Elizabeth."

That brought him to a dead stop.

Gen lifted a telling eyebrow. "The only man I've ever invited into my apartment just so I could see him naked is the David on my wall, Jack."

He at least had the grace to blush. And damn him, if it wasn't charming and sweet. Gen thought that maybe this time she *would* cry. "I didn't...I mean..."

"It doesn't matter," she said. "I wouldn't change a moment of last night. I hope you wouldn't, either, no matter what we have to say this morning."

He lifted those spectacular, sweet eyes to her, and Gen saw exactly what it was costing him to walk away. It should have at least salved her pride. It just made her all the more sad, because after what they had shared, he still refused the best she had to offer.

"I don't regret it. You have to know that."

For the first time since she'd met him, Gen caught him in a lie. He regretted every moment, every moan and sigh and shudder, and she wasn't sure how she was going to be able to stand it.

"But I can't do this, Gen. Not now. Not with you. You should know that better than anyone."

Oh, she wanted to argue. She wanted to challenge every cowardly word he said. But she'd known last night, from the very first moment, from the first feel of his mouth on hers, that this was how it would end.

So what was the point in bludgeoning herself with it?

"You're right," she said, in what she desperately hoped was a rational voice. "What we need to do now is talk about Elizabeth."

"What about her?"

But Gen could still smell him on her. She could still feel the ghost of those devastating climaxes he'd lit in her, and the terrible regret that had crept over her later as she'd lain in the dark with him. The regret that now ground in her chest like shattered glass.

"Not now," she said.

For a second he just watched her, obviously disconcerted by the sudden shift in focus. Gen just shook her head and pushed him toward the door.

"In daylight," she suggested. "In a neutral corner. Check your schedule and let me know."

"Is it important?" he asked just before he reached the door.

Gen did everything in her power not to betray just how important. It was selfish, she knew, but she wanted to keep the wonder of what had happened to her the night before safely contained in these rooms. Let the pain happen somewhere else. This was all she was going to get for herself of Jack O'Neill, and she wanted it to stay unsullied.

"Yes, Jack," she said easily. "I think so. Like I said, let me know."

She did—finally—manage to get him out the door and hoped he didn't notice her watching from the window as he climbed into his sensible, safe Volvo and drove away.

Gen sat there on her window seat for a long while after he left, hording up her memories like a miser. Then she walked on into her bathroom, where the silent, somehow pale David waited on the wall, and she washed the scent of Jack O'Neill off of her.

Gen didn't hear the key in her lock. She was sitting in her window seat watching the rain chase pedestrians down Barton Avenue. She knew she should be getting back up. She should clean the apartment, pay her bills, maybe just go to a movie. She sat in the window in her robe and wet hair, though, and couldn't seem to manage a forward motion.

But then, she wasn't responsible for anyone today. She had a week off, and then she would walk back onto the hall as a full-fledged attending emergency department pediatrician. Beyond all expectations, she had made it.

Too bad it had all happened exactly twelve hours too late.

"Gen?" Lee demanded from behind her. "Good God, what are you doing up? I figured you'd be lounging around in bed till dinnertime, at least. After all, you're a free woman."

Gen smiled at the idea but kept watch out the window. "The storm woke me. They're not quite as fun here as they are in the mountains, are they?"

Lee walked up alongside her sister and stared down at her as if trying to decipher a code. "No, but then, Chicago doesn't have any mountains for the thunder to roll around in for hours."

Gen just nodded.

"You okay?"

Lee's voice sounded oddly young. Vulnerable. Lee was one of those people who could do anything in the world, as long as her lodestars were fixed. And Gen, being Mom, had been one of her lodestars since she'd turned five. Uncertainty from her older sister did not sit well with Amaryllis Lee Kendall O'Connor.

"Yeah, sure. Just thinking."

Trying hard to get her stomach to unclench. To make the future look better than it did. She'd washed like Lady MacBeth, and she swore she could still smell citrus. But then, she hadn't had the courage to change her sheets. One step at a time. One small treasure after another to let slip through her clenched fingers until none were left.

"Well, if you're sure," Lee said, staring out the window herself. "But then, even if something were wrong, you wouldn't tell me, anyway. You never have."

"I have so."

"No. You tend to handle things alone."

"Did you need to borrow something?" Gen asked in an attempt to forestall that line of questioning.

"Well...yeah. Rock and I are going on a picnic. I'd invite you, but..."

Gen did manage a grin at that one. "Thank you, no. The last thing I want to do today is act as third wheel at a romantic picnic in the rain. Be my guest. Just what is there I have that you might need? I thought you already had a raincoat."

"Well...uh, I know you have some...well, good wine."

Gen looked over. "You don't drink wine. You drink Kool-Aid." Even Gen had to admit that the tone of her voice held an entire editorial comment on choices and taste in only one word.

''But Rock does like wine. And it's been so stressful lately, and we haven't seen that much of each other, even though we haven't been married that long, and well, you know, I thought...''

Gen knew. Since the two of them had married, Rock had finally quit his job with the police department to finish a degree that would allow him to teach. Lee had been completely immersed in her theater season, and the two had met at odd hours, like clandestine lovers.

''I think a little one-on-one time with the man you love is a great idea. Take the Côte du Rhône.''

No problem. It still left Gen with about twenty bottles of nice wine with which to assuage her pain.

''See?'' Lee countered brightly, already bent over the wine rack that stood alongside the doorway to the tiny kitchen. ''I knew you'd have the answer. You always do.''

''Not always,'' Gen retorted.

Lee straightened. ''Always,'' she insisted quietly. ''It's what you do best.''

All in all, a nice epitaph. Gen didn't bother to comment as Lee scampered over to give her big sister a quick hug and kiss. ''Enjoy your time off. After all the years you've put in, you deserve it. And if you finally decide that you can actually let somebody else in on your problem for once in your life, well...'' Lee shrugged, offered a wry smile. ''Call me.''

''Thanks, honey,'' Gen told her, reaching out to squeeze Lee's hand. ''But this one's all mine. It's okay, though. I'll find the answers, just like you said.''

''If you're sure.''

''I'm sure.''

Oddly enough, that was all it took to get Gen off the window seat. Lee ran off to have a rainy day tryst with her husband, and Gen walked into her bedroom to change.

Lee had been right. Gen did find answers. It was what she did best. And this was no different. She was a physician. She was a big sister who had literally raised two siblings. She was a woman who wanted to help the man and child she already loved, no matter that they probably could never find enough left of themselves to return the favor.

She was a woman who had given her heart, even knowing that it would do her no good.

Nothing to do about it but do what she actually could do. And what she could do was address the problem of Elizabeth.

Gen donned her clothing like armor, as if she were applying layers of protection against the naked longing in her heart. She dried her hair and braided it, a ritual as meaningful as donning robes of office. Tidying up, buttoning down, hiding away.

It took her two hours.

And then she stripped her bed and ran the linens through the wash.

It was time to concentrate on Elizabeth.

Gen was ashamed to think that for all the suspicions she'd collected, the attempts at intervention she'd made, she'd gone about it badly. She'd just finished an intensive year practicing critical care medicine, which had trained her to realize that nothing was so important as preparation. Anticipation.

And she had anticipated nothing but the color of Jack O'Neill's eyes in the darkness.

If she was serious about approaching him about his daughter, she had to have her facts in hand. All the information available. No physician of his caliber accepted unsettling accusations without the research to back it up. Yanking on her raincoat, Gen headed off to the hospital library to begin her task.

Some vacation.

She'd expected lazy days of reading salacious novels and sipping wine at some of the sidewalk cafés that dominated the Gold Coast area. A sail out on the lake, maybe an afternoon at the Art Museum communing with the Impressionist masters. A ballgame at Wrigley. Maybe she would even find a good stables and rent a horse, even if it wasn't her horse or her stables. Even if the trails were flat and the horse somnolent. Anything to give her the illusion of freedom and fun.

Instead, she sequestered herself at one of the hospital library computer stations and worked through lunch and dinner in an effort to give Jack and Elizabeth every resource she could. She came away from those hours sad and a little sick. There had been more on the computer than she'd expected. More than she'd wanted to see. More than should have been available to fragile girls who felt they couldn't control anything in their lives but their body image.

Gen went home, poured a glass of St. Emilion and sat in the dusk listening to Allison Kraus. She thought of the music Elizabeth wanted to write for Lee's play and wondered if it would sound as lost and weary and sad as she felt. Minor keys and yearning, always a good combination to enjoy with wine and trouble.

And she waited to hear from Jack.

He didn't call the next day. She spent the morning in the museum and the afternoon out on the lake getting a sunburn. She sat out at a sidewalk restaurant with a good salacious book and tried not to think how much she would prefer to share the meal with a certain doctor. And then she woke the next day, and the day after that, intending to fill them just as full.

She spent time with Lee and Rock, and said goodbye to Jake and Amanda when they reemerged from their romantic weekend and headed for O'Hare. She and Rock and Lee went to a day game at Wrigley and watched the Cubs lose, and all of them feasted on beer and hot dogs, Lee getting positively silly over the alcohol she so rarely enjoyed.

Gen enjoyed each and every thing she did. But she did them waiting. Waiting to hear from Jack. Waiting for him to be ready to face an unpleasant truth, because she knew that he'd taken that message away with him. She waited, anxious to begin dealing with the problem, nervous that Elizabeth would slip past them before she could help. She waited impatiently, because in only a few days she would be back at work and everything would be more complicated again.

More complicated than facing the man she'd slept with and telling him that his daughter was in trouble.

More complicated than trying to ignore the fact that all she wanted to do was make love to him again and forget the pain she was bringing him, the pain she'd already brought herself.

Gen had made it through almost every one of the crises in

her life on the promise of what she'd expected this moment to feel like. The moment when she would be free of everyone else's expectations, their needs, their image of her. When she could finally be the person she'd thought she would be all those years while she'd done other people's tasks and carried other children's burdens. She'd lain in all those bathtubs over the years picturing this moment like a climber imagining himself at the crest of Everest.

Her family was grown, her training over. She should have felt happy and fulfilled and free.

She felt anxious instead. Unhappy.

Impatient.

She couldn't sit still. She couldn't focus very well. She couldn't even sleep.

For the fourth night in a row, she lay in her soft, sensual bed and stared at the play of reflected streetlights across her ceiling. She listened to the breeze tease her curtains and the trees that crowded the brownstone-lined streets that surrounded her house. She smelled rain-wet streets and a whiff of geraniums from Lee's window box a story down. She thought about anything but what had happened on that bed, and she tried to sleep.

She didn't.

And still Jack didn't call.

# Chapter 10

He looked tired. Strained, as if he hadn't been sleeping, either. Tense and unsteady, just the way Gen felt herself. Not one in a hundred people would have noticed it, because Jack O'Neill wore his worries in millimeters. Gen saw, though, the crease that had somehow grown between his eyebrows and wanted to smooth it. She saw that his hair seemed just a little dull in its perfectly groomed cap and wanted to finger it into disarray. She heard the stiff hesitancy in his voice and wanted to cry.

But she didn't cry. She did what she always did when she faced insurmountable problems.

She searched for answers.

She solved problems.

The difficulty with that was that this time she wasn't going to find any answers that would help her.

"I'm sorry I haven't called before," Jack said, toying with his water glass. Not meeting her gaze, his movements just a little abrupt, his voice a bit harsh.

They were tucked into a booth at the back of a pizza place a full two miles from where they lived, a place Gen knew could ensure their privacy and anonymity, a neutral corner that wouldn't call up unwanted memories or expectations. He'd asked to meet her for lunch, and Gen had agreed. She'd spent another hour dressing, so she was armed for the battle at hand. She'd even tucked a folder of information into her backpack to support her claim.

It hadn't helped. She still felt spun around and upended, just from the fact that he sat three feet away.

"I understand," she allowed, just as shy as he to make eye contact. "After all, I'm the only one on vacation."

She knew she didn't look a lot perkier than Jack did right now. It had been a long five days. And no matter what happened this afternoon, Gen still didn't think she was due for sleep anytime soon.

And that didn't even take into account the fact that she was suddenly flashing to that night again. The murmurs and caresses and sighs of repletion. The shadows and smiles and sibilance of satisfaction. She could feel the lightning skitter along her arms and settle into her belly again, the sudden, sharp need to be nearer to him. To soothe him and stir him and settle him into her arms where they both might be safe.

Safe.

As if anything in her life had ever been safe. As if she could ever expect it to be.

"You wanted to talk to me about Elizabeth," he said.

No foreplay, then. No pretense of civility from a man who had made her scream not five nights before. If she hadn't been saddened by the strength of his defenses, Gen would have been angry.

Instead, she nodded and ran a hand over the manilla file she'd pulled out of her bag, as if seeking support. She pulled herself away from those dangerous memories and dropped her gaze away from his, where, at least for a moment, it was safer. She struggled to distance herself from him, physician to parent. She took a deep breath in an effort to maintain her calm, and she faced him, praying for wisdom, for strength, for perception.

Knowing she would settle for this just being over.

Jack gave her no encouragement. He just sat there, bemused and careful.

"I wanted to talk to you before I said anything to Elizabeth," Gen said quietly, praying her voice wouldn't shake as much as her hands. "But I think she knows I want to talk to her."

"Did she do something wrong?" he asked, brows gathered. "When she was at your house?"

That actually got a smile out of Gen. "Elizabeth? Impossible. I've never known a child who strove harder to please."

A nod, a quick pursing of his mouth, as if the words he wanted tasted bad.

"Then I don't understand. What's the problem?"

"This is difficult, Jack," she said quietly, forestalling any more guesses. "Please hear me out, if you will."

His face grew more taut. Gen could feel it, as if the temperature suddenly rose; as if someone had just taken a wrench to her chest. He was afraid of what she was going to say, and she wondered if he knew why.

There was nothing for her to do but get on with it. "I'm worried about her, Jack. I...uh, I'm afraid she may have anorexia."

Jack started like a man who'd been shot.

"What?" he demanded on a laugh.

Which meant he hadn't anticipated that one at all. Gen steeled herself against his disbelief and waded right in before he could just laugh her concerns away.

"I've been watching her since she was at my house," she said, leaning closer, trying her best to ignore his wide-eyed astonishment. "And I've noticed a familiar pattern. She's never hungry when you offer food. She usually says she's just eaten something. She tends to wear bulky clothing, although she's quite insistent that she wears size-two jeans. She has an absolute obsession about exercising and about the size of her clothes, but her bones protrude."

"She's only twelve," he blurted out, his eyes suddenly glittering.

"She's not eating, Jack."

He straightened away from her, from her accusation. "That's ridiculous."

Gen saw the walls rise and couldn't believe it. It seemed she hadn't prepared well enough after all. She'd gotten all the information she could on anorexia and failed to anticipate the fact that she wouldn't be allowed to present it.

He was a doctor, she thought, suddenly desperate. A brilliant clinician with the instincts of a street thief. He had to know. He had to understand.

"Jack..."

"No!" His voice was quiet, slashing, his eyes hard. "I told you before. Her mother was thin."

He was a doctor who was a father. A father of a child who had survived too much already. It was all Gen could do to drag in her next breath, but she did. She fought because she knew she had no choice.

"Do you see her eat?" she asked, suddenly in a defensive position and hating it. Not knowing, suddenly, how to get Jack back onto a logical track that could help Elizabeth. How to get him to listen with an objective ear to something he'd never signed on to be objective about.

There was not a trace of amusement left in those magic eyes. He sat rigid and cold and imperious, and Gen was suddenly very afraid.

"Of course I see her eat," he retorted in icy tones. "I'm at dinner every night I'm not hip deep in an ICU crisis. What do you think, that I watch my daughter starve herself and ignore it?"

"No, I don't," she said, her chest suddenly on fire. Somebody had dropped that rock onto her again, and it weighted her like grief. "I think she's learned to be very smart about it. I think you don't see what you don't want to see."

"And *you* saw it?" he retorted, suddenly leaning in, suddenly, terribly, furious. "After what, four days in your house? Four days when her father was in the hospital? And you think she's going to eat normally?"

"I think she'd already established the pattern."

Gen's voice kept getting softer, her position smaller. She kept thinking of him inside her, deep inside her, detonating explosions and ecstasies. She kept thinking of those moments he'd slept, quiet in her arms.

She kept seeing his smile and hearing his laughter.

But it had been an illusion. This was the real Jack O'Neill, the man who couldn't come to grips with his wife's death, with its cost to his family. The man who would try his best to negate the magic of what had happened on her marshmallow bed because it made him feel guilty.

"Please, Jack," Gen begged, reaching across the table. Knowing how much more difficult this was because she'd waited too long to tell him. Now the darkness was between them, the sighs and murmurs of passion that couldn't be repeated.

He flinched from her, and Gen felt worse.

"I collected some information," she said, struggling to keep her voice even. "Research and treatment. And I think there's some really good news, because a very promising new treatment fits Elizabeth like a glove. I have the information with me. Won't you even look at it?"

For the first time since she'd met him, Gen saw a look of disdain cross Jack O'Neill's features. "You intend to instruct *me*, Dr. Kendall?" he demanded. "I wouldn't think I'd have to remind you that I am chief of critical care pediatrics at the hospital where you haven't even spent your first eight hours as a practicing physician."

"You are also the person who is famous for saying that any doctor who thinks he knows everything is a doctor who's a fool."

She was frantic. She could hear it in her voice. She could feel it in the tremors that shook her. She knew he saw it, too. But he discounted it. He stood and made a deliberate motion of pulling out his wallet and tossing a ten-dollar bill on the table.

"You have been a great help to my family," he said, his voice rigid. "You were very kind to Elizabeth. But that doesn't make you more of an expert on her than her own father."

Frustrated, frightened, Gen gambled on every kind feeling he had left for her and stood, as well. "Then tell me this, Jack," she said, just as quietly, so no one knew that they were hurting each other. "What do you think of Elizabeth's music?"

That stopped him in his shoes, that crease deepening between his eyebrows. "Her music? What about it?"

"Her talent as a pianist and a composer. What do you think about it?"

He blinked a little, as if trying to bring a picture into focus. "I don't think anything of it. Elizabeth enjoys it. She says it helps her with her math skills."

Gen nodded, bent to pick up her bag and faced him down. "Then you don't know anything about Elizabeth at all, Jack."

And then she walked past him out the door.

What had she done? Gen railed at herself as she strode along the sidewalk. What exactly had she accomplished? She'd set Jack's back up, force-fed him information about his daughter he wasn't ready for, and then walked out without proving it.

She'd been irredeemably impulsive.

She shouldn't have just dropped it on him. She should have found a better way to ease into the subject. To soften the blow. To better prepare him for what was coming.

She should have told him the truth. She should have told him why she was so sure about Elizabeth.

But she'd never told anybody.

So she walked up LaSalle toward her apartment with a bag full of useless research material and the fear settling in her chest that Jack was going to go home and force an issue that had to be finessed. Or, worse, that he would simply ignore it like bad manners.

She'd never even asked him if she could talk to Elizabeth. She'd never had the chance to tell him that she was acting out of love. Now she would probably never get the chance.

It was that thought that stopped her dead in the middle of the sidewalk. Not having the chance was not an option. This wasn't cheating on school tests they were talking about. It was, quite possibly, Elizabeth's life. No matter what it cost Gen, she had to convince Jack to get his daughter some help.

No matter what it cost *her*.

Standing there on that bright windy street, she thought again of the silence of night, when she'd nestled Jack O'Neill against her heart. And thought of how, for the very first time in her life, even among a family who loved her, she hadn't felt somehow alone.

She thought of how hard it was going to be to give that away again.

But she had to.

There was nothing Gen could do about Jack's inability to move on. There was no way to entice him back to her bed, even if she thought that would make a difference to his bruised and battered heart.

But she could do something for Elizabeth. She could help pull her away from the swamp she'd stumbled into.

She had to.

Hitching up her backpack, Gen Kendall sucked in a breath and set off again, because that was the only thing she could do.

Who did she think she was? Jack wanted to know. What the *hell* did she think she was doing?

He stalked back to the hospital in a red rage, not even greeting the volunteer at the information desk as he swept past. He stepped into the elevator and struggled to control himself, not noticing that the people around him, people who normally delighted in chatting with him, separated themselves a little from him.

He didn't notice because he was seething.

Raging.

Trembling.

He stuffed his hands in his pockets and stood perfectly still so that he wouldn't simply splinter into tiny shards of fury. He wedged himself against the back wall of the elevator and kept his eyes fixed on the floor numbers until the doors opened onto the seventh floor.

The intensive care units took up most of the seventh floor. His world. His domain to protect and govern and improve. His chance to order the chaos of illness into health.

He knew it would be better here. It always was. Some days he won. Some he lost. But at least he always tried. At least he recognized his foes and fought them hard.

And it made him feel better. More in control. He didn't feel that wild, helpless feeling that caught him unaware in the deepest hours of the night when he woke to his empty bed. When he looked up at the wall to find Meggie smiling down at him, Elizabeth still a butterball of a baby in her smooth arms.

Here he could force life to make sense.

And Genevieve Kendall had done her best to sabotage that. How *dare* she?

Hadn't he spent the past five nights sweating in his bed, wanting her with a sickness he couldn't control? Hadn't he spent his days waiting to hear her laughter, the slightly off-key magic of her singing Barry damn Manilow? Hadn't he battled it every inch of the way, because he knew better?

Passion doesn't last. Obsession only creates destruction. He needed direction. Order. Action.

He needed to know that he had done his best each day to put the pieces of the earth a little bit more into a recognizable shape, and Gen Kendall was no shape he recognized.

But, oh, God he wanted her. He wanted her passion, her devotion, her hunger. He wanted the sure empathy in her eyes and the silly humor of her betting with her brothers about her future. He wanted…

But he couldn't have.

He had more than he could handle now, and he didn't need the distraction. He needed to know that he'd kept his promises. Atoned for his failures. He needed to know that the life that was left him after that stormy night five years ago remained in acceptable shape. He needed to know that Elizabeth was happy and secure.

And Gen Kendall had come to him after knowing his little girl for only four days and told him that he'd failed again? That his little girl was somehow eating herself away on the inside?

As if Elizabeth hadn't had enough to cope with in the past few years. As if she hadn't made it through with a beauty and grace and purpose that still startled him.

As if he would *ever* let anything else happen to his little girl.

"I said get that chest X ray, you stupid cow! What the hell are you thinking?"

Well, that brought him out of his reverie. The new critical

care fellow, a woman with sharp features, sharper intelligence and an absolutely surgical tongue, was haranguing one of the ICU nurses, who looked as if she was about to go for her throat right in front of the family.

Well, this he could take care of.

He never would have had to take care of it with Gen, he thought as he waded into the fracas. She would have had the whole damn unit singing by now.

"Dr. Spizer, I assume you're an intelligent woman," he said, his voice soft and reasonable.

The woman spun on him, recognized him and bristled. "How do you deal with this incompetence?"

"Odd," he said, reaching over to pick his lab coat off one of the hooks by the front door to the ICU. "I've rarely had to deal with incompetence here. But then, I've never seen the need to flay a nurse just because she's busier than I am."

"Wish Gen were still here," the nurse groused and turned away.

So did he, Jack thought. In too many ways entirely.

But he couldn't. Not anymore. Not with his little girl's peace of mind at stake.

Gen spent the rest of the day back at the library, on the computer and then on the phone. She talked to support groups, and she talked to psychiatrists, and then she talked to Amanda, who was back at the ranch trying to write her next book surrounded by children and ranch hands.

"Would you mind?" Gen asked, sitting there in her shadowy apartment watching the curtains shiver in the wind like impatient ghosts.

"Your trunk in the attic. You want me to send the whole thing?"

"No. There's another box in there. An old cardboard box that's tied up with string. If you'd send that."

"Is there anything in there I should worry about breaking?"

"Nothing. It's just some old papers of mine I need."

Any of the Kendalls would have lifted an eyebrow and said something like, *You need papers from high school to be a big-*

*city doc?* Amanda just made a humming noise in the back of her throat, which Gen knew meant she was curious as hell.

But all she said was, "Of course I'll send it. Is there anything else I can do?"

"No, thanks. That's all."

"Everything okay?"

Gen smiled now, a sad, wry kind of smile that disappeared into the darkness where she sipped her wine and watched her windows. "Everything's fine."

A minute pause met that clanker. "Uh-huh. Well, I know that you're the big sister and all, but if there's anything I can do, just let me know."

"No, no," Gen said instinctively, having been what she was for too long to be comfortable confiding in anyone. "Everything's fine."

"We're here anyway."

Her throat was burning again. "I know."

The mountains, she thought almost desperately. If only I could get to the mountains.

I could find the silence and distance and freedom to solve this dilemma. I could salve myself on the sound of streams and comfort myself against the shoulders of granite.

If only I could go home.

But she couldn't.

Not yet. Not while she had Jack and Elizabeth here, who needed her.

So she said goodbye to her sister-in-law, and she sat alone in the dark, wondering how she could feel any worse.


She was wrong, Jack thought as he stood over his daughter's bed. A gilt, four-poster confection Meggie had bought only days before her death, it cocooned Elizabeth amid eyelet lace and sky-blue sheets, her thick hair a halo around her beautiful still face, her limbs splayed in a child's haphazard sleep.

Jack bent, as he had done every night of his daughter's life, and kissed her forehead. He gave thanks, as he had every single night of her young life, that he and Meggie had been blessed with her.

He remembered that moment so well, like a bright photo pinned to a black scrapbook, the soft lights and gentle music of the birthing room, Meggie sweaty and smiling, the nurses laughing and Jack stunned to silence. Dumbfounded. Tumbled headfirst into love within the space of a heartbeat with that little scrap of life the nurse had placed in his arms.

She'd looked up at him with those dark, wise eyes of hers and frowned, as if sizing him up. And then, seeing the senior pediatric resident who was her father, yawned in perfect disinterest. Tiny ears. Tiny feet. Tiny, tiny nose. And long, delicate fingers that had seemed to instinctively stretch into impossibly graceful patterns.

He'd loved her fingers. Meggie's fingers. Meggie had called them a pianist's fingers. Jack had seen them holding scalpels. A virtuoso in a surgical suite, because his daughter was going to get every advantage. A genius with Meggie's eyes and long, delicate fingers, his daughter was. And with him as her father, there would be no door closed to that genius.

Not one.

He saw Meggie in Elizabeth more and more as she grew. A tilt of the head, a sweet kind of smile, a natural grace and dignity that was already breathtaking. He saw her blooming into a flower of unspeakable beauty.

In spite of what had happened.

And Gen Kendall wanted to ruin it all for her.

Even so, he looked not at Elizabeth's hands where they lay alongside her head in perfect, childish abandon. He looked at her wrists. At the knob of an ulna, the parallel shadows of radius and ulna. Then up to the carpals, the metacarpals and phalanges, the perfect, miraculous geometry of the hand. And instead of celebrating the wonder of creation, he calculated the angles of shadow.

Were the knobs too protuberant? Were her cheekbones too sharp, her clavicles too prominent? He looked, but all he saw was Meggie. Meggie, who had been so deceptively delicate.

Gen Kendall was wrong, and he wouldn't let her hurt his little girl over it.

"Daddy?"

Jack started a little. He hadn't even noticed that her eyes had opened, as mysteriously dark in the shadows as that night she'd been born.

He settled on the side of her bed and reached up to brush a damp tangle of hair off her forehead. "Yeah, Mouse. I just came in to say good night."

"You're home really late tonight. Everything okay?"

Everything but the new fellow, the disturbing number of teen suicide attempts they'd been getting recently and his own inability to get his mind off Gen Kendall.

"Yeah, honey. Just busy. How was your day?"

Her smile was sleepy and dear. "Last day of French for the summer. You have to take me to Paris now so I can practice."

He grinned. "What a good idea. Then you can terrorize me by ordering my meals so that I end up with calves' stomachs and quail brains."

"You guessed."

"What's next on the agenda?"

"Science camp next week, then lacrosse camp. In the meantime, Mary and I thought we'd go to the Art Museum, if that's okay."

"What could I possibly find to complain about in an art museum?"

"There are naked pictures there, ya know."

He chuckled. "There are naked pictures in most of the books in my library. Big deal."

"There are naked pictures in Gen Kendall's bathroom."

Jack scowled with every ounce of parental outrage. "I was hoping you'd forget that."

And his daughter giggled. Jack realized, watching her, that he didn't hear her giggle much at all anymore, and it made him frown a little.

"I don't think so," she assured him with a very conciliatory pat on the arm. "But since it's art, you should be happy. I got cultured when I was there."

"Only yoghurt gets cultured, brat."

"And pearls."

She looked so much like Meggie at that moment, Jack

thought. Impish and sly. Jack ached, but it was a different ache than usual. It wasn't an acute Meggie ache, which meant he couldn't identify it. That didn't mean it felt any better.

So he tousled Elizabeth's hair and gave her another kiss. "See you at breakfast?"

"No," she assured him. "*I'm* on vacation."

"Fine," he said, standing. "Everybody's on vacation but me."

"That's because you never take one."

"Of course I do."

She just lifted a very expressive eyebrow.

"I guess that means we really will have to go to Paris," he said, sighing. "Sometime."

"Uh-huh."

Jack heard the instinctive disappointment Elizabeth probably didn't even know had seeped into her voice and turned back to her. He heard again the accusation Gen had made, the question she'd asked.

"Elizabeth," he said, not even knowing what to ask. "How's the piano coming?"

And saw, that quickly, his daughter pull back.

It wasn't obvious or huge. It was nothing more than a flattening of her gaze. A caution he hadn't noticed before.

"Oh," she said in airy tones, "it's fine. Mr. Wilkinson said he thought I was ready for the Conservatory."

Suddenly he wanted to leave. Did he hear something in her voice? Something he hadn't expected? Something he didn't recognize?

"Do you want to go?"

"It is the best training in the city."

"Do you think it'll be fun?"

"Fun?" Jack saw an even further retreat. He saw it because he was looking so hard. Listening to the tone of her voice, which was suddenly a little strident. "I think it'll look great on my college applications."

He couldn't say why he did it, but when he finally left Elizabeth's room, he walked downstairs to the back bedroom into which he'd exiled the upright he'd bought her to practice on. A squat, serviceable piece of furniture without embellishment or much grace, truth to tell, it was tucked into a room with few amenities. A bench, a chair, for Mary McGregor when she listened to Elizabeth, he guessed, a side table.

Jack looked around, but he didn't see evidence that Elizabeth inhabited this space. Where her room was a tumble of personal possessions, this room was spare and neat. So neat, in fact, that it echoed.

Not sure why, he walked over to lift the lid of the piano bench. He wasn't sure what he'd expected, but he knew he didn't expect what he found. He sure as hell didn't understand it.

The bench was empty.

Jack knew that Elizabeth practiced her music. Mary McGregor assured him of it. Estela regaled him with it in two languages. Elizabeth's music teacher affirmed him of it with his eyes closed, as if he were listening to her even as he reported to Jack about her progress. Elizabeth was diligent about it, as she was with everything else.

Why didn't she keep her music here? What did it mean?

Did he really want to know?

Flipping off the light, Jack walked back up to his own bedroom, to where Meggie still lived in the bright oils on his wall, and he climbed into his empty bed. He lay there in the dark, where the shadows were silent and cold, and he ached.

And he still didn't know why.

But, he thought, just maybe it was time to get his mouse a better piano.

# *Chapter 11*

Two days later, Gen walked into the emergency department and took up her duties as the newest, most junior emergency pediatrician on the staff of Memorial Medical Center. Several people commented on the fact that she was quieter than she had been before, but they all laughingly put it down to the fact that she was growing into the gravity of her new position.

Nobody noticed that she'd lost some weight. Nobody mentioned the fact that she kept looking down the hallway as if expecting to see someone. Mostly they were just glad to have Gen back on the floor, since she was not only a good doc but a fun doc, the rarest of combinations.

Gen did her best to fulfill their expectations with only half a heart. She spent the rest of her time trying to find ways to bridge the distance she'd created with Jack O'Neill so she could at least manage to help his daughter.

Gen finally met up with Jack on the day they let Jacob Edward Christian's father out of the psych unit. Gen had been working a normal shift, treating summer colds, ear infections and a vast array of sport and summer-vacation injuries, when she got in a kid with asthma. A kid with an attack they couldn't seem to break.

Gen threw every combination of drugs, breathing treatments and positive attitude she could at Andy Young. When the ten-year-old still couldn't get a good breath past his stricken airway, even the nurses started looking worried.

It was time to call in the big guns.

There was, of course, only one big gun worth getting. Nobody worked those all-important miracles with asthma kids better than Jack O'Neill.

The first problem with that was that Gen went cold just at the thought of paging him. The second was that he brought his newest fellow along.

"Good God!" Dr. Spizer snapped as she sailed in, coattail gently flapping behind her. "You planning on *killing* this kid? Who the hell told you to use that setup?"

For a second Gen could do no more than gape. Much as the mother and child were doing, even as the little boy struggled to get air into his compromised lungs. Lungs that wouldn't work any better by having their owner scared to death by Cruella De Vil.

"I don't suppose you know anything by Barry Manilow?" Gen asked gently. She'd been sharing her repertoire with Andy while he was getting his latest breathing treatment.

"What the hell does *that* mean?" the fellow demanded, hands on hips.

"It means that you're not going to have much of a private practice if you scare all your clients to death. I find singing makes everybody feel better."

"That's what *you* think," Jack retorted with a wry grin as he walked in the door on the heels of his fellow.

The nurse laughed. The fellow fumed. Gen fought a rush of longing that almost brought her to her knees at the simple sight of Jack O'Neill and turned to Andy.

"Everybody's a critic," she mourned to the ashen little boy, by now her stock line.

"Everybody's…right," he managed.

Even he laughed this time. And Cruella the Fellow was silenced in high dudgeon. Gen was still shaky and hot and aching to touch Jack, but she prided herself on keeping a calm face as they worked together to see Andy through the worst of his crisis so they could get him upstairs to the unit.

Jack touched her in passing. She didn't flinch. Jack leaned near her to check the chart. She didn't run away. She laughed and smiled and gave quiet orders as if Jack were just another attending physician, not the man who had so thoroughly upended her life.

She barely made eye contact, hoping with all her heart that the sharp-eyed nurses were too taken up with Andy to notice how stiff their newest pediatrician was with their chief. She laughed and sang and did her job, just as everybody would have expected. And nobody but Gen knew how much it cost.

Jack, damn it, looked perfectly at ease. Smiling, gentle, patient Jack, he defused the worst of the newest fellow's antisocial personality and calmed Andy and his frantic mother, subtly weaving calm and purpose into the near panic that had almost taken control of the room before his arrival.

He could at least have looked unhappy, Gen thought as things began to settle down. He could regret what he'd thrown away. He could ache and want and sizzle with sudden bursts of need the way she did.

But Jack exhibited no emotion other than satisfaction when he listened to Andy's lungs to find them easing. He seemed to think nothing of being in the room with her, with brushing by her and talking to her, as if nothing had ever transpired.

As if Gen had never fallen in love with him.

As if she hadn't felt him come apart in her arms and then been flayed alive by his disdain.

It would get easier, she vowed. She would will it to do so.

She had to, or else she could never work here long enough to get those loans paid off. She could never figure out a way to convince Jack that Elizabeth wasn't all right.

But, she thought as she finally walked out of the room to check on her other patients, it wasn't going to happen today.

Gen hadn't even made it into the next room when she was paged to the phone.

''This is Dr. Kendall,'' she said, leaning her hip against one of the hall desks.

Silence.

Gen straightened.

''Hello?'' she asked, knowing somehow that there was somebody on the other end of the phone. The hair was beginning to stand up on the nape of her neck.

''They let me go.''

Gen knew that every corpuscle of blood pooled in her feet. Not today, she thought in real panic. She just couldn't take any more today.

''Mr. Christian?'' Not really a question. She would have know that voice no matter what. ''I'm glad to hear it. How are you doing?''

There was another silence, as if he were weighing his answer.

''Doing? I'm sitting at my son's grave. That's how I'm doing.''

Oh, God. Nothing was changed. Nothing except the fact that Jacob Edward's father sounded even worse. Strident, as if the rage in him stole his breath.

Gen squeezed her eyes shut, desperate for calm. For control. For a wisdom beyond her.

''You know I'm sorry,'' Gen all but pleaded, her hand clenched so tightly on the phone that she thought it should bend beneath her fingers. ''You *know* it.''

''I know my son's dead. And you can't be sorry enough.''

''Mr. Christian…''

''But you will be.''

Click.

Gen felt a hand on her arm and jumped like a scalded cat.

''That was the father,'' Jack said quietly. ''Wasn't it?''

Gen caught her breath and fought for control, knowing there were tears in her eyes that would never fall. Desperate suddenly to feel the comfort of Jack's arms around her.

Frantic for something she could never have.

She straightened, sucked in a couple of calming breaths and caught that damn scent of citrus.

She wasn't going to make it through this, she thought. She just wasn't.

"I don't know what to do," she admitted to the floor. "He's so angry. There must be something I can do."

Jack didn't say anything. He just took hold of her arm. Gen felt it in every nerve in her body. The heat of him, the strength of him, the solid, certain comfort of him. Again, nothing but his touch and his silence, and it was enough. It was so much that the tears threatened again.

The jagged-edged fury of Mr. Christian couldn't hold against that kind of comfort, and Gen stood there, soaking it up to save her.

She soaked up Jack. She prayed for a little time to cherish him, just standing there in the middle of the work lane, just breathing past the distress of that phone call.

And then, finally, she looked up. His gaze was on her, his soft, sweet gaze. Gen instinctively sought there what she hadn't been able to find no more than ten minutes earlier.

Of course it was there. Comfort, support, the bittersweet afterglow of their shared moments and silent solace. The unbreakable bond that had been forged in spite of everything. In a moment, a blink, Gen felt as if he'd put his arms around her and held her up.

"You can't make everybody okay," he finally said.

Gen sighed. She looked down at the phone, as if calling up Mr. Christian. "I know. But it hurts when I can't."

For a long moment Jack just stood there. Just watched her, as if searching for something. Then he took in a breath and let go of her.

"You should call the police, you know."

Gen's brief laugh was harsh. "You can see how well that worked last time. When I have a chance, I'll call his wife."

"I can do it if you want."

Gen gathered all the courage it took to face those beloved eyes and smiled. "No, thank you, older doctor. I'm an official big girl now."

She was immeasurably relieved when he scowled. "There you go again, making me feel ancient."

A truce then, she thought, gathering her composure. A careful, light bantering that would stay absolutely in sight at all times.

She understood. For now, she agreed. So she laughed. "If I thought you believed you were ancient, I'd smack you around. Thank you for the offer, though."

"Anytime."

He meant it, she knew. And looking up once again, she saw the cost of the offer in the brief flare of real pain she saw there. Oh, God, she hurt for him. She hurt for herself. Then she did the only thing she could until he let her do more, which, damn it, he wouldn't. She did her best to ignore the hallucinatory feeling of unreality this bantering set off in her and patted him on the arm like an avuncular uncle.

"Don't make rash promises. I think you're going to have your hands full with your brand-new fellow of pediatric critical care."

Another scowl, this one broader, easier. "I don't suppose you want to come back. The nurses in ICU miss you."

"I appreciate the offer," she said with her best grin. "Really I do. But, you see, I make money down here. And—" she leaned in, as if sharing the world's most weighty secret "—they let me go home at the end of the day."

He huffed. "Fine. Be selfish."

"Besides, I think you've had it too easy in your medical career. Youngest pediatric critical care chief in the Midwest and all. Time you hone your talents on something really difficult."

"Well, I can't think of anything more difficult than Dr. Spizer."

Gen patted away again, rigidly ignoring the sizzle of contact every time she did. "Well then, I think you'd better be getting to it. Besides, you need to be upstairs in time to accept the grateful praise of Andy Young's mother. That little boy was getting mighty sick until you walked in."

"I think he was just getting sick of the music."

Gen chortled. "Okay, that's it. You've officially worn out your welcome in my emergency room."

"*Your* emergency room? Didn't take you long to become territorial. How long have you been here, a week?"

"Eight days and five hours, thank you."

He bowed. ''My apologies. I will leave it to your most capable medical skills and far less commendable musical ones. Let me know if there's any way I can help with that father.''

''I will. Thank you.''

For just a moment, a fraction of a breath, she faced him once again and told him in silence what she couldn't in words. And he answered. Briefly, before hiding away again behind bonhomie and competence. And then, before he had to follow up on what he knew she'd seen, he left.

Jack stepped into the elevator on shaky legs. God, it wasn't getting easier. He still felt flushed and uncertain and impatient, just as he had the minute he'd seen Gen again.

He couldn't help but smile. She was wearing her Snoopy scrubs again, along with a wrinkled, oversize lab coat, and tendrils were pulling free of her ubiquitous French braid. Not a look designed to incite passion. It had incited his. He'd damn near had to walk right back out of that room, and that wasn't something to even consider.

He couldn't imagine how she'd managed to look so calm and collected in there. The perfect, composed doctor holding terror at bay with her smiles and silly songs. She'd looked so clean and sweet and able, especially when compared to the brilliant but unamusingly erratic Dr. Spizer.

He'd wanted to wrap Gen in his arms. Hell, he still did.

He wanted to ask her why she'd said what she had about Elizabeth.

He was going to have to figure out how to deal with this and fast. There was no way he was going to be able to work with her in the same hospital if he couldn't. And if he couldn't do that, he would fail. He would fail the children he cared for, he would fail himself, and, most of all, he would fail Meggie.

He simply couldn't fail his Meggie.

Not again.

So he would straighten up, assume a smile of indifference and treat Gen Kendall just like any other young attending who, on occasion, needed his help.

As if he hadn't let down his defenses with her.

As if he hadn't lost himself in the deep, dark sweetness of her.

"Do you want to continue the aminophylline on that kid, or are we about finished with it?"

Jack blinked at the strident tones to find himself in the unit. He was going to have to stop that, too. He'd probably insulted half the attending staff by ignoring them on the elevator as he wrestled with the problem of one young doctor with questionable musical taste. Before him stood Dr. Stephanie Spizer. Badly named, he thought, for the person she was. Too soft a name, too romantic. His new fellow was all brain and no empathy. She was the kind of doctor who'd managed to get through med school on the strength of her test scores without once proving she could talk to another human being, much less a sick, frightened one. And she wanted to be a pediatrician.

Tall, angular and unblessed in looks, she had drab brown hair and a mouth that always seemed to be pursed with impatience or displeasure.

"You and I are going to talk," he said, facing the snapping black eyes.

That seemed to stop her for a minute. "About what?"

"Dr. Genevieve Kendall."

Spizer stiffened as if he'd slapped her. "Not her again. For God's sake, you'd think she'd invented pediatrics, the way people talk about her. Well, she screwed up this morning, didn't she?"

"Did she?"

"Of course she did. She had to call us, didn't she?"

"No," Jack said quietly. "She had to call *me*. You were along to learn. But it seems you didn't, did you?"

"I had no problems following you."

"You had a problem figuring out the most vital element in treating any condition that is affected by stress or anxiety. Which, come to think of it, in kids, is mostly anything."

Spizer looked sincerely confused. Jack sighed. Lord, he wished he had Gen starting with him this summer instead of this human misfit.

No, he thought quickly. He didn't. He would never make it through September.

"You are brilliant, Dr. Spizer. There's never been a question about that. But unless you learn that you're treating humans instead of diseases, might I suggest you go into research? Petri dishes rarely have their feelings hurt."

She snorted, stuffed her hands in her pockets. "Oh, now you're talking about the nurses. Well, if they're too stupid—"

"Dr. Gen Kendall," he interrupted as calmly as he could, "can shorten the time on a patient interview, a crisis or a treatment, by the simple fact that she listens. She smiles. She cares."

There went that lip again, curling in disdain. "Caring's not going to do you a damn bit of good if you don't know what you're doing."

"Ah, but you see, she does. That's why she got the highest recommendation ever seen at this hospital, from every chief she ever served with. Because she knows how to be both. You, Dr. Spizer, don't. And if you don't figure out how to set your ego aside long enough to *care* for your patient, you're not going to be recommended by me for lab janitor."

Again that startled look of incomprehension, which meant that Jack's little speech wouldn't do any good. Dr. Spizer had to already have it in her to be caring, for his words to make any impact. She had to instinctively think of her patients first.

Like Gen.

Who was devastated not so much by the fact that that little boy's father had lashed out at her but because he'd been so shattered by little Jacob Edward's death that he'd been driven to attack her.

What had she said? That it hurt when she couldn't make everything better?

He'd seen it in her eyes, that dark, lost look.

He'd heard it in the thready pain in her voice.

The same pain he heard every time she couldn't help one of her patients or take their parents' grief away.

The same pain he'd heard when he'd stood up at the restaurant and thrown her concern back in her face.

For a few long minutes Jack just stood there in the middle of the work lane and thought about that moment. The moment she'd told him how worried she was for Elizabeth. The moment he'd taken her words as an accusation.

She'd never meant them that way. He knew that. He'd known that the moment she'd said it. The moment he'd spewed out his own venom like the very kind of pompous ass he most despised.

She was wrong. He knew that. But she hadn't meant to hurt him or Elizabeth. She'd wanted nothing more than to help.

He should tell her.

He should ask her pardon.

He couldn't. Hell, he could barely be on the same work lane with her. Better she thought he was unforgivable than have to face the sweet sympathy in those eyes without any kind of protection.

"Hey, Dr. O'Neill," he heard next to him.

"Yes?"

It was one of the nurses. A good one.

"I don't suppose we could throw Dr. Spizer back and wait for a bigger fish?"

Jack finally managed a smile. "Heck, no. What's the challenge in that? Our job is to *make* her a big fish."

"As opposed to a big—"

"Yes."

She scowled. "Sure wish Gen Kendall were back."

There was absolutely nothing he could say.

Gen shouldn't have been surprised to find Lee waiting in her apartment for her.

"Need more wine?" she asked dryly as she set her work bag on the scarred oak table that was supposed to seat dinner guests. Instead, it held her computer, her notes and a good three weeks' worth of laundry.

It also held that cardboard box she'd received the day before. The box she hadn't had the courage to go through yet.

Lee looked up from the medical journal she'd been flipping through. "Do you actually *look* at these pictures?"

"Kinda defeats the purpose of learning how to recognize disease if you don't."

"You really think you're going to see leprosy in Chicago?"

"Hansen's disease. And the way the world's shrinking and a goodly portion of it's ending up here, very possibly."

Lee stood up and stretched. She was letting her hair grow this month. A part in a play, probably. Lee did everything for either her theater or her husband. And since her theater was in session and her husband should have been home, her appearance in Gen's living room meant some kind of problem.

"What?" Gen asked, short of patience.

She'd had to call Mrs. Christian. She'd had to call Mr. Christian's psychiatrist, only to find out that that worthy had considered Mr. Christian "just a little depressed." She'd had to work the rest of her shift dodging Jack O'Neill and his very large, very shrill shadow. She wasn't in the mood to take on anybody else, even if it was her favorite sister.

Lee faced her. "I've met with Elizabeth O'Neill a couple of times about those tunes she promised me."

Gen stalled to a halt. "Yes?"

Lee's brow crinkled, making her look like a little girl trying to decipher long division. "This may sound really stupid..."

Gen waited. Lee looked up, still frowning.

"It's okay," Gen said. "It's not stupid."

"I just have a feeling," Lee said.

"About her music?"

"About the fact that she seems too skinny. I laughed about it when she was here, but I'm beginning to think it isn't so funny anymore."

Gen sat on her overstuffed couch, not sure whether she wanted to hear this or not. Wondering if she really wanted to be so right. "What have you seen?" she asked.

Lee perched on the arm of a chair. She took a moment, as if trying to put her best words to it and simply failing. Finally she shrugged. "I've seen that she's awfully obsessed with weight and exercise. She's dropping twenty push-ups when we're talking key transpositions because she says she ate a doughnut. Don't you think that's a little much?"

Now Gen was absolutely still. "Yes," she said. "I do. What do you think?"

Lee looked up. "She makes me nervous, Gen."

"Have you said anything to her?"

Lee scowled. "Like what? 'Hey, kid, there are refugees in the Sudan who eat more than you'?"

Gen smiled. "No, not that."

"Have *you* said anything?"

Gen sat very still. It was very important to her to maintain a neutral expression, even when she wanted to cringe. When she wanted to look over at that box on the table. "Yes. Kind of. I'm trying to talk to her dad first."

"And?"

"He's not ready to hear about it yet."

That wasn't what Lee wanted to hear. Lee who solved all her problems on the page of a play. Fiction was easy to control. Life was messy.

"What do we do?"

Gen sighed. "What have you seen her eat? All I saw was salad."

"That. Fruit. Dry cereal."

"Well, we're still lucky, I think. At least she's not trying to get by on paper and water."

Lee stared. "Paper?"

"Oh, yeah. I have lots of research you can read. My favorite is the fact that there are Web sites out there started by anorexics to show other young girls how to starve themselves to death. I learned a lot more than I ever wanted to. I ended up wanting to smash the damn computer into dust."

"So we can't force her to just start swallowing hamburgers, huh?"

Gen's smile was sad. "Not just yet. The first thing I have to do is try and get through to her father that Elizabeth has problems. In the meantime, if you'd continue being Elizabeth's friend and foster her music, I think it's the best ace we have."

"What do I say?"

Gen could manage no more than a shrug. "I don't know. I'm not the expert. But if you're worried about her, tell her. One thing a person can never get enough of is people who care about her."

Lee sighed, suddenly looking very tired. "Poor little Mouse. You can hardly blame her, though, with what she's gone through. I'm just surprised one of *us* didn't end up puking in a toilet on a regular basis."

"Yeah."

Lee hadn't noticed, Gen thought. Nobody had. Even so, after all this time, Gen's palms were sweating.

"Well," Lee said, climbing to her feet. "if music will help, music she'll get."

"Did she play her songs for you?" Gen asked, following her up.

"Oh, God, yes. They're wonderful. I want to send them out to be arranged."

Gen nodded. "Then I think I may have something. But I won't get a chance to try it out until I can get her father to see past his own guilt and grief to what's in front of his face."

"You always do take on the easy jobs, Mom."

Gen scowled. "Yeah, don't I just?"

"I guess I was lucky," Lee mused, giving her sister a hug. "I had a passion for something that was more important and a family who loved me. This kind of thing never occurred to me."

Gen hugged back, savoring the real security of her own family. "It's the path I hope we can take with Elizabeth. Keep good thoughts. And do some reading if you want to help. You're going to be on the team."

Lee's smile was sad. "It's so much easier just to write about it. After all, if I want to, I can make everything come out all right."

"But you so seldom do."

"I keep trying."

"Yeah, well…"

It was after Gen let Lee out that she finally walked over and opened up the box on the table. And when she finally read what she'd hidden there so many years ago.

Jack wasn't sure how he felt about this. He was standing in the music room of his house looking at the brand-new baby grand piano he'd just had delivered for his mouse. It gleamed like temptation, he thought, a frivolous distraction from what a serious scholar should concentrate on. A serious scholar who had been born to hold a scalpel in her hand.

But Elizabeth had talent. Everybody said so. And she'd been right. A proficiency in music looked exceptionally good on med school applications. Why shouldn't she polish her already remarkable skills on a good instrument?

At least, he assumed her skills were remarkable. They were at everything else she tried, earning her every high grade and accolade by dint of hard work and concentration. And the new piano teacher at the Conservatory had lapsed right into his native Italian when he'd heard her play.

Jack didn't understand it. He liked music, of course. He'd played some himself once, more for the camaraderie than anything else, truth to be told. But Elizabeth seemed to have some ear that made the music special.

At least he knew that she wouldn't waste a penny of this piano.

He couldn't wait to show her. To see her eyes light up. To hear her run those delicate, graceful fingers over the keyboard.

"Daddy?"

Oh, good, she was home. Jack took a deep breath and backed out of the doorway.

"I'm here, Mouse. Come on back."

She did, padding down the oak-floored hall in her tennis shoes like a sprite let loose from the forest for the afternoon, her face pale against the dark umber of her hair. She was smiling, her head tilted.

"You're home early."

"I have a present for you."

Her smile slipped a little. "You do?"

"Uh-huh. Come here."

He guided her by the hand right to the door of the room. The empty, echoing room that held nothing more than a huge piano and bench, a hard chair and a small table. A sterile, concert hall of a room saved just for her.

And he lifted his hand to show her the scope of his love.

Elizabeth froze. Her mouth dropped. Her face seemed to pale.

"I thought it was time to get you a real instrument," he said, turning toward the piano, suddenly nervous. "For the Conservatory."

She didn't make a sound. Jack finally looked away from the piano so he could see her excitement.

He didn't see it. She looked shocked, stark. She looked...grief stricken.

Jack's stomach slid. "Mouse? Don't you like it?"

Longing. Such powerful, dark longing that it was almost painful to see.

"Mouse?"

It was as if a switch had been thrown. She turned to him, and he could have sworn he saw tears in her eyes. He heard her draw in a breath that sounded almost painful. He saw that her eyes looked quiet and controlled and almost dead.

"It's beautiful."

At least she sounded sincere. He'd heard women speak in that very tone of voice the first time they'd seen their newborns.

Then why should she look as if she'd just lost everything?

"What's wrong?" he asked. "I thought you'd like it. Dr. Spinelli said you needed an instrument worthy of your talent."

Her breathing hitched. Jack could have sworn she was holding in a sob.

"Nothing's...uh, nothing's wrong, Daddy. It's beautiful. I just don't deserve it. I mean, how am I going to do it justice when I have to focus on school?"

Jack wrapped her in his arms and smiled. "You don't buy a piano to do it justice. You buy it to play. And I know you'll play on it. Nothing else matters."

Elizabeth stayed there for a minute, her head against his chest, her young heart fluttering. Jack closed his eyes and wondered why he suddenly felt afraid, standing there with his daughter in his arms. But he did.

Finally she slipped out of his embrace and backed away, smiling up to him. "Daddy, thank you. Really. I'll play something for you tonight, okay?"

"What about now?"

"Oh, now I have research to do. Big paper due for science camp. It's the last day tomorrow, ya know."

"After dinner, okay?"

She seemed to flinch, to straighten. She still smiled, but somehow it wasn't right. "If it's okay with you, I think I'll skip dinner. I had pizza with one of my friends after camp, and I'm not really hungry."

"Nothing? Estela made beef stroganoff."

She actually took a step back. And smiled. "Thanks, no. I'll be down later. How 'bout Mozart? You like Mozart."

"Of course. Go on up and make Einstein look like a fool."

She started for the stairs, then stopped, gazing at her father with an expression he simply couldn't read. "It's really beautiful, Daddy. I'll take really good care of it."

Jack smiled. "Just enjoy it, Mouse."

Her nod was just a tiny bit sharp. Then she turned for the stairs.

"Mouse?" he asked as she stepped up.

"Yes?"

"What do you do with your music? I couldn't find it when we changed benches."

She didn't even face him. "Oh, I lock it up in my room. Okay?"

"Okay."

But it wasn't.

Jack didn't sleep that night, either. He ached and he sweated and he pretended that he wasn't the blindest fool in the western hemisphere. Gen was most likely wrong. He had to believe that. But something was wrong with his mouse, and he couldn't sit by and watch it get worse.

The next day, when he got to the hospital, he walked right by the elevator banks that would have taken him up to his ICU. Instead, he headed for the ED. He went looking for Gen Kendall.

"Gen," he said when he saw her standing in the work lane with a can of soda in one hand and a bagel in the other. "Will you do something for me?"

She stopped cold. "Anything."

He sucked in a breath. "Would you tell me about Elizabeth's music?"

# *Chapter 12*

Gen closed the door to the doctors' lounge and took her seat across the table from Jack. He looked so tired, so taut. So rigidly controlled as he spoke, as if terrified of what might happen if he gave rein to his emotions. And Gen couldn't touch him. Couldn't hold him against her chest and rock him like a child. Couldn't tell him they were wrong, that Elizabeth was just fine.

But Elizabeth's reaction to the piano said it all. God, she even locked her music away, like a filthy secret. Gen couldn't bear it.

At the same time, though, it gave Gen hope. That locked box might just prove the key to Elizabeth's treatment, if they could get the right person to help them.

Certainly not that ass who was treating Mr. Christian.

But that was another problem for another day.

"Where do you want to start?" she asked quietly, keeping her hands strictly to herself, where they wouldn't get her into trouble. After all, they were still in the hospital, where anyone could walk in the room, where gestures could be misconstrued and reputations lost.

Where any progress Gen made could be blown to hell on the weight of a rumor.

Jack faced her without flinching, his lovely eyes dark. "You said that I didn't know her because I didn't understand her music."

Even his voice sounded lost, as if his very foundations had been shaken. Gen imagined they had been.

"Do you go to concerts?" she asked.

He stared at her a moment. "What does that have to do with anything?"

She smiled. "I'm working my way toward the answer you want. Do you?"

He shrugged. "Not really. Not for a long time. My wife was the musician in the family. She played the concert harp, of all things."

"I heard that you played the banjo."

"Badly. And late at night."

Gen nodded, praying with all her heart she had the right words for Jack. For Elizabeth. For her.

"I think maybe that's the reason you haven't figured it out yet."

"Figured out what?"

"I love music," she said. "And not just Manilow. Everything. I go to concerts when I can. I have season tickets to the Lyric Opera. I listen all the time. If I could wear headphones to work, I would. It soothes me, and it excites me, and it keeps me sane on a bad day. I'm envious of people who can write music and play music and appreciate music."

"Elizabeth said you played the piano."

"Kind of the way Arnold Schwarzenegger acts. I'm competent. Nothing more. But I can see talent. I can recognize brilliance."

He became very still. "What do you mean?"

"My sister, Lee, is brilliant. You saw the play she wrote. She's almost better, even, as an actress. My sister-in-law, Amanda, who writes books that make you weep, is brilliant. My brother, Jake, who trains cutting horses. Watching him on a horse is like the most primal, breathtaking ballet you've ever seen. He's brilliant. A master, a genius, a glimpse of heaven that simply robs you of breath. I don't have those kinds of talents. I think my talent is being able to recognize it in others. Especially people with musical talent.''

''Are you saying that Elizabeth is one of those people?''

Gen took a breath and looked away, gathered the rest of the words she needed right now. Then she faced him. ''Yes, Jack. She is. She…oh, I don't know how to put it. She should be playing symphonies. She should be *writing* symphonies. She wrote some songs for Lee, did you know? Lee said that they're stunning. Your daughter, at twelve, has genius in her, Jack.''

He looked so confused, so left behind, as if he were trying to interpret a strange language. God, she wanted to hold him, to smile for him and stroke him like one of her children.

''That's ridiculous,'' he said with a small, bemused shake of his head. ''She's only a little girl.''

Gen lifted a wry eyebrow. ''Do you really need me to quote all those clichés about Mozart writing symphonies at seven and Stevie Wonder being a superstar at ten? The word is *prodigy,* Jack, and Elizabeth is a prodigy. She needs desperately to have the kind of training to support that kind of talent, and she needs it now.''

''But she doesn't want it. She wants to be a doctor.''

Gen watched him a minute, gauging his readiness.

Who was she kidding? He would never be ready. She just had to get on with it before they were interrupted.

''Ah, well, this part involves the second half of the genius equation, Jack.'' He moved to object, but Gen wouldn't let him. She just kept on talking, so she could get it all out. All the words that would eventually break him, right there in front of her.

''What she has isn't just the talent, Jack. And remember, I have geniuses in my own life, so I recognize this part even better than the brilliance. What Elizabeth has is the obsession, the passion, the absolute blind devotion to what she does that geniuses have. It sets her apart from the rest of us. It makes her hear things we don't hear, see things we don't see, feel things she can't yet explain. It makes her die a little bit when she has to be away from it.''

"You can't see all that in a twelve-year-old."

"Of course I can. I did the very first time I saw her play. You *have* to have seen it in her. She just glows. She becomes otherworldly, and the sounds that pour out from those fingers make us simple mortals weep."

"That's absurd. Of course I haven't seen anything like that, and I would have. She's my daughter, for God's sake. Why, she's never even talked about music except to say that the work will look good on a med school application."

"She's writing music for Lee's play. Lee says it's good enough to be published."

For just a second he allowed a stricken look to cross his eyes. But that fast, he covered it. "She didn't..." He stumbled to a halt, looked away. Took in a breath, as if girding himself. "All right, let's say you're right. What does it mean?"

Gen sucked in her own breath. Squared her shoulders. "How much do you want to hear, Jack? Because from here on out, it's going to start to hurt."

She got a real grimace for that one. She'd hurt him already, and she knew it.

"What do you mean?" he asked.

"I mean she doesn't say anything because she doesn't want to fail you. I think she probably feels like the worst traitor because she wants so badly to play, and she knows she should be a doctor like you want her to be."

"Like *I*...?"

On his belt, his beeper trilled. The regular trill of a message, not the two-tone emergency alert. He ignored it.

"Like *you* want her to be," Gen repeated. "At least in her mind. She's only twelve. Her mother's dead, her father is suffering, and she can't do anything to help him. She can't do anything to make her family what it was before that terrible night. But maybe, if she makes you proud, if she does everything you want of her, she can replace her mother in a way for you. She can take away some of your grief and guilt."

Jack actually came to his feet. "What the hell are you talking about?"

Gen faced him square on now. Stood up, straightened, challenged him as if she had the right. "Jack, it's the talk of the hospital. Jack O'Neill is still grieving over the wife he couldn't save from a drunk driver. Do you really think your daughter's not going to get a hint of it?"

Again the beep. One of the other doctors leaned in the door. "There you are, Jack. They need you up in the unit. Seems your fellow is about to be lynched."

Jack just stood there, frozen, stark, his hands clenched at his sides.

"Jack?"

"Yeah, Ahmed. I'll be there."

Ahmed left. Gen held her breath.

"We'll continue this conversation later," Jack said, getting to his feet.

"It can't wait long, Jack," Gen warned him. "Please."

He turned, and she saw the cost of his control in the pallor of his face, the harsh lines at the corners of his mouth. "Why?"

"You know why."

"You really think Elizabeth is anorexic."

Gen prayed for the right words. The words that would propel him to action. The words that wouldn't crush him instead. Oh, she hurt so badly for this kind man.

"Until we can talk again, watch her. At meals she'll rearrange her food, cut it up into tinier and tinier bits so that she won't have to put anything substantial in her mouth. She'll maybe drink diet soda or water, never milk. She'll turn down almost anything that has fat in it. Lettuce. She might eat lettuce. No calories in lettuce. She'll work one person against another so everybody thinks somebody else knows she's eaten. She'll be obsessed about exercise. I saw her get almost frantic when she couldn't run just one day. Watch her. Please, watch her."

"I can't just watch her. I'll talk to her."

"Then know this. She'll lie to you. She'll be the most facile liar you ever faced."

"Elizabeth would never—"

Gen shook her head, certain. Frantic herself. "She will. She can't help it. Please, Jack, let me know the minute you can get

away someplace quiet where we can talk. I have the information.
I think I know a way to help her. But we have to talk."

"Why?" he demanded, his voice anguished and angry. "Why
are you so sure?"

Gen's smile was so sad, so afraid, so full of her own guilt
and grief. Yet she faced him, because she knew it was the only
way. And she gave away her own secret.

"When you're ready, I have a box of writing I'd like to share
with you from when I was a girl."

"Why?"

"I was a twelve-year-old girl who lost her mother, too."

He looked stunned. "You mean—"

Another beep, but this one was two-tone. No chance to ignore
it.

Jack grabbed the beeper and read it, already heading for the
door.

"Later," he commanded. "I'll call you."

"You do that, Jack," Gen said to the empty doorway.

And then she just sat back down and looked at her shaking
hands.

He lasted three days before calling Gen. In those three days
he cut short his hours to get home every night for dinner. He
watched his mouse play with the food on her dinner plate instead
of eating it, cutting the portions into more and more precise
geometric patterns and spreading everything around so that it
looked as if something happened to it.

Nothing did.

Except for the salad. Lettuce and carrots. And one lousy cu-
cumber.

He talked to Estela, and he talked to Mary McGregor, and
from both he got the same story. Elizabeth ate mostly in her
room, nibbling while studying, she said. She ran at least five
miles a day and did stomach crunches and the Stairmaster. Mary
smiled and said that Elizabeth should be in prime condition for
lacrosse camp. Estela clucked and said she was too skinny.

He tried so hard to talk to Elizabeth. He asked her once why
she wasn't eating dinner, because it seemed that ever since he'd

brought that piano into the house, she'd stopped eating even the little she'd eaten before. She smiled brightly and talked about the pizza she and Mary McGregor had shared. The pizza Mary McGregor didn't remember eating.

He asked Elizabeth to play for him in the evening after dinner, and she did. And by the third night, she lost that tight, controlled look and the mechanical actions of her fingers. By the third night, Jack realized that Gen Kendall was right. When Elizabeth could no longer bear to control herself, magic spilled from her fingers. Glorious, glistening sorcery that stole his breath and rent his heart.

And her eyes...

He couldn't tear his own gaze away from her eyes, glazed and soft and so sad he thought he would weep. Not the deep, almost spiritual glow Gen had talked of seeing, but the kind of look a person sees on someone who is saying goodbye to a lover. The look that must have been in his own eyes that dark night in February.

Seeing the thing you loved the most and knowing it didn't belong to you.

When she finished, he held her. Nothing more. Wrapped in his arms, her glorious Meggie eyes closed against his chest, her small heart stuttering like a bird seeking flight.

His beautiful, sweet mouse.

He didn't wait any longer. The next day was his day off, and Elizabeth was at her fourth day at lacrosse camp. He walked over to Gen Kendall's flat and knocked on the door.

Gen had just walked out of the shower after completing her three-mile post-junkfood-binge-penitence run on the hottest damn day of the summer. At least she was finally out of Girl Scout cookies for the year.

She was toweling her hair by the front window when she heard the knock on the door. She didn't even worry about answering. Nobody but a tenant could have gotten up without buzzing, and she knew the two tenants. Lee and Mrs. Moffitt, the previous landlord.

Gen threw open the door, smiling. She stopped.

"What are you doing here?" she demanded.

He didn't so much as smile. "Lee buzzed me. She said to tell you she's on the way to the theater and won't be here for you to yell at."

He was here to talk about Elizabeth. Gen could see the weight of what he'd realized on his shoulders, in the incremental tightening of his features. She knew it was time. It was past time. She should be relieved.

She was devastated.

Jack looked like a disaster survivor, and it made her chest clench. He stood at her doorstep, and it made her want to sob. He had come to her, and yet he would not reach out any further than he had to. It made her want to die.

And he was bringing this into her apartment. Here, where she could still hear his whispers in the flutter of her curtains, where the night held his scent, even if only in her memory. Where he'd brought joy and completion and comfort. How could she so taint those precious few moments?

How could she not?

"I'm not going to yell at anybody," she said, stepping aside. "I was just surprised. Come on in, please."

He did. He walked in and stood in the center of her living room, staring at Emily the piano as if she'd personally betrayed him.

"Jack?"

He turned on her, and Gen caught the jagged pain in those sweet sea eyes of his and almost wept.

"I bought her a piano," he said, his voice almost raw. "I thought she'd like it."

Gen could just imagine. "Come on, let's sit down. Would you like a drink?"

Even though it was no later than noon.

He shook his head, sank into the overstuffed couch that faced the windows. "No, thank you. Nothing."

She nodded, embarrassed. "Oh, yeah. I forgot."

Gen briefly thought of taking up a seat in a facing chair. Keep herself at a safe distance where she could hold her wits in order. But, of course, she couldn't. She couldn't be that far away from

Jack when he hurt. She couldn't make him hurt worse without being close enough to help.

So after he settled, she claimed the cushion right next to him and turned to him, her feet curled up beneath her. She just hoped she survived the next few minutes.

He didn't even look up. "Would you tell me about…about your…"

"About the time I tried very hard to starve myself to death?" she asked. "Yes, Jack, I will. Did you watch Elizabeth?"

He was picking at his slacks, his attention on his restless hands. "I did. She did everything you said she would."

"But she did eat something."

"Yes."

"And you didn't hear her throwing up later?"

His head came up like a shot. Gen grimaced at her own lack of foresight. "I'm sorry. I don't think it's that. But we'll talk about it later, if you want."

He stared at her for a long moment, looked away out the window into the hazy sunlight of another hot summer day. "Can you imagine how criminally stupid I feel right now?"

"My family *still* doesn't know," Gen admitted. "So you can't be that stupid."

He looked startled. "No one in your family was a board certified pediatrician."

"You're also a father. The only reason I noticed was because I recognized myself in her. Remember what I told you about Jake? Not one of us realized he couldn't read, and we lived with him every day. Amanda knew because her favorite uncle was illiterate, and she recognized all the tricks. It's much the same thing, Jack."

He nodded, his eyes closed with pain. "Tell me about it. Please."

Gen laid her arm against the back of the couch when she wanted to hold his hand. She faced him when she wanted to close her eyes against her own failures. She wished desperately that she could just hand over that box of old writings so she didn't have to actually give voice to all those old feelings of failure.

"I was another little girl who lost her mother, who felt responsible, who felt as if she'd lost all control over her life. Who felt she had to be an adult—and felt she failed at everything she did. Who finally found one thing she *could* control."

"Her food."

"Her body."

Gen couldn't help remembering that time fifteen years ago when she'd cooked the meals and then made sure hers weren't eaten. When she'd run up to the high meadow and back at least once a day, or ridden her dun up the mountains just to exercise off those love handles. At twelve. She'd almost run that horse into the grave.

"But why would Elizabeth feel that way?" he protested. "It wasn't something I taught her."

"You never had to. It's something the media is teaching her, Jack. Her friends. You know that perfectly well. And it's not just that, anymore. I found some Web sites...." She still felt sick at the photos and advice on those sites. "There are Web sites out there that teach a girl how to starve herself. I've seen them. I think you might want to check your computer and see if Elizabeth has bookmarked any."

"But why?" he demanded. "She has never had the responsibilities you did. I've done everything I can to make sure she gets over what happened. How could she think this made sense?"

"She's twelve. She's trying to be thirty. She's taking on guilt that isn't hers. She has a feeling that somehow, if she'd done something differently, she might have helped save her mother. Now she's beginning to forget what her mother looks like. She thinks she's letting her down. And she thinks she's letting *you* down because she can't be the person she thinks you want her to be, because she can't make your grief any better."

"It's not her job to make my grief any better."

"You can't tell her that, Jack. She won't believe it. It's the way a teenage girl's mind works. And now that you're all that's left to her, she's trying to live up to the example you've set, of being a humanitarian, a top doctor in your field, a true caregiver.

She's going to seven school camps this summer, Jack, just so she can excel. So you can be proud of her and feel better.''

"But I would never ask her to do that!"

"Of course not. But she would ask it of herself if she thought it meant she would be a better person for you. She asks a lot of herself. She feels deeply. You only have to look at the Save the Whales and Nine-eleven posters on her walls to know she's taking on the problems of the world. It's kind of classic.''

"Classic in what, anorexia?"

"Classic in anorexia. Girls who are too empathetic, too perfectionist, too uncertain of themselves. Girls who look in the mirror and can't see how special they are, only how ugly they are. Girls who need something, some one thing, they can look toward and say, 'There, I did a good job.'"

"She *always* does a good job."

"Stop being a father for a minute and see this from her viewpoint. It's the only way you're going to help her.''

For a very long moment he just sat there, just watched her as if sizing her up, as if letting all her words tumble and spin around in his brain until they could fall into some kind of recognizable pattern. He sat, so rigid and separate, as if nothing could touch him, as if he wouldn't let anyone touch him.

Especially her.

Oh, how she understood that. They were so alike, the two caregivers who didn't know how to be cared for.

"Will you tell me about you?" he asked.

That caught Gen right in the chest. It had been so long since she'd talked about it, even to a professional. It was such an instinctive reaction to hide it away, like the dirty secret it had been back when she was twelve and the world was coming apart.

"It's such a frightening thing," she said. "For a while you know it's wrong. You don't feel good. Your energy's down. You get sick a lot. But you feel ugly and fat and useless, and it drives you to starve. I starved.''

"How did you stop?" he asked, his voice hushed.

"I was lucky enough to have a teacher who caught me."

"She didn't tell your brother?"

"God, no. I would have run away if she'd tried. Jake already had enough on his plate."

"It does seem a familiar theme, doesn't it?" he retorted, his eyes wry and sad.

"Very. I was lucky, because my teacher found the one thing to target that would motivate me. I began passing out at softball games. Got violent headaches and couldn't play. And a softball scholarship was what was going to get me to college. Considering how Jake felt about education, I couldn't let him down yet again. She got me to understand that I couldn't keep starving and play. I wouldn't have the stamina to last. And she paid for me to see a specialist in Bozeman all the way through college."

"College?" He looked panicked.

"Anorexia isn't chicken pox, Jack. It's more like post-traumatic stress syndrome. It's a stress response. Each time I faced a new major stressor, I saw a counselor, just to work through the destructive impulses."

"But you're through it now."

She so wanted to hold him, to ease this terrible truth for him. "I haven't needed the counselor since my first year of med school. That doesn't mean I never will again."

It took him a second to ask the next question, a long, fraught second of silence. "How lucky do you think Elizabeth will be?"

This time Gen did reach over, she did make the contact she knew he needed, no matter what it cost. She saw that deep, searing grief in Jack's eyes and knew she would do anything to ease it. She knew how frightened she'd been when she'd realized how much she'd compromised her own health. She couldn't imagine how a parent would feel to know that his daughter had done the same.

Or maybe she could, and it was why she'd never told Jake.

So she took hold of Jack's hand and held on for her life.

"I think she's very lucky. I knew a lot of kids with the syndrome, and the ones who couldn't seem to overcome it had terrible underlying family problems. Elizabeth has a father who would die for her. A father who gives her absolute, unconditional love. It will help her understand that she doesn't have to do or be anything special to be loved. And, if you'll let us, she has all of the various and assorted Kendalls to be her extended family. We may be mad, but we're very supportive.''

"You said…you said you might have found a treatment option.''

Now Gen could really smile. "I did. Remember I said that my teacher had used my softball to concentrate on instead of the anorexia? Well, I've been reading some of the latest treatment options, and that's one of the things they're finding success with. Focus on something the girl loves that isn't her body image. Something important to her.''

"Her music.''

"Her music. There has been some excellent success with this kind of program, and I just happened to talk to the people at the Eating Disorders Unit here and found out that one of the docs is working in this very area.''

"But we have to talk Elizabeth into it.''

"Yes, we do. But I've been thinking. Would you mind if you and I sat down together with her? It might make a difference if she knows I've been through this. And then she has to know that it isn't going to be a secret anymore. Everyone will watch her. I actually found it comforting that somebody was watching over me.''

"You've got the research in your bag?" he asked.

"As much as I could put together. You want to read it?''

He shook his head. "Not now. Not…I just want to soak this in. I want to have a moment to believe we can actually make a difference here.''

So they sat, side by side on the overstuffed couch. They sat in silence, Gen holding his hand, Jack stroking her palm with his thumb. They sat hip to hip, and Gen could almost feel their heartbeats match. She felt her own hands grow damp, her chest tighten with the electricity they couldn't help but spark. But she felt, too, a newer, fuller silence between them. A sharing that didn't need words.

She felt the first flutterings of hope.

Jack's beeper trilled. The message trill. He didn't even look down.

"I should leave," he said. "I should answer that.''

"I know."

Yet he didn't leave. He sat alongside Gen stroking her hand. And then, as if he couldn't help himself, he turned and gathered her into his arms, and Gen went. She closed her eyes at the feel of his heartbeat against her cheek, his hand in her hair.

He kissed the top of her head.

"Oh, Gen," he whispered. "How do I thank you?"

And tucked against his heart, Gen smiled. "You don't."

They rested there for long, silent moments punctuated by the distant rhythm of street life, the sun slashing across them, the hollow silence of the room a pleasant companion. Gen shouldn't have been surprised when Jack laughed, even if it was a sore, tired sound.

"You have a lot of courage, ya know."

"Why?"

"You stood toe to toe with the chief of your service. Do you know what I could have done to your career?"

Gen felt like smiling again, her eyes closed, her cheek nestled against the crisp cotton of his shirt. "How could I do less for the man who braved my brother Jake to tell him he wasn't considerate enough of his little sister?"

Another silence. Fuller. Deeper.

"I'm sorry," he said softly, stroking her hair as if salving himself with the feel of it. "For what I said in the restaurant."

This time Gen laughed. It was so easy to forget that terrible moment right now. "I know. It's hard, though, isn't it?"

"What?"

"Accepting help. We're very much alike, you know, older doctor."

She felt it again, that sweet, deep rumble in his chest. "You figured that out, huh? I'm just so used to solving all the problems myself. It's what I'm good at."

"That's what my sister, Lee, insists is going to be on my tombstone. I was completely panicked when I walked into that surprise party."

Now Jack backed away to stare at her. "Why?"

She shrugged, less comfortable with honesty when he could

see her expression. "I've never had a surprise party thrown for me before. I wasn't sure what to do."

His smile was infinitely sweet, exquisitely gentle. "At least you didn't call me names and stalk out."

She lifted an eyebrow. "Not when I'd gone to all the trouble of putting on panty hose. I wasn't leaving that party until I had some of those pot stickers."

It was as if a light had been switched on behind those Caribbean eyes of his. "I'm glad you stayed," he whispered and bent to brush a soft kiss across her lips. "You're a great dancer."

She leaned up, reached a palm to cup his cheek, that harsh, strong cheek that held the most wonderful dimple in the world. "Barry Manilow," she assured him with a grin. "He taught me everything I know."

He kissed her again, more slowly, more thoroughly, until her toes curled and she thought her heart had stopped beating. "Not everything," he assured her. Then, his mouth no more than a breath from hers, he paused. Frowned, his gaze on her lips, his breathing harshening a little.

"What do I do now?" he asked, almost as if to himself.

Gen knew that the question wasn't about Elizabeth.

*Love me,* she wanted to say. *Hold me here where we're both safe from the rest of the world. Let us both hold each other up in the face of the terrible things we must confront.*

Instead, she kept quiet and simply held him. Simply met him, eye to eye and lip to lip, her challenge as much plea as invitation. She held herself there, held him in her hand, and she waited, because it would have to be his decision. He had to know just by looking at her that she had long ago made hers.

Gen almost stopped breathing, so quiet did she want to stay, so he wouldn't startle away. So he wouldn't suddenly remember that he had no business being in her arms. She tried with all her heart to believe that this day could make a difference to them both.

For a while they just sat that way, together, alone and wrapped tight, eye to eye and heart to heart, taut with possibility, sharing warmth and breath and the respite of silence. And then, almost imperceptibly, Jack's hands began to move. To stroke. To soothe. Gen held still only by force of will, by dint of the fact that she'd simply stopped breathing.

He couldn't mean it. He couldn't know what he was doing. He'd told her right here in her living room that he wouldn't return to her. He wouldn't return to her marshmallow bed and her outstretched arms. But he was coaxing her body to life as surely as he'd done before, and she wouldn't stop him for the world.

Again his beeper trilled. His hands never stopped. He lifted one to her chin and raised it to him, and Gen saw the fire that smoldered in those eyes, the smoke that almost hid that deep, abiding pain, the sorrow and grief he carried for a dead woman and a frail young girl.

But for now his eyes spoke volumes of need and want and desire, and Gen couldn't help but answer.

He kissed her, a deep, sweet communion that set the fire loose in her. He teased her with his tongue, with his lips, with his teeth. With his hands. He managed to undress her there on the couch, and she did the same. Slowly, savoring every touch, every murmur and sigh. Stopping only long enough to seek protection, like magic, so that she wouldn't be hurt.

And there in the sun-drenched living room that should have been in Sienna, he took her on the couch, thrusting deep into her, joining with her, smiling down at her, for that precious moment hers and no one else's. He stroked her and soothed her and stoked the fire he'd built until it consumed them both, leaving them shaken and smiling.

And then, neither of them saying a word, he took her into her marshmallow bed and they made love again.

Gen heard the beeper trilling again, that reminder of the other world that lay beyond her fantasy rooms. She saw Jack pause, felt him shake his head. Then he whispered in her ear, "This once, the hospital can go to hell. I need you, Gen."

Gen had no answer. She needed him, too, right there, inside her, around her, above her. She needed the scent of him, the sight of him, the rough, strong feel of him against her hands and against her heart.

She was so afraid that this was only a brief respite. That he merely needed a little joy, a little comfort, a little life to offset what he had to go home and do that night. He needed to believe that there was more than grief and duty in his life.

Even if that was all it was, though, it didn't matter. She needed the same.

But oh, how she wished it were different. She wished that this was where he would come home. Where he would rest and play and work, here in her sunny, bright Tuscan rooms where they could make all the magic they wanted.

She needed to believe him when he murmured, spent and sweaty and smiling, "Do you think it's possible to start again?"

For a long time she didn't answer. She didn't know how. She didn't know if he wanted to hear what she had to say. But she had to say it anyway.

"Oh, Jack, I hope so. I really do hope so."

And he held her, just as he had in the deepest hours of the night, both of them dozing and weary as the hot breeze blew in to make the gauze dance around them. He lay as if he didn't want to ever move again, and Gen finally let that small seed of hope grow.

Maybe, just maybe, she thought, her eyes closed, her hand splayed out across Jack's flat belly. Maybe, given time and attention and patience, Jack could forgive himself for the fact that his wife had died and he hadn't. Maybe he could allow someone else in his life.

She was almost asleep, curled around the man she loved, almost happy with the thought that maybe they could be a family after all. Maybe they could all three work to help Elizabeth get through her problem and Jack walk past his pain.

Maybe she would finally have those things she'd never dared dream of.

Again Jack's beeper went off. This time, though, it was the two-tone emergency alarm. Both of them bolted up out of instinct, as if all they had to do was run down the hall.

"It's my day off," he groused, padding into the living room to retrieve his pants. "What the hell could they want from me?"

Gen followed, much too distracted by the sight of his tight, delicious tush to worry about the hospital. She wanted that tush in her hands again, not to mention everything else. Those taut, muscled thighs, that flat stomach. *Everything*.

"Can I use your phone?" he asked. "It's the ED."

"Of course."

He made the call from the kitchen, standing there blithely naked on her Italian quarrystone floor, phone in one hand, pants in the other. Gen watched from where she leaned against the bedroom door, but she didn't really listen. Not until he straightened.

"What?" he demanded, and suddenly the light went out of the room. Gen listened now, but he didn't say any more. Just "I'll be right there."

She'd stopped breathing. Suddenly she didn't want him to turn around. She didn't want to know what he was going to tell her, because she could already see by the sudden panic in his movements that everything had changed again.

"It's Elizabeth," he said without even facing her as he yanked on his pants. "She collapsed at camp. She came into the ED in cardiac arrest."

# Chapter 13

Gen slammed through the ED doors right behind Jack. The place was a zoo: screaming, shrilling kids everywhere, parents making demands, ambulance sirens and radios adding background counterpoint. But trauma room one, where Elizabeth O'Neill lay, was completely silent.

Gen stuttered to a halt just inside the doorway, her heart skidding to her toes. A good half of the day-shift staff was clotted around this room. Equipment was torn open, and trash littered the floor. Monitors and IV machines and a respirator took up most of the available space, and yet movement came to a complete halt the minute the staff saw who had come storming into the room.

But worst of all, worse than Gen could ever have imagined in her lifetime, Jack's beautiful little girl, with her nimbus of earth-colored hair and her freckles and her pianist's hands, lay splayed on the trauma cart, a breathing tube supported her lungs, a nest of IVs replaced fluids, and a dozen staff members watching her like a science experiment. At least the monitor at the head of the bed was beeping with some regularity.

"She came back with a couple of shocks, Jack," the ED

physician said the minute he saw his chief. "But her electrolytes are in the toilet, and she's ketoacidotic. What the hell's been going on with this kid? Is she diabetic and she doesn't have a tag?"

"No," Jack said, his voice strangled as he stared down at his baby girl. "She's not diabetic."

Gen stood right behind him, her own gaze frozen, her hands clenched in impotent frustration.

"The camp said they tried to page you, Dr. O'Neill," one of the nurses said. "They thought it was just heat exhaustion, since it was so hot out there today and the girls were working so hard. But Elizabeth got worse."

"Is she on any medication, Jack?" The doctor asked, stepping up. "Anything…unusual we should look for?"

"She doesn't do drugs," Jack rasped as he tried to walk over to where his daughter lay breathing through a tube. He didn't make it two steps. Shaking so badly he shouldn't have been able to move, he simply fell to his knees onto the step stool alongside the cart.

Every person in the room looked stricken. Some looked away. Gen couldn't breathe. Jack reached out to Elizabeth's pale, slack face with a trembling hand.

"Oh, Mouse," he whispered, harsh tears in his voice. "Don't do this. Come back to me."

Gen couldn't bear it. She crouched right down alongside him, wrapping her arm around his shoulders. "She's better, Jack. They got her back. It's going to be okay."

She lifted him, and he came to his feet like a sleepwalker.

"Come on," she urged softly, not caring who heard her. "Let's move someplace out of the way so they can work."

Jack spun on her, his glistening eyes stark with fury. "No. I'm not moving."

"It's okay," the other doctor said. "Just tell me if you know anything that can help."

Gen met Jack's gaze and held it in silent challenge. She saw him breaking apart, could almost hear the keening grief he couldn't let loose. She hung on to him as if he were a drowning man and desperately wished she could hold his face in her hands right then. To hold his eyes to her where she wouldn't let these people hurt him.

"Anorexia," he finally rasped, and looked away. "I've just begun to believe she might be anorexic."

"Bingo," the doctor crowed, then turned to dispense orders at machine-gun speed.

Gen didn't move. She just held on to Jack. Held him up. She stood there, knowing damn well that her place in the hospital would never be the same, that all the rumors and snickering and suspicions would begin. She didn't give a damn. Jack's mouse was fighting for her life, and that was all that mattered.

Oh, God, Elizabeth was so pale. So still, that bright gypsy girl who spun miracles in the sunlight. Gen couldn't bear it. She couldn't stand to see those grubby legs stretched out bare beneath a haphazardly applied patient gown.

So she let go of Jack just for a minute. Just long enough to get Elizabeth properly covered, warmed and tidy amid the frantic care the staff was giving her. Then she wrapped her arm around Jack again and shared that same warmth where he stood cold and silent and bent with anguish.

"They tried to call," he muttered, and suddenly Gen felt even colder.

"Jack, you couldn't have…"

"They tried to call, and I didn't answer."

That hope, that frail, friable thing that had tried to take root in her such a short time ago, failed. She heard its death in his voice. Accusation. Self-loathing. She saw it in his stance. His daughter had almost died, and instead of being there to prevent it, he'd been in bed screaming Gen's name.

He'd failed his little girl. Which meant he'd failed his dead wife.

Which meant that Gen was the one who lost.

She would think about that later. Right now she had to help him get through this crisis. She had to help Elizabeth. She held Jack, who had one of Elizabeth's delicate, long-fingered hands in his. She laid her other hand against Elizabeth's hair, just as she'd seen Jack do all those times. Touching, stroking, connecting with that small life force and doing her best to will her own to reinforce it.

She'd done it many times, more times than she thought she could count. But not since she'd done it for her own sister, Lee, so long ago in another ICU, had she thought she wouldn't survive it.

"We're gonna get her up to the unit, Jack," the doctor said. "Uh, Dr. Spizer's on up there. You want...?"

"I'll take care of Elizabeth," he snarled.

"No," the doctor said without hesitation. "You won't. You know better."

Jack looked away from his daughter with a glare that should have frozen the doctor in his toes. The doctor, his eyes understanding, didn't flinch.

"You will not treat your own daughter, Jack," he said. "You know you can't."

"She's not *my* daughter," Gen offered quietly, trying so hard to hold perfectly still, as if none of this mattered. "I can take over for the fellow if you'd rather she not help. And Tony Martin is up there to be her critical-care-attending. Who's her pediatrician, Jack?"

She got the glare now. Gen never knew blue could be such a deadly cold color.

"Who, Jack?"

He pulled his hand away from her, and she thought she would crumble to her own knees. She straightened instead.

"Abe Beilstein."

"I'll call him," the doctor offered, and headed out of the room.

"I'm staying with her," Jack said unnecessarily.

"I can come with you, if you want," Gen offered, her voice still quiet, still calm, no matter what she felt like inside.

Jack looked at her for a moment. Then he turned back to his little girl. "No," he said in a dead voice, "that's okay. We can take care of ourselves."

And that was that. What had begun with just a faint trace of promise, a joke about two people who couldn't ask for help, died in the brevity of a dismissal. Gen fought down the urge to scream, to pummel Jack for his obstinacy. To simply wrap herself around him until he couldn't ignore her anymore.

So he and Elizabeth would be their own complete circle. Gen wasn't needed anymore. Not her help, nor her information, nor her care.

Certainly not her love.

For a moment she just stood there, held outside Jack's magic circle by his silence. Then, somehow straightening even more, as if assumed dignity would better protect her from the pain, she simply nodded.

"When the time comes," she said quietly, "the doctor you want to talk to is Theresa Peterson."

He nodded, nothing more. Elizabeth was beginning·to stir.

Gen wasn't needed here anymore.

As she walked out into the work lane, she saw Tony Martin heading her way. One of the other critical-care-attendings, he was short, squat and furry from one end to another. The kids tended to call him Bear.

"Gen, what's going on?" he asked when he saw her.

"The ED guy can tell you," she said with a travesty of a professional smile. "I just happened by. But since you're here, I might as well make my offer. Jack's little girl is in there, and she's pretty sick. He's not going to be able to do much work. If you'd like, I'll pick up extra time in the units till he feels comfortable coming back."

Tony's eyebrow lifted. "On top of your schedule?"

Gen did smile then. "I just got off a residency. You might as well take advantage of my offer while I still can't remember what it is to sleep more than three hours a night."

"You're on."

She nodded. "That's fine. Take good care of her, Tony. She's really special."

"She's Jack's kid," he retorted, heading for the room. "Of course she's special."

Gen stayed through the evening as Elizabeth began to wake up. She stayed through two more episodes of cardiac arrhythmia that taxed everybody's professional calm, and she stayed through a screaming tantrum from Jack that had every person in the unit slack-jawed.

But she remained on the sidelines. She helped out on the floor when Tony was busy with Elizabeth, and she helped the ICU nurses when Dr. Spizer pulled a fit because she wasn't allowed near the chief's kid. Gen even faced down the big, overbearing doctor and sent her into retreat.

"You're not going to finish this residency if you don't shut up right now," Gen said, her voice deadly quiet.

"Who are you to—?"

"Your guardian angel, you stupid cow. That's the chief of your service in there with his critically ill child. Every stupid, shrill word out of your mouth is putting nails in your professional coffin. At least act like you understand."

"I'm supposed to understand that he won't let the critical-care fellow near his kid?"

"You're supposed to understand that he's frantic. Everybody else knows exactly why he doesn't want you near his daughter. You'd scare her to death."

"Well, at least I'm not getting death threats."

That stopped Gen for a moment. "Jack's getting death threats?"

Spizer laughed, and it wasn't pleasant. "No, you stupid *cow,* you are. It's all the talk of the hospital. Not caring enough, I guess, if a parent wants to blow your fat head away."

Still Gen stood there, trying hard to concentrate on something other than Elizabeth and Jack. "How does everybody know?"

"Because he's been calling. I got to talk to him once. Smart man. You killed his kid, huh? Not well done, I'd say."

And then she just walked away.

Right before Elizabeth's alarms went off. Gen forgot about the conversation almost before it ended.

She spent the rest of the night waiting to make sure Elizabeth was stable before she went home. She only had four hours before she was due for her next shift. It didn't really matter, though she wasn't going to get any sleep.

Gen wasn't sure what good it would do, but when she returned to the hospital, she brought her bag of research material with her. She carried it up to the unit where Elizabeth was at least off the respirator and sleeping, and she left it with the unit nurses to give to Jack when he was ready.

She didn't say anything in response to their raised eyebrows, and she didn't walk into the room where Jack lay asleep with his head on the side of Elizabeth's bed. She just watched for a minute and prayed. She watched and prayed and hurt so hard she thought she would never be able to breathe again, because she wasn't allowed in there to help, and she knew damn well Jack wouldn't let anybody else in there, either.

So she worked her shift, and she helped out the shorthanded critical-care docs when they needed her to, and she kept track of what Elizabeth was doing. And for the next four days she kept offering. It seemed, though, that Jack, the perfect doctor, had decided that he had to get back to his job. So in between his time in with Elizabeth, he ran the units and consulted and calmed frantic parents whose children weren't as ill as his own.

Gen worked her ED shifts and slept in the call room in case she was needed, and she fought the urge to stop eating, herself.

Well, she'd told him. Stress brought back the feelings of inadequacy, of ugliness, of worthlessness.

And who could feel more worthless than a woman who couldn't comfort the man she loved?

"You okay?" Abbie Viviano asked the next morning when they walked onto the ED hall together at seven.

Gen felt as if she had broken glass in her chest. She felt raw and frightened and alone. So, of course, she smiled and patted Abbie on the shoulder. "Just a little tired. I've been trying to help out the good chief, but it seems he'll have none of it."

"I can pick up some shifts, if it'll help," Abbie offered.

"You have three children and a husband to corral. I have a piano that's much happier when I'm not the one playing it."

Abbie chuckled. "How's Elizabeth?"

"Out of the unit. Sleeping a lot, I hear."

"You hear? You haven't been up to see her?"

"I will."

When hell froze over, it seemed. She'd tried to talk to Jack, to ask about Elizabeth. He'd just gotten that frayed look on his already-drawn face and done a few more steps in the "need more distance" dance.

And Gen had gone off to the call room to lie on the lumpy bed and stare at the ceiling some more.

Lee caught up with her at lunchtime, storming into the ED lounge like a diva in high dudgeon.

"I thought you'd been awfully quiet upstairs," she accused, pointing a finger.

Gen didn't want to face her, either. "I didn't know that was a reportable offense."

Lee huffed like a little steam engine. "You weren't even *there!*"

"I know. I've been here, mostly."

"And you didn't tell me about Elizabeth!"

That brought Gen to a stop. "Oh."

Lee plopped into one of the plastic chairs and sighed. "I had to find out from Estela when I called about more music…. Elizabeth wrote the most wonderful tune that she just tossed in with the other stuff. She calls it 'Song for the Wise Woman.' It's the most beautiful thing. But then I find out…and you can imagine how easy it was with Estela sobbing in incomprehensible Guatemalan…."

"I think that language is called Spanish."

Lee looked up from her diatribe, real distress in her eyes. "You didn't *tell* me."

Again, Gen could think of nothing to do but sigh. "I'm sorry, Lee. I…" She tried, she really did. But she ended up just shaking her head and tamping back that burning, tears-on-the-back-of-her-tongue feeling. "I forgot."

Gen couldn't seem to look up from the half-eaten hospital salad she'd scattered over her lunch tray. She couldn't face her own sister.

"You okay?" Lee asked softly.

That brought Gen's attention up. It straightened her spine. "Sure. Just tired."

Such a strong instinct. Such a certain answer.

Lee's gaze was sharp and discerning. Gen had a terrible feeling that she wasn't fooling her sister at all. It made the glass grind a little harder against her sternum.

But Lee nodded, slowly, and got to her feet. "Can I visit her?"

Gen shrugged. "I'm sure you can. Room 715."

Lee opened her mouth, as if there was a lot more she wanted to say. "I'll say hi for you."

Gen nodded, reached over to hug her sister. "You do that, squirt."

Lee hugged back and wandered away, leaving Gen alone. Alone with her fear and her longing and her sadness. Especially her sadness. Damn it, she should have known better. She *had* known better, since she'd been no more than twelve. Nothing lasted. Nobody stayed. No one out there really wanted anything more from her than her competence and her management.

She knew she was tired then. She'd just spent ten minutes more in self-pity than she ever had in her entire life.

But then again, in her entire life she'd never been in love. And she'd never seen the man she loved deny her in favor of a memory and a load of guilt.

Taking one last look at the salad that was beginning to look wilted and sad itself, Gen straightened her lab coat, checked her instruments and walked out onto the floor where she did belong.

It was one of the floor nurses who told Gen what was going on. Gen had been sitting at another cafeteria table trying to interest herself in lunch when the nurse sat down and just stared at her.

Gen really wasn't that surprised. She figured that the nurse was coming to settle a bet. After all, the entire hospital knew Gen had been trying to talk to Jack. She'd tried so hard that she was fast becoming the daily entertainment for the entire staff. Some of them were even starting betting pools.

She'd checked a couple of times on Elizabeth, only to find her asleep, and she'd tried to wait until Jack could be there to talk to Elizabeth about what was in store for her. And the only thing she'd managed to do was give herself a burgeoning reputation.

"You looking for lunch?" Gen asked the nurse. "I don'
recommend the fare here. It tastes like a hospital cafeteria."

"I want you to do something."

"Me? What? And why?"

The nurse, a sharp, storm-trooper-mother kind of floor nurse
who took every one of her kids home with her, huffed as if Ger
were the most stupid person on earth. "Dr. O'Neill is transfer
ring his little girl to a treatment facility for eating disorders."

Gen brightened. "Wonder—"

"In Minnesota."

Gen was on her feet without knowing how. "What?"

The nurse didn't budge. Her scowl grew absolutely fierce
"It's a national leader in the treatment of eating disorders."

"That's fine. Is he going with her?"

"It's not that kind of unit."

Gen didn't even bother to wait for more. She went straigh
into battle.

It shouldn't have surprised her that she didn't find Jack any
where. The coward was probably avoiding her. Probably throw
ing a tantrum somewhere because somebody else had tried to
help him. Well, let him be a petulant brat if he wanted. But she
was not going to let him compromise his daughter's well-being

When she couldn't find him anywhere else, Gen decided to
beard him in the proverbial lion's den itself.

Room 715.

He wasn't there, either. Elizabeth, however, was.

Gen found her sitting alone in a private room that overflowed
with flowers and stuffed animals, her hair ratty and her eyes red-
rimmed and anxious. Gen's heart went out to the child, who
reminded her so much of herself. But this one was stuck with
the father who didn't need any help.

The idiot.

Well, Gen thought, sucking in a huge breath to calm herself
might as well just wade on in. It was what she had wanted to
do for the past four days. Shoving open the door, she smiled a
Elizabeth's wary surprise. And then she just settled herself dow
on the side of Elizabeth's bed.

"It's scary, isn't it?" she asked very gently.

Elizabeth could barely look at her.

Gen kept a careful distance, merely taking gentle hold of Elizabeth's restless hand. "I mean the fact that everybody knows," she said. "It was your secret. It was something you had power over, and now they want to take it away."

This time she got a very startled look.

"And they *are* going to take it away, Elizabeth," Gen said, never moving away, never moving closer, letting Elizabeth make that decision. "You know that, don't you, honey?"

Tears welled up in those sweet blue eyes that were supposed to be her mother's but reminded Gen of Jack in the most ferocious way. Gen wasn't sure she would ever get a good breath again as long as she lived.

"I screwed up *everything*," Elizabeth whispered, the tears tracking down her cheeks.

Gen couldn't bear it a moment longer. She leaned over and gathered that little girl into her arms, where she could find at least a brief moment of rest. Where there was safety and comfort and respite.

"You have screwed up nothing," she said in her surest voice, her head bent tight over Elizabeth's. "You just tried to take on jobs that should never have been yours."

"What do you mean?" she heard muffled against her scrub top.

"It's not your job to make your daddy feel better, Elizabeth. He's a big boy. He's got to figure that out for himself."

Good advice for herself, too, Gen thought with a wry smile at her own pain.

"Your job is to be twelve," she said, her heart full of the frightened girl in her arms. Oh, how she wished she belonged there.

"That's what my daddy says."

"He's right."

"He also said that you...that when you..."

Gen backed away, brushed the damp hair from Elizabeth's face and wiped away the tears. "That I stopped eating when I was your age. Yeah, I did. My mother was dead, and suddenly I couldn't remember what she looked like. I didn't think I was helping Jake enough, because he was always exhausted and sad, and I didn't know how to make him feel better. Yes, Elizabeth, I quit eating. Just like you.''

Those eyes were so expressive, huge pools of grief and fear and insecurity. "I don't...I..."

Gen waited, but Elizabeth couldn't manage any more, so she nodded for her. "It's so hard," she mused, "being told you have to give up the one sure thing you really think you have a hold of.''

She heard a hiccup and a gasp. Those eyes got wider.

"If you want," she said, "I have some things I wrote back then. Things that might seem familiar to you. Sometimes it's just nice to know you're not the only one feeling this way.''

Elizabeth couldn't seem to do more than nod.

Gen nodded back. "In that case, I'll tell you the good news and the bad news," she said, stroking again, touching. Keeping contact. "The good news is that you do have something else to hold on to. You have your music, and that's a mighty powerful thing, isn't it?''

For a second, Elizabeth looked away, looked down, as if ashamed. But Gen wouldn't let her be ashamed, never again.

"Do you think Lee is talented, Elizabeth?" she asked.

Elizabeth's gaze immediately lifted. Her shoulders straightened in pure defensive posture. "She's a genius. Don't *you* know that?''

"Of course I do." Gen smiled. "Well, that genius thinks that you're a miracle. I'm a doctor because I could never be a musician. You should be a musician because you'd never be happy as a doctor. And because I'd never be happy if you were a doctor, either. I need your music, Elizabeth. I desperately need that kind of magic in my life.''

"But Daddy wants me to be a doctor.''

Gen shook her head. "He wants you to be whatever *you* want to be. I promise. You just have to be brave enough to tell him what that is.''

"I don't know.''

"Elizabeth," Gen said, stroking her hair again. "Your daddy

loves you too much to see you sad. Haven't you realized that these last few days?''

Tears rose in those lovely eyes, and Gen wanted to cry, too. ''I hurt him so much.''

''No, baby. He hurts because he loves you, and when we love somebody, we can't stand to see them in pain. But you'll both begin to hurt less when you start sharing what's wrong.''

She hoped. She prayed.

No, she thought, she knew. Jack O'Neill might be stubborn and blind and stuck in a morass of guilt, but there was no question that he would give his life gladly just so the light would return to his daughter's eyes.

There was a pause. A shaky breath. ''I'm just not sure.''

''It'll take a while for you to believe it, honey. I know. But you will. You'll discover what gives you joy, and you'll move past this place.''

''What's the bad news?''

Gen smiled. ''I told your dad, and I'm telling you. These feelings don't go away just 'cause we want them to. They come back when we're stressed. I'm stressed now, and I've caught myself eyeing the lettuce again.''

''Still?''

''Uh-huh. The good news is that I recognize the feelings before they get bad, and I talk to somebody. And so will you. But asking for help is the hardest part. Just ask me and your daddy.''

''Ask me what?''

Gen looked up to see Jack standing in the doorway, his legendary cool visibly missing. He looked furious in that tight, controlled way of his. He looked frightened, as if Gen would somehow steal his daughter away from him while his back was turned. He looked desolate and absolutely alone.

He needed to ask for help, Gen thought, instinctively furious. He needed to share.

Then she almost laughed. Just the way she'd shared with Lee and Abbie. The way she'd let anybody else help her anytime in her life. They *were* a pair, weren't they?

''That the hardest thing for some of us to do is ask for help,'' Gen said. ''But it's the most important.''

"I didn't ask you to…"

Gen deliberately turned back to Elizabeth as if just the sight of him weren't destroying her. "I didn't offer. This is between Elizabeth and me. How 'bout we go in and wash your hair, Elizabeth? I think you'll feel better."

Elizabeth, once again tossed about by the unspoken tension in the room, simply nodded. Gen got her robe and got her to her shaky feet, and walked her toward the bathroom door, just next to where Jack was standing.

"Gen, I thought I told you that we'd deal with this."

Gen stopped right in front of him. "Elizabeth is my friend. I came to see my friend. Is that all right, Dr. O'Neill?"

There was nothing he could do. For just a moment, a flash of a moment, Gen saw the pain rear in his soft eyes, but then he shut it away, just as he'd shut her away. Then he turned to his mouse and tousled her already-knotted hair.

"And when Elizabeth and I are finished," Gen said, "I need a word with you, Dr. O'Neill."

That put the steel back into his spine. "Is that right, Dr. Kendall?"

Not only did Gen not back down, she faced him like a recalcitrant child. "Yes, Doctor."

Thirty minutes later she found him no farther away than the hallway outside Elizabeth's door. She shut the door on a now-sleeping Elizabeth and stalked over to him.

"You want to go someplace private to talk?" she asked, hands shoved deep in her lab coat pockets as she struggled to keep control of her temper.

He straightened from where he'd been leaning against the wall, and Gen saw that he didn't look appreciably better.

"No. We'll talk here. I have a lot to do."

Gen glared at him, frustrated and frightened and so furious she could have screamed until the alarms went off.

"Fine," she agreed. "Please tell me you aren't sending Elizabeth away for treatment."

He stiffened like a shot. "You saw her downstairs. You know damn well that we have to catch this right now."

"I didn't say we shouldn't treat her," Gen said. "I said you shouldn't send her away."

"It's the finest facility in the country."

"Her mother's dead and now her father's throwing her away. That ought to make her feel loads better."

Gen wished those words back as soon as she'd said them. Jack went paper white, his eyes as dark as death.

"You're treading on thin ice, Doctor," he hissed.

Gen could hear the staff working along the hall. She knew they were listening to every word. But Jack had been the one to stay here in public, probably hoping it would keep Gen's mouth shut.

Well, some things were just too important.

"So fire me," she retorted. "You haven't even told her yet, have you?"

"She's not ready."

Gen damn near laughed. "When will that happen?" she demanded. "When you drive her to the airport? When you walk away? You know damn well this isn't what's best for her, or you would have told her already."

He stood so rigidly that Gen thought he might shatter. But his eyes, oh, his eyes were cold as death. "I told you how much I appreciated your help. Now leave this to us."

She was trying so hard, and she had so few words to convince him. Lifting a hand, pulling back, she struggled for calm. "Jack, you can't do this to her. Not when she's this fragile. *Please.*"

"I've weighed the options—"

"Did you read the information I gave you? Did you talk to Theresa Peterson?"

"The unit here is too new for me to take the chance. I am not losing her, no matter what you say. I'm not taking a chance with her life!"

"But that's what I'm trying to tell you," Gen insisted, all but tearing her hair out. "Right now, the most important factor in Elizabeth's treatment is *you*. Not the finest facility in the country, not the best doctors on the damn planet. *You*. If you send her away, she's going to feel as if she failed again. She'll never stand a chance!"

"I've made my decision, and that's all there is to it. Now I suggest you stop interfering where you aren't wanted and go back to your own patients."

He was turning away. She couldn't let him. She was frantic, she knew. Probably irrational. But she knew, knew better than Jack, better than anyone, what exiling that little girl would do to her.

"*Listen* to me!"

He whipped back as if she'd tried to assault him. "I've lost too much already," he grated. "Elizabeth is all I have left."

Later, Gen thought, she would think about what he said, and she would hurt. She would probably die, at least a little.

Right now she ignored it.

"Then don't send her away. Please."

"Why?" he demanded. "Why should I listen to you when I've had experts in the field tell me differently? What makes you so special?"

She could hear that silence behind her, that vacuum of complete attention that made her words echo and spin down the hallway.

"Couldn't we *please* go someplace else to talk?"

"No. Finish this here, so I can get back to what's really important."

"I can't."

"You can't?" His eyebrow curled. His posture straightened. "You can't tell me why I should listen to you?"

"You *know* why you should listen to me."

"Because you know what she's been through."

"Because I love you."

Oh, God, she hadn't meant to say it. She hadn't even meant to think it. Not here. Not in front of a rapt audience, when the last thing Jack O'Neill wanted on his overloaded plate was a futile vow of love.

She went still now, too. Perfectly, utterly still, only the racing thunder of her heart giving her away. And then she began to crumble. Because Jack O'Neill of the Caribbean eyes and the gentle hands, Jack O'Neill who delighted and challenged and compelled her, pulled away. He stepped back and straightened even more, and suddenly his chief of staff armor was back on.

''Well, don't,'' he said.

And then he walked away.

# Chapter 14

Gen wasn't sure how she found herself in Lee's apartment. But suddenly she was there, and she was pacing, and she couldn't seem to stop. Round and round the room, skirting trunks and saddle trees and a bazaar of mismatched furniture. She didn't even notice the things she bumped into, or the things she missed. She just kept moving, first in one direction and then another, bouncing around the room like a random ion.

And from her position on one of the big chintz couches she preferred, Lee just watched. Actually, she stared. Open-mouthed and, for once in her life, stone silent.

"Bullheaded, idiotic…"

Gen made another turn. Lee watched.

"Jerk?" Lee offered.

Gen didn't notice.

"He's so full of himself, he can't see what's right in front of him. He's gonna…he's gonna…"

"Blow it?"

"I can't…"

"Stand it."

Gen knew she was being irrational. Frantic. Frightened, like a rabbit caught in a box. She couldn't breathe. She couldn't calm. She didn't know what to do, and she couldn't seem to get her brain in gear enough to figure it out.

She couldn't get past that moment when Jack had lifted that disdainful eyebrow at her.

"Well, don't," he'd said, as if he were chastising a young student for throwing spitballs.

"I'm going home," she muttered, hands wrapping around themselves like snakes. "That's it. I'll go home."

"You just started your job," Lee said from her couch.

Gen shook her head. "I just started my job. They'll never let me go."

She felt as if she were going to explode, there was such pressure in her chest. She felt as if she were going to fly apart.

He couldn't do it. He couldn't hide his daughter away like dirty laundry. He couldn't tell Gen she had no right to love him.

He'd done it.

He was going to send Elizabeth away, and there wasn't anything Gen could do to stop it. And yet she couldn't stand by and watch him shatter what was left of his family.

Not the way he'd already shattered her.

Enough, she thought brutally, skidding to a halt and then heading in another direction. Self-pity again, and there's nothing more useless in the world than self-pity.

But oh, God, she hurt. She hurt so much she thought she would splinter beneath the weight of it.

"I have to…"

She slammed into a rolltop desk and kept moving.

"You have to what?" Lee asked, her eyes wide.

Gen didn't hear her. She didn't notice that the bright-blue door opened and Rock walked in. She was making a circuit over by the sari-draped bay windows and trying to figure a way to spirit Elizabeth away before her father could send her off.

She was frantic and panicked and devastated.

His eyes.

His eyes had been so cold. So empty and final and dismissive.

She never should have told him. Should never have admitted there in the crowded work lane that she loved him. Stupid her, she'd had the idiotic idea that if he knew she only wanted what was best for the both of them for the best of reasons, that he would see she was right.

Now he never would. He would burrow into his safe hole and cover his head with guilt to keep her away. He would circle the proverbial wagons and keep her out.

And she would have to go on with her life as if he'd never taken it apart.

But she couldn't just wander anymore. She wasn't doing any good here. She had to go somewhere else. Somewhere productive, she thought. So she headed for the door.

"Thanks, Lee," she said, not really seeing her sister. Not seeing her brother-in-law where he stood behind his wide-eyed wife. "I've gotta go."

She walked out the door without hearing the dialogue she left behind.

"Good God," Rock said, his attention on the still-open doorway as the sound of Gen's footsteps faded away. "What happened?"

Lee shook her head as if coming out of a trance. "I don't know," she admitted in hushed tones. Then, unwrapping her legs from where she'd been tucked up on the couch to stay out of Gen's way, she climbed to her feet. "But I think she's fallen in love."

Rock looked upward as if tracking Gen's movements. "Is that a good thing?"

"Not from the looks of her just now. I think I'll go upstairs."

The two of them listened for a second until they heard Gen's footsteps match the same pattern they'd followed in Lee's apartment.

Then Rock nodded. "I think you'd better."

Lee went up. She opened a suspiciously unlocked door to find Gen skirting her own furniture. Lee didn't want to admit it, but she was afraid. She'd never seen Gen like this. Heck, she'd never even seen Gen break a sweat, not when she'd come home to Lost Ridge to find Lee in a hospital, not when she'd landed in a hospital herself after the fire that had almost taken her life.

Not when they'd found out that Jake couldn't read, or when they'd buried their mother. Gen just didn't fall apart.

Gen was the one in charge. She was Mom. She was impervious.

Obviously not.

The universe was definitely out of order.

"Honey, you want to sit down?"

"No," Gen said, not seeming to notice that it might be odd that Lee was now in her apartment. "I don't think so."

"What do you have to do?"

"Save Elizabeth."

"From what?"

"Her jerk of a father. Her jerk of a stupid father who can't seem to forgive himself for not saving his wife, so he holds on to Elizabeth like a lifeline, and he's gonna strangle her before we can save her."

"Oh."

Lee realized that her sister was shaking. She was picking at her clothes as if they suddenly didn't fit anymore. Her hair was a mess, and her face was puffy. Lee really didn't know what to do.

Maybe she should call Jake. Jake was the other person who always knew what to do. Or Amanda. Amanda had known what to do when Jake hadn't. Maybe she should get Rock up here to just hold Gen down long enough to get some sense out of her.

"Why do I even bother?" Gen demanded of the front windows.

"Bother what, honey?"

"Loving the son of a bitch."

Well, Lee thought, at least that issue was settled. Gen, her calm, collected, supremely rational sister, had finally tumbled off that big I-love-you cliff. Which, at any other moment in time, would probably have been endlessly amusing. It certainly would have set up some memorable bets among the family.

But Lee had the terrible feeling that Gen was flying apart right before her very eyes, and that wasn't in the least funny.

"Can I give you some Amanda advice?" she asked.

"Sure."

She wasn't sure Gen was really listening, but she tried anyway. "She said if you love a man who has big problems, you do everything you can to help him."

Gen skidded to a halt not three feet away. "And if that doesn't work?" she demanded.

"You walk away."

That seemed to freeze Gen solid. "You're kidding."

"Nope. As she said, no woman gets gold stars in heaven for beating her head against a wall her whole life for a guy who isn't going to change."

Gen huffed. She shook her head. Her eyes grew suspiciously moist, but no tear fell. Lee suddenly wanted to see some tears. She wanted, oddly enough, sobs and storms of weeping and the catharsis of grief. She wanted Gen, for once in her life, to have the luxury of it, and she didn't know how to give it to her.

That was something else Lee suddenly realized. She'd never, in her entire life, seen her sister Gen cry. Why in God's name hadn't anybody noticed that before?

"Would you have walked away from Rock?" Gen asked, her voice tight and small.

Lee shrugged. "I guess I'll never know. My lovely, hard-headed husband finally saw the light. He had to get shot to do it, of course."

Gen grimaced. "I'm sure it could be arranged again."

"Wouldn't help your career much."

"The hell with my career. I'm more worried about Elizabeth. I thought we'd finally gotten a breakthrough, and that jerk is setting up to ruin everything."

"Want to tell me about it?"

They were like magic words. Gen literally pulled herself together, like the Scarecrow being restuffed after the flying monkeys had eviscerated him. Lee saw it happen and wondered just how many times Gen had accomplished it in the past. Tucked away in her room maybe, or the bathroom, where nobody could see what her life was costing her. What her courage took from her.

"Didn't I see Rock downstairs?" Gen asked, her voice deliberately bright, her eyes not meeting Lee's. "I thought you two were going out tonight."

"We don't have to."

"No, honey, go ahead. I'm fine."

Lee got to her feet and faced down her sister. "No, honey," she said. "You're not. And I think it's my turn to do the helping." Oddly enough, that made Lee laugh. "Wow," she said with a giggle. "Who'd ever have thought I'd be the one saying that?"

Gen didn't let her help, of course. But she let her hug her. And they stood that way for a long time, survivors who understood better than most what life cost, what it was worth.

And when Lee left, Gen gave her a parting shot that made her feel a bit better. "I hope at least the son of a bitch can't sleep."

The son of a bitch couldn't so much as sit still.

He couldn't breathe. He couldn't find quiet. He couldn't escape the voices in his head. Voices of memories that always followed him but today seemed to flay at him without cease.

He couldn't stand any more. He simply couldn't go on this way, and he had no idea how to change it.

He'd told Elizabeth.

He hadn't even waited until he'd calmed down from the lecture he'd gotten from Gen Kendall.

The lecture that had somehow involved her admitting she loved him.

Not that he really should have been surprised. He'd known, really, that first time he'd tumbled with her onto her dream-soft bed. He'd understood, deep in his gut, that Gen Kendall didn't tumble with just anybody. She didn't offer that much of herself anywhere. She didn't open herself to hurt and disappointment and despair.

She'd had enough of it in her life already to make her more wary than even he was.

But she'd let him past. She'd let him in, welcomed him with smiles and sighs and off-key songs. She hadn't really had to tell him there on the work lane where he'd ended up humiliating her in front of half the staff. She'd told him every time she'd taken him inside of her. Every time she'd stood toe to toe in an effort to help Elizabeth. To help *him*. Every time she'd made him laugh and made him think.

She'd told him with her eyes and her hands and her quick, sweet wit.

And he'd thrown her away.

And not kindly. He'd done it in a way to provide maximum damage. He'd made sure she would never come back, for any reason. He'd shamed her for the sin of loving him, and he had no right to believe he could ever gain her forgiveness.

And then he'd done the same to Elizabeth. Walked right back into that little girl's room and told her she was being exiled to Minnesota for her own good, whether she liked it or not.

And he'd found that Gen had been right all along.

"What do you mean?" Elizabeth had asked, her voice suddenly small and unsure, her posture painfully careful, her eyes wary and dark and wide.

Her beautiful blue eyes. Her mother's eyes.

Her mother's eyes that he couldn't face anymore. Not in the daytime and not in the nighttime, and not in her beloved daughter.

"I mean that I've found this great place that has a wonderful success rate with eating disorders, Mouse. They don't even think you'd have to stay long."

"You want me to leave," she said, her voice grown impossibly small.

Jack climbed onto her bed and took her into his arms. "Of course I don't want you to leave. But I want you to feel better."

"I do," she protested, her thin body tense and tight against his embrace. "I really do. I don't think I have to go."

Jack leaned back so he could face her. "No, Mouse. That's not an answer. You know from what Gen told you that we can't beat this thing by ourselves. We need the help of professionals. Just as if you have appendicitis. I can't take out your appendix, so I'd have to ask somebody else to help us."

"Isn't there anybody else here?"

He let her go then, backed away as if he were afraid of her.

Afraid of his little girl. "Not anybody as good as at this place in Minnesota."

"Does Gen think this is a good idea?" she asked.

And Jack had snapped at her. Jack, who didn't even snap at Cruella De Vil Spizer.

"Gen doesn't have anything to say about this," he retorted. "I do, and after doing the research, I think this is best."

He might as well have murdered her on the spot. He saw it, right there in those glorious blue eyes. The light in them winked out, and they went flat. Careful. Compliant. Right before his eyes, his Elizabeth became the perfect little girl, the girl who would never disappoint him again, never fail him, never make him sad.

The little girl who would end up starving herself to death in the hopes that it would somehow please him.

"If you say so, then, Daddy," she said, not even looking at him anymore. "I'd be happy to go."

He'd walked out of her room and into the nearest bathroom, where he'd vomited everything he'd eaten that day into the toilet.

He couldn't change his mind, he kept saying to himself. He couldn't chance making another mistake. He had made so many already. He'd made mistakes he could never take back, never negate, never atone for.

How could he chance making another with the most precious person in his life?

What had he said to Gen? The only thing left to him? He could still see the anguish in her eyes, the swift, lethal hurt that she hadn't let loose at his hard, cold words.

But it would have been worse if he'd told her the truth. That he'd fallen in love with her the first time he'd seen her sing to a baby. That he ached hard for her in the dark of night when his defenses were down, because she was the best thing that had ever happened to him or his little girl.

He didn't deserve her, after all. He never had. Hell, he hadn't deserved Meggie, and he'd proven it.

How much more damage could he do to a woman as fragile and brave as Gen Kendall?

He didn't want to face it.

He didn't want to face any of it.

Which was why, he knew, he was sending Elizabeth away.

Because, in the end, he was a coward.

He took a minute to dunk his head under the cold water in the sink just to settle himself. He ran shaking fingers through his hair and checked to see he had his mantle of calm around him before he stepped back out onto that work lane.

And then he just stood there. Just stood in the harsh white hospital bathroom looking at the door back to the work lane, back to his life. Back to the world where decisions had to be made.

He just stood there.

Gen knew that her composure was held together with baling wire and chewing gum. One good shove and she would shatter into tiny, sharp fragments of pain. She knew she shouldn't so much as walk out her front door before she had herself better put together, but she had a shift to cover, and they wouldn't understand that kind of excuse. The "I'm in love with the boss and he spurned me" excuse. Or maybe the "I made a fool of myself in front of everyone who might have respected me and now I can't face them" excuse.

She had no intention of giving them the real one. The one that involved not being sure if she could make it through the day carrying such a load of grief and loss in her chest.

She wasn't unacquainted with the feeling. She'd survived an awful lot, after all. And she'd gotten through it every time. She'd buried the people she'd loved and done her work, cared for her family and faced her world with her shoulders back and her eyes dry. Well, she would do it this time, too. No matter what happened. No matter what it cost.

She had to.

After all, if she were honest with herself, she'd done nothing but anticipate this moment from the first sight of Jack O'Neill on the ball field. She'd been preparing for it. Girding her loins, so to speak, against that time when he walked past her in the other direction and she had to keep moving in her own.

She'd survived before.

She'd survived death and hunger and despair. She'd survived disappointment, and she'd survived isolation.

Then why wasn't she sure she could survive this?

Gen was still stiffening her spine for her walk onto the work lane when she was intercepted right at the triage desk.

"Gen?"

Gen blinked as if she were hallucinating. But no, there was Abbie Viviano's husband, Michael, in his police lieutenant's uniform, standing foursquare in front of her with another officer, hats in hands.

She came to an uncertain stop. "Michael?"

He smiled briefly.

Gen liked Michael a lot. A good cop, a great husband and father, a legend around the hospital, where he'd met his wife during a hostage situation. But Gen had only seen him at social functions. Never in uniform unless it was to come pick Abbie up from work.

Which, of course, scared Gen. "What's wrong?" she demanded, trying her best to remember where everybody was who mattered to her. "Abbie? Somebody in my family?"

Michael's hands came up in defensive position. "No, no, Gen. I swear. It's nothing like that. Can we talk a minute?"

Gen glared at him. "You promise."

His smile grew to a grin. "On my kids' lives."

So they followed her into the staff lounge, where everybody was milling about before the next shift.

"So you killed him, huh?" somebody asked her. "Not that he didn't deserve it."

"Who?" Michael instinctively asked.

"Our new chief of critical care. Asshole."

Gen straightened like a shot. "Yeah, Terry," she said quietly. "I'm sure if one of your girls came in in cardiac arrest, you'd be the most sensible person in the world, too."

Terry had grace enough to blush, and the rest had the sense enough to leave before anything more was said. But at least Gen knew the mood of the hospital. Poor Jack. He was going to have to face a lot of cold shoulders today.

"Would you mind answering some questions?" Michael asked, settling himself onto one of the hard-backed chairs.

"Yeah. Sure."

"William Christian," the other officer said.

Gen want numb. Oh, hell. Now what?

"His little boy died here," she said, her attention swinging between the two. "But I think you know that."

It was Michael who nodded. "One of the hospital administrators called about the threats you've been receiving, Gen. I promised to look into it."

"Abbie strong-armed you, ya mean."

His smile was wry. "Everybody's worried."

"He's a grieving father. He has to blame somebody."

"He's disappeared," Michael said bluntly. "Right after his wife caught him making pipe bombs."

Gen had been right earlier. She wasn't going to make it through this.

She made it through another forty-eight hours, though she didn't make it through well. The police had brought dogs into the apartment building to sniff for explosives, and the hospital had stationed one of the security officers full-time at the triage desk just in case a crazy man happened to walk in wielding a pipe bomb. It was still summer, which meant that her workload was crippling, and she hadn't heard anything more from Elizabeth or Jack except that the entire staff of the hospital had evidently sided with Gen.

By noon the first day, Gen had called Theresa Peterson herself for an appointment and tried not to throw up the ham sandwich she'd shoved down at lunch. By noon of the second day she'd counted an even dozen times she'd walked over to the elevators to the seventh floor and then walked away again.

She hadn't done such a good job the first time she'd interfered with Jack and Elizabeth. If she tried going up again, Jack would probably just toss her out one of the windows.

She tried to go home to sleep in her apartment. She really did. But somehow it wasn't hers anymore. She kept seeing Jack there. She kept hearing his low laughter. His harsh cries of climax. She kept thinking that maybe she should sublet her apartment and move someplace else.

She kept thinking that she was an idiot to let one man so destroy her.

Lee was right. If Jack O'Neill didn't want her love, the hell with him. Let him wallow in his little trough of guilt for the rest of his life. Heck, let him just paint Martyr on his forehead and get it over with. She had a job to do, and she was going to do it. She had a year to get through, and then she was going the hell home.

It sounded so easy in her head. It was so very, very hard to do in her life.

She'd made it through two days. There was only another hour to go before she could go home again, before she didn't have to worry about ignoring all the staff comments and the possibility that she would run into Jack somewhere and embarrass herself. She was standing at the elevators on four after helping bring a kid up to the units when she got stopped.

"Oh, no," came her instinctive and heartfelt reaction.

It was the same nurse who had stopped her in the cafeteria. Marian Thurson. Blocking the elevator doors with her stout little body, her arms across her chest.

"Oh, yes," she said.

Gen shook her head and tried to shove her aside.

"No," Gen insisted. "Not again. You go find a priest or something, girlfriend. I am not welcome among that family."

"The little girl is staying here."

Gen swung around, suddenly hopeful. Then she saw the look in the nurse's eyes and knew that for some reason it wasn't good news at all. Gen was not used to seeing Marian Thurson scared. She was scared now.

"Staying here is a good thing," she assured the nurse.

"That's not the problem."

Gen sighed. "Why did I know you'd say that?" She tried her best to ignore the sudden fire in her chest. "All right," she said. "Then what is?"

"It's Dr. O'Neill..." Marian Thurson managed, her hands lifting aimlessly, as if wrapping themselves around an undescribable problem. "He had an appointment to talk to the social worker from the eating disorders unit today, and then he just didn't come back. I'm really worried."

"Have you tried to page him?"

"I know where he is."

"I was afraid you were going to say that, too. What do you want from me?"

Marian actually looked unsure of herself. She couldn't seem to hold still, which made Gen even more anxious.

"Somebody needs to talk to him," she insisted. "I think something happened when he talked to those people. Something…"

"Something what?" Gen knew she sounded strident. She didn't much care.

The nurse faced her. "I don't know. It's like he's just reached the end of his rope. He's…he's falling apart."

Jack O'Neill, who prided himself on nothing more than his professionalism. On his brilliance and his calm. Falling apart. And if Marian said it was true, it was.

"Where is he?" Gen asked, because she had no choice.

"The last I heard, he was tearing apart the call room on three."

Marian knew damn well what kind of reaction she would get with that kind of statement.

Gen gaped. "Tearing apart?"

"You heard me."

"You should have told me that first."

She didn't even pause to say goodbye. She just got her sorry self to the stairs and ran down.

By the time she reached the call room, there was a small crowd clustered around the door, as if wanting to do something but afraid to go in. Gen heard something smash against the door and understood.

"I thought they kept breakables out of there so they wouldn't tempt the residents?" she said dryly.

To a person, they turned on her, anxious and uncertain. No matter how mad they might have been at how Jack had treated her, they didn't want this.

Who would?

"Yeah, yeah," she said, shooing them with her hands. "I'll beard him in the lion's den. Go tell the kids somebody had *Jerry Springer* on too loud, so they don't get panicked."

They didn't move quickly, but they did move. And when she was certain they were far enough away, she tried the call room door.

To her astonishment, it opened.

She simply couldn't imagine taking the chance of having somebody walk in on this kind of rage. Especially if the person allowing anybody to walk in on him was Jack O'Neill.

Not that she would have recognized him.

Dear God, she thought, he's…he's…

But she couldn't even put words to it. It was as if everything she felt in her chest, he had succumbed to. As if he really had simply splintered into a million sharp pieces of pain and rained down on this small room.

There was debris everywhere. Some fool had left a pile of dirty dishes from the cafeteria up here, and Jack had thoroughly demolished them. He'd hurled a lamp at the wall and evidently ripped apart several medical texts. And now he stood there in the middle of the room panting. With tears on his face.

Tears.

Gen swore her heart stopped beating.

She couldn't take her eyes off him. His face was ravaged. Old, sallow and sagging, as if he'd aged twenty years in two days. She could hear the wind rasp in his lungs as if he'd run all the way up here carrying a weight. She could see the tremor in his hands, as if the terrible emotions in him were leeching out of every pore.

She didn't know what to say. She didn't know what to do.

So she locked the door behind her, and then she walked up to him. And as gently as if it were one of her babies, she wrapped herself right around Jack O'Neill and brought his head to her shoulder.

He stiffened. He fought her. He cursed her.

She held on.

"You don't...you don't even *know*..." he rasped, his voice terrible, "...why I'm..."

"I don't need to," she whispered, and edged them both over to the bed in the corner. "Is Elizabeth all right?"

"She's here. She's right here where you wanted. You should be happy. You should be satisfied. She's safe from me now."

Gen never let go as she stripped the shard-littered blanket from the bed. She didn't say another word as she eased Jack down onto it, so that his back was against the wall. So she could hold him in her arms and soothe him.

So she could soothe herself with the solid feel of him here where she could help him.

She felt the hitch of his breath, the terrible struggle to maintain control when it was just too great a burden to bear. Her heart had started again. She knew, because every beat hurt her like a gunshot. Every breath seared her lungs.

She shouldn't be here. She should let him face this himself, because she simply wouldn't survive it when she helped him again and he walked away from her. Again.

She didn't leave.

"What happened?" she asked very quietly, holding on more tightly.

"What happened?" he echoed, trying to pull away. *"What happened?* Just what I thought would happen."

"You let Elizabeth stay."

"I let her stay, and they came after me. They came after me, and they kept after me and they...they accused me..."

Gen pulled back just far enough to face him. "Tell me."

His eyes were a wasteland, and she knew, looking at them, that there would be worse. She held on as if against a high, terrible wind, for whatever would come.

*"You* should know," he accused her, his eyes harsh and unforgiving. "You of all people should know what they accused me of in there."

"You mean that a percentage of girls with eating disorders have suffered sexual abuse."

"They asked me!" he spat. "They asked me, in that *concerned* tone of voice they perfect so well, could I tell them anything? Did I have a *healthy* relationship with my little girl? Did it change after my wife died? They wanted me to tell them that I'd hurt her! They accused me of something that *unspeakable,* and you knew they would!''

''They had to, Jack. You know they had to. How could you ask them to overlook anything that might help Elizabeth heal?''

''Not that! Not that I'd hurt my little girl.''

''I'm sorry, Jack. I didn't think it would bother you, because I knew you'd never hurt her, so the question was moot.''

''You knew!'' he echoed, his voice so tight and shrill that Gen couldn't imagine how he held on to his sanity. She couldn't even imagine why this would so upset him.

''Are you sure you knew?'' he demanded, shaking her. ''Are you absolutely sure? Are you sure you didn't want them to force me to admit that I'd hurt her? That I'd hurt my Elizabeth? My Meggie's baby? You didn't *want* that?''

''Of course not. It was all in the literature I gave you, Jack. I thought you'd read it and understand. I told you. I could never believe you'd do anything to hurt Elizabeth.''

He laughed again. He laughed so hard and so sharply that Gen flinched. Then he shoved her so hard that she fell backward off the bed.

''Well, isn't that the best joke of all,'' he said with another terrible, harsh laugh. ''You know why?''

''No,'' she managed, holding very still, suddenly so very afraid.

''Because for all your blind faith, young doctor,'' he snarled, crouched down over her, ''you were wrong.''

''I don't believe you, Jack.''

Gen thought she'd never seen a more terrible anguish on a human's face. ''You thought everything would be *fine* once she got to treatment here. You thought they'd just pat her on the head and point her to a piano and everything would be okay. That you wouldn't cause any more hurt to us. Didn't you?''

He was shouting now, curled so tightly over her that she was frightened. Her heart was stumbling around inside her like a wild thing, and she couldn't seem to breathe. She didn't know what to do. How to answer him.

"Jack, they just want to talk...."

"They want to *know...everything!* Well, I'll give you everything, Gen. I'll give it to you, since you prodded and poked and pushed us to this point." And then, his face so close, the poison spilling out of him in a torrent, he did just that. "I did hurt Elizabeth, Gen. I hurt her in a way that I can never forgive. I hurt her so badly that it'll take the rest of my life to make up for it."

"Jack, you didn't—"

"I did! I know it, they know it, and now you know it. Remember that drunk driver who killed Elizabeth's mother? That unforgivable bastard who was so selfish and callous and remorseless that he left my Meggie bleeding to death by the side of the highway?"

"Yes," Gen answered, choking on the word. Terrified of the manic light in Jack's eyes.

Jack straightened. Swept his arms out wide, an exhibit of himself. Laughed. "Well, meet that bastard, Gen. I was the drunk driver who killed my wife."

Then he bent to her again, and Gen cowered before his grief. "And now I get to tell my little girl."

# Chapter 15

Gen froze. Literally. Stunned, silent, shivering. Crouched against the wall in the smallest ball she could manage.

She tried to speak. She couldn't. She tried to breathe and didn't do much better. She simply couldn't push the air past the grief that had lodged in her chest. She tried to close her eyes and couldn't. She felt as if she were simply imploding, and she didn't know what to do about it. She didn't know what to do about Jack.

She didn't know what to do *for* Jack.

He just stood there, tears coursing down his cheeks and soaking his scrub top, fists clenched, face ravaged, back bowed. She could hear the rasp of his breathing. She could see the unbearable strain on him. She could almost smell the self-loathing on him.

Oh, God, she thought over and over again. Oh, God.

And then, before she realized what she was doing, she was on her feet. She was reaching out to him, because she couldn't survive his pain when it kept her apart from him.

"Oh, Jack," she whispered. "Oh, Jack, I'm so sorry."

He pushed at her again. He straightened and glared.

"No," he demanded, the breath catching in his throat. "No! Don't you dare comfort me! Don't you understand? I murdered my wife, damn it! Don't you dare try and tell me it doesn't matter!"

"Of course it matters," she retorted, toe-to-toe with him. "It obviously matters so much that you've changed your whole life to atone for it."

"Atone!" he demanded, leaning in again, fierce and furious and so very fragile. "You think I can atone for something like that? You think I can *ever* make up for what I did to her?"

He gasped, as if he simply didn't have the strength for what he had to say. He said it anyway, his eyes as bleak as death, his hands shaking where they fisted by his sides.

'She tried to get my keys. She even had them once, but I got them back. *I* was the one in charge. It was *my* Porsche, my brand-new Boxter, and nobody but nobody was driving it but me. I was in control, wasn't I?"

Gen could do little more than shake her head. "I'm sorry."

"Yeah," he said, the abhorrence thick on his tongue. "So am I. I used to have a family. Now I have a wife who only exists in a painting on my wall and a little girl who's paying for my sins by starving herself to death. And I have a *mission*."

"A mission?"

He glared at her. Gen so wanted to touch him, to ease the anguish on that dear face. "Just what do you promise your wife as she lies dying in your arms, younger doctor? Just what do you say that will take away all your sins?"

Gen couldn't help it any longer. She had to reach for him. Only her hand, cupping his cheek. His wet, hollow cheek that felt oddly warm when his eyes were so cold. So deadly, deeply cold. And the tears still fell, even though he didn't realize it.

"Did Meggie really ask you to give up your life to pay for that sin?" Gen asked.

"She didn't have to. There is no way I can ever make it up to her now, is there? I can only do what I think is right."

"The same way Elizabeth is doing what she thinks is right?"

He backed away again, his lip curled in derision. "Don't you dare play amateur psychologist with me, Genevieve Kendall. Better people than you have tried.''

''Why don't you tell me?'' she said as simply as she could. ''Just sit and tell me, Jack.''

''Why the hell should I do that?''

She motioned around the room. ''Physical exertion doesn't seem to have helped any.''

''I have an entire house I haven't even started on yet.''

''And you have someone here to talk to. You've never had that before. Why not try it? As the old cliché is wont to say, 'Burdens are easier carried by two than one.'''

''Because you *love* me?''

She faced him, the tears that had been building for days now lodged right in the back of her throat, closing her chest, burning her eyes. ''Because I love you. Because I know what it's like to take the world's responsibilities on my own shoulders without sharing them. Because I'm strong enough to share yours without crumbling to pieces.'' She reached up again, just to brush a few tears away. ''Because you need to talk to someone else who understands before you talk to Elizabeth.''

''How could you understand?'' he demanded. ''Haven't you heard what I said?''

''Yes. You had too much to drink at a party and had an accident. As a result, your wife is dead.''

''I *murdered* her!''

She didn't so much as flinch. ''You made a mistake. You've been paying for it ever since. Do you want me to tell you that it was your fault? Then yes, Jack, it was your fault. You made the decisions that put you in that place on that road where your wife died. But prison sentences have their limits, and I think it's time you walked out of yours. So sit down and talk to me about it.''

To Gen's eternal surprise, Jack sat. He simply folded up and landed on the bed, his hands in his lap, his head down, as if he simply couldn't hold himself up anymore.

Gen took the first good breath she'd had since walking into that room. Oh, God, she wanted to hold him. To just wrap him up in her arms and nestle his head against her chest. She wanted to be able to just pull all that old, hardened pain out of him and into herself, where she could disperse it somewhere. Anywhere. Anywhere that would save him from this.

She was going to sit on the floor, just that. Just settle at his knees where she wouldn't crowd him. She really was. Then she saw his shoulders tighten. She saw his head bow even farther. She heard the sob building in his throat as if it had been caught there for years. Which it probably had.

She didn't have to think about it anymore. She sat down alongside him and simply gathered him to her. She wrapped her arms so tightly around him that he couldn't get loose, and she pulled his head down to her, close, tight, safe in the haven of her arms.

And he didn't pull away. He didn't fight her. He simply wept. Racking, shuddering sobs that seemed to tear him apart as he curled in her arms, as she murmured to him, soft words meant to soothe.

She held him as the poison spilled free, as the grief and anger and guilt fractured that hard, careful wall he'd built around himself so that he would never again have to come face-to-face with what he'd done. Even though it had been eating away at him from the moment it had happened.

He was such a good man. Such an intrinsically honorable man. If he hadn't been, he wouldn't have battered at himself for so long for the one terrible mistake of his life.

Well, Gen thought in an odd dispassionate corner of her brain as she rocked him and murmured to him, at least he finally made sense. He made utter, complete sense. She should have known that the world didn't know everything about a man. That there was something darker, something more destructive, that drove Jack O'Neill to the limits he reached.

After all, critical-care physicians knew better than most that even best efforts didn't always save patients. They knew that sometimes, no matter how hard they worked, no matter how much they cared or gave or did, people died. A critical-care physician would have grieved, would have fought and railed and raged at his wife's death. But after four years, he would have moved on. Because he knew better than anyone that that was the way things had to be.

He wouldn't have redirected his entire life into a kind of holy mission simply because his wife had died.

He would have if he'd killed her, though.

He certainly would.

Gen wasn't at all sure how long they sat there together, both of them wet with his tears. She wasn't sure how long the silence that followed lasted. She didn't really care. She would stay here as long as Jack needed. As long as he would let her.

"It was why I tried to send her away, you know," he finally said, lifting his head from her shoulder. Pulling away, just a little. "Elizabeth."

Gen loosened her hold so she could see him. What she saw was that he watched his clasped hands as if they would offer answers.

"She never knew at all?" she asked.

He laughed, and the sound was so sad, so sore, it broke Gen's heart all over again. "I've spent the past five years trying to protect her from the truth. I mean, wasn't it hard enough losing her mother? Did she have to know about me?" He shook his head, lifted his hands, as if warding off his own selfishness. His own fallibility. "When I had the choice of treatments for her, I thought that if Elizabeth were at a place far away from me when they started mining for the reasons that set this terrible thing off in her, maybe I could...I could keep...fooling her."

"Fooling her about what? Into believing that her father is a decent man?"

He briefly met her gaze with disdain. "Yes. Into believing that her father is a decent man. I thought maybe they wouldn't ask. Wouldn't force me to...to admit what I'd done."

"Nobody forced you, Jack," Gen said as softly as she could. "It was time, and you know it. You simply couldn't hold it in any longer."

"Not with you badgering me, I couldn't."

She hurt so badly. "I'm told it's my finest talent."

"I wouldn't consider that a compliment."

Silence. Taut and heavy and fraught with secrets. Gen waited.

She waited as quietly as she could, because she was afraid he would bolt if she didn't.

He wasn't used to this. He probably didn't know how to do it any better than she did.

So she waited.

"The worst part," he said, sounding almost bemused, "is that I got away with it. The highway patrol guys knew me. I'd helped save one of their kids. And the other driver in the accident wasn't any more sober than I was. So…they made sure that I never saw a breathalyzer. They made sure the good doc didn't have to pay when he wrapped his brand-new Porsche around an SUV on an icy road."

"The other guy went to jail?"

"The other guy was dead on the scene. He wasn't just drunk. He'd decided he didn't need a seat belt."

"Oh."

"Yeah. Oh. Everybody expected me to file a civil suit against the drunk driver who killed my wife. Now, how delicious is that?"

"Does *anybody* else know?"

"Meggie's parents. They almost sued for custody of Elizabeth. Instead, they moved as far away from me as they could. Florida."

"And you moved to Chicago."

"And I moved to Chicago. I just couldn't live in Boston anymore. But after this, I'm not sure I can live here, either."

"You can't just keep running, Jack."

"I hate Chicago."

Gen closed her eyes for a moment, only long enough to get her heart started again. Just how many times would she survive his telling her that she had no place in his life?

"Well, you're here, at least for now. What are you going to do about it?"

That got him to lift his head a little, to stare at her as if she'd just bitten him. "What do you mean?"

It was all she could do to keep from reaching up to wipe the rest of his tears away. To kiss them away. To rock him in her arms again. But she had an idea that wasn't what he needed right now.

"I mean that there is an entire staff outside that door terrified that you've killed both me and yourself in here. A staff who are really afraid for you. There's a little girl upstairs who needs to hear what you have to say so you can both start to move on. And there are not only a Guatemalan housekeeper and a nanny back home but a whole slew of Kendalls who worry about you two on a regular basis. What are you going to do now?"

His head went back down. His hands locked together. He sat there for what seemed like an eternity, and Gen held her breath. Again. It seemed to be all she did anymore.

"I don't know."

"Do you plan on doing yourself bodily harm?"

That got his head back up again. "No."

She tried to smile. "Do you plan on doing *me* bodily harm?"

"I'm considering it."

She reached up again, because she simply couldn't help it, and because this time he let her. "You do need to talk about this to somebody who knows what they're doing, Jack. You know you do."

An eyebrow lifted. "Are you telling me that you don't think you're qualified?"

"I didn't say that," she said with a slight grin. "I'm saying that you'd feel better talking to an objective professional. There's nothing in my contract with you or Elizabeth that says I have to be objective."

Better. He was looking minimally better. Gen felt herself relax just as fractionally.

"Soon," he said, sighing. "Soon. I'm just not…ready."

"Maybe you should just get a little rest for a while," she suggested, holding on to him. "You haven't had a whole lot of it recently, and it might help."

"No," he said. "I need to go up and talk to Elizabeth."

"Uh, Jack," Gen demurred, "I'd rethink that if I were you."

He stiffened. "Why? Don't you think she's heard by now that I've been in here making a fool of myself?"

"Nope. I think the staff would protect her. And I think that even if she does hear, she'll be worried. If she sees you in the state you're in right now, she'll be terrified.''

Finally, finally, she got a smile out of him. A small smile, a wry, brittle smile, but a smile nonetheless.

''Why haven't you run from me screaming like a banshee, Gen Kendall?'' he asked.

*Because I love you.*

But she couldn't say that. Jack wouldn't allow it. He didn't want it. Too bad. There was nothing she could do about it.

So she huffed as if he were an idiot. ''You met my brother Jake. At your worst, you're a pale comparison.''

She realized suddenly that he was watching her. Studying her, as if trying to read something in her features. ''I mean it. Why aren't you more upset? Why haven't you told me what a worthless piece of garbage I am for what I did?''

Gen could do little more than shrug. ''I don't know, Jack. Maybe I will when I think about it for a while. Maybe I would have if I'd been there when it had happened. Nobody who works critical care has any affection for a drunk driver. Nobody wants to see a beautiful, bright young woman die for no reason. But don't forget, I've seen what you've tried to do as penance. I've seen the man you are. Ask anybody in this hospital and they'll tell you that they don't have a doubt in the world that it was the accident that was the aberration in your character. Not what you've done since.''

''I just tried to be the man she wanted me to be.''

''There's nothing wrong with that. But I also think you're being the man you are. And don't forget, you're a hell of a daddy. I can't tell you how I envy Elizabeth.''

He was shaking his head at that, but Gen could see that he wasn't really fighting her anymore. He'd spent all his ammunition. He'd drained his own reserves.

He was exhausted.

''Lie down now,'' she said, standing up. ''Get a little rest. I'll go with you later to talk to Elizabeth, if you want.''

''No,'' he said, even as he lay down under her pressure. ''I should do that alone.''

"You can if you want," Gen said, shaking off the cover to lay it over him. "But I'm here if you want. I'm happy to help."

She was just about to turn away, back to the real world, when Jack took hold of her hand.

"Don't go," he begged.

Gen stopped. She turned back to see the need in his eyes, to see that for now, for just now, he didn't want to be alone. He didn't want to be without her.

Gen knew that this was nothing more than compassion. Another service she could offer, like prescriptions and child rearing. She lay down next to him, anyway, and she wrapped him back in her arms. And there in the call room, with the rustle and clatter and chatter of the hospital hallway outside the door, Jack O'Neill fell into a deep sleep, and Gen Kendall held him while he did.

By the time she walked back out that door, Gen was in serious doubt she was going to make it. She was actually trembling with the effort it took to set one foot in front of the other.

Jack would be all right, she thought. A slow, careful step at a time, but he was at least pointed in the right direction. Once he and Elizabeth sorted out their past together, they stood a good chance of getting on with their lives.

As opposed to Gen Kendall.

Lee was right, she realized. Amanda was right. She simply couldn't live her life like this, constantly being there to hold up a complex and demanding man with nothing of her own to show for it. Not a look. Not a word. Not a gentle touch.

She was walking away again with nothing but leftover grief to weigh her down. Old, hard tears that were going to calcify at the back of her throat would one of these days cut off her airway completely.

She had to get on with it herself. Walk away from those two as if she'd never met them and focus on what she'd always wanted her life to be.

Who cared if it suddenly wasn't as much as she'd once hoped for?

"Dr. Kendall?"

Gen seriously thought about not answering. She'd pretty much given everything she had, back in that little room.

"Please. Is he all right?"

Marian, the floor spokesperson. Probably the hospital spokesperson. Gen stopped where she was, but she didn't so much as turn around.

"He's fine. He needs to be left alone for a while, I think. This has all just been a little much for him, with his daughter and all. He needs some sleep."

"That's good. That's…um, good."

Gen took another step.

"Um, Dr. Kendall?"

Gen kept walking and heard Marian pace her. She eyed the elevator like the escape hatch on a stricken submarine, wondering if she could make it. Punch that button, shut those doors and run like hell for some kind of safety. For her apartment.

No, not her apartment. Not till she got the smell of him out of it.

A hotel. Yes, that was it. A nice, anonymous hotel where she could burrow into somebody else's sheets and sleep the rest of her life away where nobody could ask anything else from her.

"Dr. Kendall?"

She came to a halt, no more than ten feet from escape. She sighed. "Spit it out, Marian. What do you need?"

"Well, it's Dr. O'Neill. He's supposed to be on shift, and we can't find Dr. Martin to replace him till he's feeling better."

So Gen was supposed to fill in for him, too. She just couldn't. She wasn't sure she was going to be able to look at one sick kid without bursting into hysterics.

She couldn't do it.

For once, damn it, she should think of herself.

"I can cover a couple hours," she said, still not facing the nurse. "Who needs me?"

"First? Elizabeth O'Neill."

Gen shut her eyes and leaned against the wall. "She heard?"

"Kinda hard not to. Would you mind?"

Yes. Yes. Yes.

I'm just so tired. Tired of the O'Neills and tired of the hospital and tired of always being the girl in charge.

I want to go home.

"No, I don't mind."

She'd actually managed to take two steps before Marian stopped her again.

"Dr. Kendall?"

"Yes, Marian."

"Thank you."

Gen swung around to see that that stout, efficient little woman knew exactly what it was she'd asked Gen to do this afternoon. She knew, too, what it was costing her.

Gen almost managed a smile. "You owe me a drink."

"I'd say the whole hospital does."

Gen turned back for the elevators. "I just might take them up on it."

She did get in to talk to Elizabeth. She got her calmed down and talking about the people she'd met at the eating disorders unit, and the fact that her father had let her stay close. They talked about various Kendalls, and they talked about music.

And they talked about Jack. Gen knew perfectly well that Elizabeth could see the lies she was telling. Elizabeth knew that her father had suffered some kind of reaction that had never been seen on a hospital floor before. But she let Gen lie about the cause, and she believed her when she said that he was feeling better now. She even let Gen get away with telling her that most of her father's problem had been exhaustion from trying to be too nice a man.

In the end, the two of them reached a tacit agreement that Elizabeth would get her final answers from her father when he felt better. And then, after dispensing another hug and kiss, Gen trudged on out to her next assignment.

She spent the next two hours in the unit trying exceptionally hard to keep her mind on the crises at hand. She allowed herself to rely on her nurses, and she asked Dr. Spizer for advice on a couple of arcane matters. She even sang to one chubby little boy with Down Syndrome who had come in to have the deformity in his happy heart corrected and purportedly loved music.

He must have. He loved Barry Manilow. It was the only thing that kept Gen going.

"ED's looking for you," one of the techs informed her, leaning in the door.

"Just a minute," Gen cautioned.

Right on cue, the little boy swung into the last verse of "My Baby Loves Me," and everybody in the unit applauded.

He applauded right back, laughing and happy, and Gen hugged him, just for herself. For her own sore heart that couldn't be healed with sutures and grafts. And then she headed on to the next thing.

She should have known. They didn't need her in the work lanes. They needed her in the staff lounge, where Lee waited with Abbie Viviano.

"Ah," Gen greeted them. "The Greek chorus."

Lee stood up and just looked at her sister. Abbie didn't budge from where she sat.

"Yes," Gen told them both. "Jack was throwing a massive temper tantrum. He has completely redecorated a call room—not that it didn't need it. But I'm not sure the administration was thinking of retro frat house as the decor of choice. He's better now, because he finally wore himself out from that caregiving marathon of his, and I think he'll be much more rational after this. All right?"

"What about you?" Lee asked.

Gen had been feeling better. Microscopically, admittedly. But she could still see that little boy's bright, unfettered smile, and it had carried her all the way downstairs. Now those damn tears were back, and she just wasn't going to deal with them.

She wasn't.

"Me?" Gen retorted with a shrug. "My work is done here. I think I'll just slip back into the role of rookie trauma pediatrician and leave the superhero stuff to somebody else."

"I thought maybe you'd like to go home," Abbie offered quietly. "Your shift has been over for a couple hours, after all."

"*My* shift has," she admitted, shoving her hands into her lab coat pockets before they betrayed her. Fortunately, she'd long since changed out of that soaked scrub top that would have marked her own role in Jack O'Neill's startling lapse of control. "I'm finishing up Jack's until he gets a little rest."

Abbie lifted an eyebrow. "You gonna cook the ED dinner, too? Maybe clean up OR when it's finished?"

Lee looked at her friend as if her hair was on fire.

Gen just lifted her own eyebrow. "Nah. Nobody'd pay me extra for that. I can always use overtime toward my loans, though. Get me out of town faster. I wonder if I could demand Jack's scale for this time. I'd be out of here a good month earlier."

"You want to leave so badly?" Abbie asked.

"Yes," Gen said, revealing more than she'd ever intended. "Oh, yes."

For a second there was silence. Another uncomfortable silence Gen felt obliged to fill. Anything to avoid acknowledging the despair that dragged at her, the disintegration of dreams never admitted.

She wanted to be alone, because she was terrified of what caring people would do to her.

She was afraid of letting go when there were no walls to protect her.

"Well," Abbie announced. "I hear they finally found Martin. He should be here in about ten minutes. And Jack is up on the eating disorders unit talking to his daughter. So, in fact, your work *is* done. Why don't you change out of your cape and go home with your sister?"

Gen felt her shoulders sag, as if she'd been bracing herself for the past four hours. The past twenty-eight years.

"Yeah," she said, turning for the door. "Why don't I?"

She didn't because she walked out of the staff lounge and ran right into William Christian.

Gen stuttered to a halt.

He was just standing there, hands in his coat pockets, waiting. Watching for her. Calm and patient and quiet. Little Jacob Edward's father, who had sworn to kill her. To make her hurt as much as he had.

Gen should have run.

She should have started screaming and locking doors and

shoving him out toward the driveway. Instinctively she knew that. Physically she was so drained and so distraught that her own reactions were slowed.

"Dr. Kendall," he greeted her, his voice flat.

"Mr. Christian," she greeted him back. "Your wife's looking for you. She's worried."

He didn't even react. He just stared at her.

Gen felt the import of that crawling over her skin like lice. She knew that tone of voice. That stance. That dead, empty look in the eye.

It was the look of someone who had nothing to lose.

Somebody who had made his final decision and didn't have to think anymore.

Which was when she realized what she should have noticed sooner.

He was wearing a full-length raincoat.

In June.

And not twenty feet behind her, Lee and Abbie were about to step out of that lounge to come looking for her.

Right now, Gen wasn't sure she much cared whether William Christian shot her. She just didn't have the energy left to be outraged.

But the people on her work lane were now at risk.

Her *sister* was at risk.

"Okay," she said, the energy surging back. "This is enough. You and I are going to walk outside and deal with this, Mr. Christian. I'm going to talk to you about Jacob. You're going to get help for this rage you feel, and we're going to stop tormenting your wife."

"I don't think so, Dr. Kendall."

Which was when he pulled open his coat.

"You don't give a damn, Dr. Kendall. So I'm going to make you."

It was then that Gen saw that underneath his full-length coat, Mr. Christian had strapped a dozen pipe bombs to his chest.

# *Chapter 16*

Jack felt as if he'd gone ten rounds in a boxing gym. He knew he looked like hell. He'd been getting sidelong looks all down the hallway. And this after he'd showered and changed and shaved. All so he could see his daughter.

So he could break her faith with him.

He was shaking. Shaking like a man going to his execution.

He *was* going to his execution, but Gen was right. He could no longer put it off. If he needed any proof of that, he'd received it not three hours earlier in that claustrophobic, cluttered little call room on the third floor. He was finally falling apart, his sinews and bones and brain eaten away by the guilt he'd carried around with him for the past five years.

He had to make peace with what he'd done.

He had to make his confession to the most important person in his life.

Well, he thought, with a sharp ache of fresh guilt, one of the two most important people in his life.

How could he have let her offer so much? How could he have taken from her, drinking from her life force, her compassion, her boundless love, without so much as thanking her? Without letting her know the truth?

How had he let her walk away with no word from him?

Oh, Meggie, he thought, as he stopped at the door to his little girl's room. How did I get so far from where we started? Have I become so absorbed with my own penance that I could so hurt a beautiful woman like that?

You'd like her, Meggie. You'd like her so much. She's the person you always wanted to be. Strong and certain and insightful. But she doesn't have that bone-deep assurance of herself you did. She never had the luxury of the safety and comfort you were given, so that you knew your own worth.

You'd like her, Meggie.

"Daddy?"

Jack stopped in the doorway to take in the sight of his daughter.

"Hi, Mouse."

Elizabeth's smile was at once breathtaking and uncertain. A woman's smile, a child's smile. A daughter's smile.

The smile of someone who was seeing her life change. Again.

Jack ached for the words he had to say to his little mouse. He wanted to run from them. From her. From the trusting, devoted light that would die in those sweet blue eyes his Meggie had given her.

Instead, he held out his arms, and Elizabeth flew into them.

"Are you okay now?" she asked.

"I'm better now that I'm here," he assured her.

Wrapped around her, protective and selfish. Hungry for that little-girl feel of her, when she still ran first to him before anyone else.

He'd almost forfeited that. Almost lost it to his blind devotion to his own pain.

"Do you have time to talk for a few minutes, Mouse?"

She looked up, and the uncertainty blossomed in her eyes. "You're not rethinking Minnesota, are you?"

Jack hugged her even more tightly to him. "And let you out of my sight? Never. I promised, remember?"

So they sat in the straight-backed chairs in her yellow semiprivate room with its chintz curtains and animal posters, and Jack held her hand.

"I've been unfair to you, Mouse."

"Daddy, no…"

He lifted a hand to silence her, and smiled. "Shhh. This is my story, okay? I need to tell it." He only waited for her nod before continuing. "I've kept something from you. For years. Something I think you should know if we're both to move forward."

Gen's words. Gen's soft hand against his cheek. Her wise, sad eyes lifted to his in silent empathy. Jack stoked himself on those things and went on.

"It's about the night your mom died." He sucked in a breath, held on to Elizabeth's hand. Sought the wisest words to give her.

*Please, Meggie. Show me how.*

*Please, Gen.*

"I was drunk, Elizabeth." As baldly as that. It seemed all he could manage. God knows he couldn't face her with it. "We'd been at a party, and I…I, uh, wouldn't let your mom drive. If I hadn't been drunk…if I hadn't…"

"I know."

"She loved you so much. She wanted so much to stay and see you grow up, and because of me, she couldn't."

"I know."

Jack had his mouth open to say more. He had the words gathered on his tongue. He was all set to use them when he finally heard her.

"What?"

She had tears in her eyes. Tears on her cheeks. "Grandma Benson told me. I thought you knew."

"She *told* you?" he demanded, distraught. The fire in his chest melted, reformed. "She *told* you that? When did she tell you?"

"Before they left. She said you were selfish and criminal and brutal. Why do you think I never want to go to Florida?"

He was simply struck dumb. "I don't understand. How could you know?"

"Daddy," she said, in that wise-little-girl voice daughters have used throughout history to their parents, "I'm not deaf and dumb. You had nightmares for a while, remember? But I wasn't sure until Grandma told me the truth."

"Why didn't you say something?"

"Because you seemed sad enough. I didn't want you to be sadder."

He was numb. Stunned and breathless with the enormity of what he hadn't seen. Of what he and Elizabeth had forfeited.

There was so much they could have shared about her mother, if only the two of them...

If only *he*...

Gen had been right. But then, Jack had found that Gen Kendall had a knack for being right about everything but herself.

"How could you still love me?" he asked anyway, because he couldn't understand it.

More tears. And not just in Elizabeth's eyes this time. It seemed that Gen had loosed that in him, so that he wasn't afraid.

"Did you try and kill Mommy?"

"Of course not. How could you say that?"

She shrugged. "You act like it sometimes. Like you believe you did. But you didn't. And you wouldn't."

And that was that. Jack was still struggling for breath, and his little girl was finished, her logic sound, at least to her.

"Attention, Dr. Thomas Strong to the emergency department, stat. Dr. Thomas Strong to the emergency department stat."

Jack was still holding Elizabeth, his tears soaking her braid, when he heard the hall announcement. Somewhere in the back of his head, he knew it meant something. Dr. Strong was the call for security. The Thomas part meant something more. But he hadn't been here long enough to know anything more than that Mr. Twister meant a tornado alert, as if anybody would be fooled by that.

He found out when one of the staff pushed Elizabeth's door open. "Excuse me, folks, but we need to leave this unit."

Jack looked up to see the strain on the normally placid black face.

"What's up?"

"We need to evacuate the floor," she said, pointing the way. "Now."

Jack grabbed Elizabeth and pushed her in the right direction. "What's up?" he asked the tech.

"Bomb," she murmured, out of hearing from the scurrying escapees. "I hear that some guy's down in the ED threatening that nice Dr. Kendall."

Jack came to a skidding halt. "What?"

"Bomb squad and SWAT team are here," she said, and this time Elizabeth heard. "We're evacuating the wing, just in case."

"That must be some bomb," Elizabeth said, eyes immense.

Gen.

Dear God, Mr. Christian had come back.

Jack had to get downstairs.

"Mouse…"

"Bring her back up here," his little girl said with a pat up to his face. "Bring her back safe, Daddy."

He dropped a kiss on her forehead. "I will, baby."

And then, more frightened than he'd been since that night he'd found Meggie lying in a heap along the side of a dark, icy road, Jack ran.


"No, you won't," Gen was saying.

She stood in the middle of the hallway, where Mr. Christian had led her, the finger of one hand on some kind of release button, his other hand full of a Glock 9mm.

Gen was way past frightened. She was in the surreal range, where nothing really registered anymore. Nothing mattered. Nothing except the fact that she had a hallway full of frightened patients and a man made mad by grief keeping them at bay.

"Oh, but I will," he insisted, a tiny spark flaring in those cold brown eyes. "I mean to make you hurt."

"Then shoot me," she said, "and be done with it. You're not going to set off those bombs, no matter what. Or is it that you want to die, too? That you can't survive losing your little boy?"

He didn't answer, so she went on, her voice pitched low, soothing, the kind of hypnotic tone used by animal trainers and psych staff the world over.

"I can understand that," she said. "Please believe me, I can. I don't feel what you're feeling. Who could? If you really feel you can't live without your little boy, that's your decision. But if you set off those bombs, how many other parents are you condemning to that same kind of pain? That same, awful grief that won't let you sleep? How many parents will you make hurt the same way you hurt just because you want to get back at me?"

"*You're* going to hurt," he insisted, lifting the gun. "I've thought about it, ya know. You don't have kids. So I can't kill your kid. But you say you care about kids. If I kill other kids, it'll be your fault. And you'll hurt. You'll hurt so much you'll know how I feel."

"So you're going to kill children, just like Jacob, just to get me? I don't think so, Mr. Christian. I think you're a coward. I think you don't give a damn about anybody else. I think you're going to kill fifteen children and make their parents go through what you're going through because you're too much of a coward just to turn that gun on yourself and kill yourself."

"I don't…" He seemed to waver, to lose focus for a minute. He actually looked around at the doorways, where Gen could hear the anxious voices and fretful cries of the patients and parents. "I have to…don't you see…?"

"You don't have to do anything. You have to make your little boy proud of you and stop this. You have to help your wife. She carried Jacob for nine months. She knew him even better than you did. Don't you think she hurts as much as you do? She needs somebody with her who understands, and you're the only one who does. But you won't be able to help her, because you'll be dead. And you'll make it worse, because you'll kill other people's children, and she'll be left behind to try and explain to those parents what you did. To feel responsible for what her husband did."

"No! No, it's not like that."

"It's exactly like that."

Gen saw the SWAT team gathering out by triage and knew she had to get this over with. She had to get him to give himself up before they felt they couldn't take any more chances with a madman and his bombs.

"Please," she begged, hands out, palms up. "Think of your wife. Think of how she'd feel with you and Jacob dead, with all those children dead. Think about it."

He thought about it. For about a half a second. Then Gen saw something she never hoped to see again as long as she lived. She saw that shattered, grieving man lift that Glock. And she saw him turn it on himself.

She didn't even think. She just lunged. She hit him in the middle like a battering ram, shoving his arm up and away from him. She heard the pop of the Glock and felt debris fall in her eyes from the ceiling. She felt all those metal pipes he'd taped to his chest scrape her ribs and wondered if she was about to become space dust from the thousands of nails he'd packed against his own body.

She skidded across the floor atop him and didn't blow up. But suddenly there was the thunder of booted feet, and a hundred hands plucked at her, pulled her away, shoved her aside. They grappled with Mr. Christian. They yanked away his gun. They lifted him and carried him and ran with him right back down the hall.

"I didn't really mean for you to kill yourself," she said to the ceiling, unable, finally, to move.

Literally.

Sprawled on the floor in an ungainly heap, her ribs aching and her head ringing and her throat finally blocked completely with the pain that had been rising in her.

She couldn't move. She couldn't close her eyes. She couldn't open her mouth. People were swarming around her like a crowd at the zoo. Friends, colleagues, Lee and Amanda, openmouthed and saying something Gen couldn't seem to hear.

And then one face. One worried, frightened face.

One dear, handsome face.

Hovering over her as if she'd dreamed him. As if she wanted him so badly at this moment when she simply couldn't take any more that he had materialized by magic.

"Younger doctor," the voice said with a wry smile, "I

thought it was your sister, Lee, who always found herself in
these kinds of predicaments.''

Gen blinked.

And he was still there.

Reaching out to her. Gathering her to him. Pulling her into
his arms, into the sweet, sharp scent of him, into the refuge of
him, where she knew she was safe.

Where she knew, if she let herself, she could fall apart.

She held herself together with nothing more than grit.

After all, she'd been here before. She'd been in those arms,
held to that strong heart, and she'd been thrown away. She simply couldn't survive it if she sought asylum there and was once
again repulsed.

She should have been stunned that Jack literally lifted her
from the floor. Carried her through that crowd as if she were
precious, and closed them both into the staff lounge alone. She
should have been speechless that he then curled up on the couch
with her still in his arms and kissed her.

Kissed her as if he were coming home, as if he were a wanderer finally blessed with a path, a message, a star to follow. He
kissed her as if he'd waited his whole life for that kiss, as if
he'd looked for that kiss through a journey that had tested him
to the edge of his courage. He kissed her as if there was nothing
he lived for but that kiss.

She almost succumbed. She almost believed. She almost relaxed into his arms and kissed him back.

She didn't.

She knew better.

''Oh, Gen,'' he rasped against her hair, his hands trembling
as they clutched her, ''what have I done to you?''

Rising. The tears were closing in on her again. Clogging her
throat and searing her eyes. They were crowding her, choking
her. They were so close, so deadly thick, that she tried to escape.

She tried to escape his arms, his safety. His promise of trust.

He wouldn't let her. He held on to her as if he could save
her, and he lifted her face to him. He smiled for her, and there
were tears in his eyes.

''How could you do this to me?'' he asked.

"Oh, I see," she couldn't help but say. "You've suddenly realized my worth now that I almost died? Quite the romantic cliché, doctor."

He actually smiled. Brushed her hair back from her forehead, and laughed as if he had discovered laughter like an archeologist's find. "Almost died?" he demanded. "Not you. I never had a moment's doubt that you'd take care of Mr. Christian."

She stared. "You didn't?"

"Of course not. You'd never let him hurt anybody else. Most especially you wouldn't let him hurt himself. That was a pretty fancy maneuver out there, younger doctor. I think it could well make you eligible for the Bears."

Still she couldn't grasp what he meant. Still the tears crowded her, confused her. Still she lay in those gentle arms and fought the urge to stay.

"Then, what?" she demanded. "What brought you down here?"

Another laugh, delighted and wry. Wise and tender.

"The fact that you had no one else around who understood what it meant to not be able to unload part of the burden Mr. Christian dumped on you. What another selfish doctor dumped on you. What it cost you." He stroked her cheek this time, gazed at her as if at a precious artifact. As if he'd suddenly discovered a diamond in a dirt pile. "As someone very wise once told me, 'Burdens are much easier carried by two.'"

She couldn't even breathe anymore.

"Aren't you going to ask me why?" he asked, touching her again, his fingers feathering along her brow, down her cheek.

"Why what?"

"Why I want to do this?"

No, she wasn't. She couldn't. She didn't dare. She'd lived her whole life without hope and didn't see where it had gotten her for the last month. She didn't dare court it again.

"Why?" she asked anyway. Because, in the end, she couldn't help it.

"Because I love you."

She struggled against him then, and he held her, gently and firmly against him, where she would have to listen.

"I've loved you since the first time I saw you sing to a baby. Since you invited me into that wonderland of a bed of yours. Since you stood up to me for the sake of my daughter. I've loved you so much that you scared me right into confessing the greatest sin of my life just so I could redeem myself in your eyes. That's how much I love you."

"No…"

"Yes, Gen. I love you so much that I realized not ten minutes ago that I can't live without you. But worse, I can't let you bear your burdens alone anymore. Please, Gen. Share them with me. Love me. Marry me."

"But…" Her voice was dying now, a rasp of a whisper that hurt. "You have a mission."

"Elizabeth wants to try out a small town in Wyoming."

She still couldn't answer.

She couldn't believe.

She couldn't hope.

"You'd do that for me?"

"I'd do that for us. Just think of it, Gen. We two problem solvers would finally have somebody else to take our problems to. We could share everything, and God, Gen, I need to share my life with you. Don't you understand that you bring me laughter and delight and peace? Don't you think I could bring you the same? Wouldn't you like to see Elizabeth grow into that music maestro your sister talks about?" He stopped stroking and took her hands. And then he simply laid them against his heart. "Please, Gen. Please share our lives with us. Let us share ours with you. Be our family."

She realized she was shaking now, as if the pressure couldn't be withstood or contained.

"What about Meggie?" she had to ask.

The tears brightened in his eyes. "Meggie wanted to leave a long time ago. I wouldn't let her."

"But you can't simply throw her away. You loved her so much."

"I still do. But now I love you. Can you live with her memory as a part of our lives?"

''Of course. She gave you Elizabeth. She helped make you the person you are.''

His eyes were so bright. It was as if the sun had struck the sea in them, and they took Gen's breath away. ''Then you'll say yes?''

She didn't get the chance. She opened her mouth. She formed the word on her lips, wrapped it around her tongue. She tried to smile.

But the tears beat her to it.

The tears she'd held in since the day since her father had dropped dead in the barn. The tears she'd sublimated, submerged, shoved down so far that she'd thought they didn't exist anymore.

The tears that had etched the terrible, constant pain in her chest that suddenly, in a flash of sun on water, began to ease away. The tears that finally bubbled free, overflowing, spilling and tumbling, in sobs and shudders and terrible, gasping breaths, in a red, runny nose and puffy, swollen eyes. Tears that soaked Jack's shirt and the three hand towels he found on an end table. Tears he kissed away and tears he laughed away and tears he soothed away, rocking her in his lap like a child, like the child she'd never been, like the child he would now encourage her to be.

Tears that cleansed and tears that surprised.

Gen couldn't stop them, and Jack didn't try. He simply chuckled and assured her that he had all the time in the world, since he knew she'd saved these tears up just for him. That he was privileged to accept them. That he was delighted that she finally felt she could trust him enough to bestow them on him.

She cried for her father and for her mother and for the small, young family who had scrabbled in the dust to survive. She cried for the lonely woman who had suppressed everything she yearned for beneath everything she had to be. She cried for the pain she'd swallowed while trying to save her children, and she cried for the pain she'd inherited when she'd fallen in love with Jack O'Neill and his little girl.

And finally she cried for the wonder of the man who held her. She cried for the happiness that seemed as unreal as a chimera in a very large desert. She cried for her future and the mountains where she would live with Jack and Elizabeth when they finished their year in Chicago. She cried for the splendor of Elizabeth and for the gifts given by Meggie Benson O'Neill.

And when, finally, Gen ran out of tears, Jack kissed her. Nothing more. A simple, sealing, healing kiss. A touching that reminded her that no matter what, she had someone else who knew her. Who loved her. Who understood what she carried with her. Who wanted to share it, and wanted her to share what he carried, too.

And then, smiling with the whimsical joy Gen had once seen on a glass photo in a window, Jack O'Neill gave Gen one more hug.

"I think it's time we gave these people back their lounge," he said. "Don't you?"

Still a little disoriented and a lot stuffy from all those tears, Gen nodded. "Well, at least I was neater about it than you were."

Jack lifted her off his lap, but he held on to her as he walked to open the door.

Lee almost tumbled in at their feet.

"Oh, my God," she whispered in awe, not moving. "How did you do that?"

Gen looked at Jack and then back at her sister. "Do what?"

But Lee had eyes for nobody but Jack. "Welcome to the family."

"You been eavesdropping again, brat?" Gen demanded, not at all concerned that Jack had his arm around her waist. She had hers around his.

"Don't be silly," Lee retorted. "It's undignified."

Jack lifted an eyebrow. "Then how are you so sure?"

"Are you kidding? I heard Gen crying in there. In fact, I think passersby on LaSalle could hear Gen crying in there. This is a Kendall national holiday. Not only that, but you've just scored yourself at least five hundred dollars."

"You're kidding," Gen protested.

"It was fifty-to-one, Gen."

Gen turned to Jack. "You sure you want to do this? You

know, it's not just your family I'm buying into. You'd be an official Kendall.''

''As long as you're part of the package,'' he said, pulling her close again, ''I can withstand any family.''

''Hey!'' Lee objected.

But nobody really noticed. Gen and Jack were kissing again, and every person in the emergency room was cheering.

# Epilogue

Dr. John Parker O'Neill and Dr. Genevieve Anastasia Kendall were married in the Grace Church on Main Street in Lost Ridge, Wyoming, on the twentieth of August. Attending the bride were her sister Amaryllis Lee Kendall O'Connor and her new step-daughter Elizabeth Margaret O'Neill.

It was a beautiful mountain day, the sky a deep, high blue with scattered clouds that chased shadows across the mountain-sides and a soft breeze that carried with it the scent of wildflow-ers. The reception was held in the VFW Post, where the ladies of the church provided a lovely buffet and the gentlemen of the valley provided alcohol.

As for the wedding itself, it was a traditional ceremony, at least regarding the service itself. Both bride and groom smiled with delight throughout, and pledged their troth with vows that, along with the usual, included the promise of laughter and shar-ing and something about painting pants on a bathroom wall, which made the congregation look to each other and made the bride's sister laugh out loud.

But all in town would remember with fondness and amaze-ment the moment Gen Kendall's new daughter stepped up to the old church organ that lurked at the side of the altar and began to play.

She played the traditional pieces demanded of such an occasion, but no one remembered them ever sounding quite so lovely pouring forth from the usually wheezy pipes.

Even more memorable to the guests—who included among their number not just every person in Lost Ridge and the surrounding ranches but medical people from Chicago, and even, causing more than one titter and sidelong glance, Ian Griffin—was the music the young Miss O'Neill provided for the reception.

She had written, she announced, two songs particularly for the couple. The first, entitled "Song of the Wise Woman," she insisted was a tribute to the Kendall women all, among whom she now numbered herself. The tune was haunting, the words a poetic tribute to a line founded among the fey folk of Ireland.

The second song she sang to her daddy. She sang it as he held her hand on the dance floor. It was called "Some Men's Dreams," and the words that resonated among more than one member of the party, were these.

"Some men's dreams do come true. Some men, I guess, deserve them to."

Dr. John Parker O'Neill was seen to weep. Elizabeth smiled. Gen hugged them both, so that people commented that they made up a perfect little circle of a family. Gen's own family began laying bets as to when that circle would grow.

Nobody bothered to mention the fact that although Elizabeth passed on the spice-cake-and-buttermilk-icing wedding confection, she was seen to greatly enjoy the ham and green beans that accompanied it. The people who knew her simply smiled and complimented her music. Those who didn't were more interested in the fact that she put ten dollars on the chance that she would have a new sibling by the next summer. The couple were, after all, honeymooning quite alone up in the mountain meadow where the first Kendalls had settled. What else, she demanded of her new relatives, was there to do up there?

It would never be recorded except in Gen Kendall's heart that later, as she and Jack stood out on the front porch of the old

Kendall cabin watching the sun set against the Wind River Range, she drank in the peace of that high meadow, the strength of the man she loved and the joy with which she faced her future. There, where four generations of Kendall women had dreamed their dreams, she had finally found some of her own.

"So you like Wyoming?" she asked her new husband, whose arm was around her waist.

"I do."

She smiled. "I like that phrase."

He smiled back, his eyes clearer than the Wyoming sky. "Me, too. You sure your brother won't mind us building here on the ranch?"

"I told you. It's a family concern. We can have the five acres of our choice and help from everybody in the valley."

He sighed, as if the words filled him somehow, had pulled her closer to him. "I really can't believe it, ya know."

"What?"

"That I've had the chance to start over again. That Elizabeth could be healing, that I could have found you. That I could really feel able to move on with my life. That after everything, as Elizabeth said, my dreams could come true."

"She didn't get it completely right, ya know," Gen said softly.

Jack raised an eyebrow. "My daughter is perfect," said he. "She would never get anything wrong."

"Oh, but she did. In her song to you, she forgot the part about how some women's dreams come true, too."

"Some women," he said to her, as a vow, as a blessing, "deserve them to."

And then, as the setting sun settled into those crystalline eyes of his where laughter and love once again lived, he kissed his new wife welcome.

"Now," he said as he rested his chin atop her head, "all we have to work out is that artwork in your bathroom."

"I only said I'd paint pants on the apartment wall," she said from within the haven of his citrus-scented shirt. "As for the house, Estela should be letting Pete Simpson in even as we speak. It's his wedding present to us, you know."

"I don't suppose I could get a *Venus Rising* in the bedroom."

"You will, Doctor," Gen promised. "Every day when your lovely wife gets up for work."

They laughed. They stood in the gathering darkness as the birds settled and the coyotes began to creep out and the stars winked on in the peacock sky, and they laughed. The sound of it echoed back from the mountains and the stream and the high, whistling meadow. It echoed well into the night, and again the next morning. Riding up to check his cattle two days later, Jake Kendall heard it once again and stopped there at the edge of the meadow to smile. It occurred to him that he'd never heard a more wonderful sound in his life.

\* \* \* \* \*

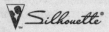
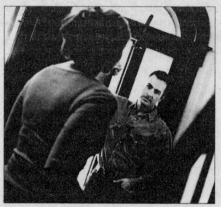

If you enjoyed what you just read,
then we've got an offer you can't resist!

# Take 2 bestselling love stories FREE!

# Plus get a FREE surprise gift!

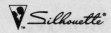

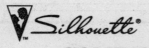

# COMING NEXT MONTH